# DISORGANIZED CRIME

## KAREN K. BREES

Black Rose Writing | Texas

ISBN: 978-1-68513-586-7
PUBLISHED BY BLACK ROSE WRITING
www.blackrosewriting.com

Printed in the United States of America
Suggested Retail Price (SRP) $21.95

*Disorganized Crime* is printed in Garamond Premier Pro

*alla mia famiglia*

# ACKNOWLEDGEMENTS

Thanks to Park, Keri, Trizbel, and Michael. I hope you like your characters. Thanks to John for his input and for catching some bloopers. Thanks to Terry for reading. Thanks to Cate Perry, developmental editor extraordinaire. And especially, my heartfelt thanks to Reagan Rothe and the crew at Black Rose Writing.

# DISORGANIZED CRIME

# CHAPTER ONE

*San Francisco*

Morrie Landow was thinking he was the luckiest guy alive. He was married to the most beautiful woman in the world, and she adored him almost as much as she adored Pierre, that ex-Mafia poodle she'd rescued from Sally "The Pipe" Puglisi. Love aside, he couldn't help questioning her sanity as he watched her stuffing toilet tissue into the cracks around the kitchen window where a considerable draft was operating. "Carla? What the hell are you doing? It's all just going to fall out when you open the window."

"Keeping it out. Or trying to." She paused, another sheet of tissue in hand. "It's been a perfect year, Morrie. Really, it has. The best year of my life." She glowered at the tissue. "I met you. I got away from my sad excuse of a life, and I'm finally going to be high class and talk like I got a education. The apartment. *Our* apartment. I never had a place like this before. It's our home. And the ballet studio." Carla heaved a sigh that came from somewhere deep in her soul. "That's the problem. It can't last." She resumed her stuffing. "I got a feeling. It's like the wind's gonna come up and blow everything away. You can laugh, but it's the truth."

Italian superstitions were not to be taken lightly. This much Morrie had learned. And there was no way to convince her that the weather wasn't made in Italy. One other thing he'd learned was when not to say another word. This was one of those times, but he gave it a shot, anyhow. "Everything's fine, Carla. Just let it go."

"Everything's fine now," she muttered. "Just wait. You'll see. It comes on the wind."

The day had been unusually warm and sunny for late autumn in the City by the Bay. The curtains hung limp at the kitchen window, but that draft that seemed to come from nowhere had Carla worried. "I know, Morrie, but I got a feeling and it won't go away." She turned away from the window to look at him. "And there's nothing we can do to stop what's coming."

"Then come sit down. You're getting yourself all worked up for nothing."

She sighed again and looked at the tissue in her hand. "You're right. This won't help."

***

The first ruffling of the curtains came at midnight. Curled up in his dog bed on the rug at the foot of his humans' bed, Pierre whimpered in his sleep, his paws twitching. Carla, unsettled, worried, unable to sleep, finally got out of bed just after one in the morning. She padded to the kitchen and looked out the window at the street below. Leaves and litter were swirling into small vortexes, the breeze pushing them along to some unknown destination. Paper tornados and gusts of dirt moved in fits and starts at the mercy of the wind. She shuddered, gripping the edge of the sink for support. Returning to bed, she moved close to Morrie and closed her eyes. An hour later, just as sleep finally claimed her, the first whiffs of smoke filtered up from the stairwell and pushed their way into the bedroom, activating the smoke alarm.

"Jesus!" Carla screamed, clapping her hands over her ears.

"Better deaf than dead," Morrie said, throwing back the covers. "Get dressed. Fast." He pulled on his t-shirt and trousers and moved to the kitchen. The smoke was now flowing in under the door that opened onto the hall that led to the stairs and the only exit. He touched the door. Hotter than Hades. Shit. No escape this way. He grabbed their shoes and ran back to the bedroom where Carla was snapping Pierre's leash to his collar. "Here," he said, handing Carla her shoes and tugging on his own. "There's no way out down the stairs. It's the window or nothing. How the hell could I have been so damn stupid?" He fumbled with his shoelaces. One entrance that was also the only exit. It hadn't registered when they'd first looked at the apartment, but then most urban apartments were laid out that way.

Carla nodded, her expression grim and her mouth set in a tight line made all the tighter since her teeth were clamped down on a couple of hair ties. Finally, with Pierre taken care of, she released him and made a quick pony tail that she twisted into a bun. "I need my pocketbook and cell. Grab your wallet. At least we don't have to tie sheets together like they do in the movies." She eyed her husband, 6'2" tall and 250 pounds, with concern. "I don't think there's a sheet strong enough to hold you."

Morrie grunted something unintelligible. He opened the bedroom window and tossed out the rope ladder that was attached to the wall studs and designed to carry a load of 500 pounds.

Carla, just about to the window, paused and looked over her shoulder. "What are you doing?"

"Tying strips of the sheet together." He jerked his head at Pierre. "He needs a harness. Something else I should have thought to get him. This will have to do. I'll lower him to the ground after you get out."

"Hurry!" She wadded up jackets for them both and a knit cap for Morrie's bald head and pitched them out the window into the darkness. She swung her right leg over the windowsill. The ladder swayed as her foot searched for the first rung. Once she'd balanced herself, the swaying decreased, and she brought her left leg into position. She began her descent, running her hands down the side ropes, matching the movements of her feet as they sought each rung. She barely felt the ropes chafing her palms, but the bricks, already heating the air outside, caused beads of perspiration to form on her forehead. She fought the urge to let go with one hand to wipe them away. Within two minutes, her left foot touched the ground, and she reached up with both arms to receive Pierre when Morrie lowered him from the window. She gave the dog a reassuring hug, then tied his leash to the rose bush, the strongest piece of vegetation in the weedy strip of side yard that separated their walkway from the neighboring apartment's fence. Morrie tossed down her pocketbook and then rappelled down the ladder to join her on the corner where a crowd had begun to gather. She dialed 911 and was told that the fire had already been called in. There was nothing left to do but wait and watch the destruction. Time stood still.

Carla wrapped her arms around herself to ward off the night chill that seemed twice as cold now that she'd left the heat of the fire behind. She went in search of their jackets. "Damn," she grumbled. "I hate being right."

Their outerwear had landed close to where the ladder had touched down. Now, with their protection from the night air clutched in her arms, she looked up at their window and felt a pang of sorrow at the loss of their first apartment. Their first bed. All the firsts. But then, a door closed in her mind, locking all that away to some safe place. The fire had not destroyed what was important. She and Morrie and Pierre had survived. That was all that mattered. The rest was just *stuff*. Still, it had been some really nice stuff. She patted Pierre on the head. "You just stay here. I'll be back in a few. It's too noisy up front. Everything's gonna be all right." She bent to touch his little nose and then returned to Morrie.

Harry Lai's *Superior Dry Cleaning* establishment on the ground floor was past saving. Their own apartment, directly above, was now fully involved, and smoke poured from the third floor, as well. Carla reached for Morrie's hand, lacing her fingers through his, and they watched in stunned silence as the flames soared skyward. The smoke alarm that had been blasting incessantly suddenly went quiet. She began to cry, and Morrie wrapped his arm around her. She scanned the crowd but didn't see the face she was hoping would be there. "Harry! Oh dear God! Where's Harry? Did he get out?"

"I don't know. Maybe. I don't see him." Morrie didn't sound hopeful, and Carla, sobbing, buried her face in Morrie's chest.

Sirens heralded the arrival of the fire engines that seemed to be converging on the site from all directions, and the noise was deafening. Carla left Morrie to check on Pierre, but in all the confusion and the noise, he must have panicked and slipped his collar. Frozen, all she could do was hold his leash and collar and call his name, over and over. On a night when everything had gone wrong, this was somehow the worst. Pierre was gone.

"There it goes!" one of the firefighters called out as flames shot heavenward, signaling the collapse of the roof. From that point on, there was nothing left to save. The crowd had swelled. Some were neighbors, but most were the curious, come to watch the disaster unfold. And Carla wondered. *Who else was in the crowd?* She had a feeling of being watched, but pushed it aside As dawn broke, the crowd filtered away, but she and Morrie stayed on, hoping Pierre would return. After a time, though, with nothing left but smoldering ruins and an overwhelming sense of loss, they gave up their vigil and walked the two blocks to the parking lot and their car.

"At least we didn't have a garage under us," Morrie said. "We've still got wheels."

Carla nodded, too tired to answer. "I don't feel like getting a motel room. We can go to the dance studio. There's the back workroom where we can throw down the mats for a bed. It's got a kitchen and bathroom with a shower. It'll work until we figure out what to do. I've still got a business to run. Tomorrow's Saturday. I got four classes to teach." She wiped away another tear. "Why, Morrie?"

"I don't know. Tonight, we're alive. The rest can wait until tomorrow."

***

"Everything smells like smoke," Carla said, wrinkling her nose. "Maybe it's stuck in my nose. And my hair. It could be there forever." She took several sniffs and her nose still disapproved. Just back from an emergency shopping trip for clothes and groceries, she kicked off her shoes, deposited the bags on the chair by the work table, and plunked herself down on the floor mat. "I went back to look for Pierre again, but no luck. So I got these." She dumped the contents of one of the shopping bags on the floor. "Markers and poster paper. I'm going out after lunch and plaster these all around the neighborhood. And I thought I'd stop by all the businesses along the street too and see if anyone's seen him. He's microchipped. He's somewhere. I just need to find out where that is." She caught herself chewing on her lower lip, a habit she was trying to break. "I'll call the Humane Society and all the vet clinics in the area, too." She picked up a marker. "He's scared, Morrie."

Munching on a cookie and occupying the only chair, Morrie was absorbed in an apartment search on his laptop and hadn't been listening, but the sudden silence alerted him that a response was in order. A year of marriage had taught him that a nod and a grunt often worked in these situations.

"I picked up the morning paper," Carla said, setting down the morning edition of *The Reporter*. "It doesn't say much. They found Harry or what was left of him. He didn't get out."

This time Morrie looked up and answered. "He was a decent guy. Bad way to go."

Carla reread the short account. "It just don't make sense. He was organic. I mean, he didn't use any of those chemicals that the other places use." She set the paper on the table, pointing at the story. "No, I mean it. Look at this. They're saying he had cans of solvent stored next to a space heater. That ain't true. I been in there enough to know. He ran a clean shop. It don't make sense."

"Don't get involved, Carla. Even if you're right," Morrie paused, regrouping, "and I'm not saying you aren't, you don't want to go down that road. If you're thinking what I think you're thinking, you're going to be opening doors that we've tried to close. And at the moment, we've got more than enough to handle here. You've got your classes to teach, the insurance guy is coming tomorrow, and we've got to find a place to live." He crumpled the paper towel he'd been using as a napkin and tossed it in the direction of the waste basket. "We both know Harry's not the first the Mafia has killed, and he won't be the last. Carla, I don't want that to be you."

Carla looked up from the newspaper and stared at yesterday's vocabulary word, *evasive,* taped to the cupboard door by the refrigerator. Her language improvement program was plowing through a section on adjectives. One word a day. The hardest part was finding somebody to talk with who already knew all these words. She wasn't high class yet, but she was closing in on it, and only cussed now when there wasn't anything else to say. This was one of those times when a whole lot of cussing was called for, but she managed to keep control and said nothing, although her eyes blazed.

Morrie groaned inwardly. Once Carla got interested in something, there was nothing and nobody who could stop her. He'd tried, but the love of his life was like a pit bull with a piece of raw meat—a beautiful pit bull, granted, with her auburn hair the color of a summer sunset and her eyes as green as a martini olive, and a body with all the curves in all the right places, but her full lips were pursed and there was that frown line between her eyes that told him everything he needed to know. He gave up.

"I was in there just last week," Carla said. "Harry had a piece of cardboard taped to the window. Why do you suppose he did that? I know and you do too. Somebody had smashed that window, and that *somebody* came back to finish the job because Harry wouldn't ante up. Seems kinda over the top for some regular jerkoffs."

"Carla," Morrie began, but Carla waved his objection away before he'd even had a chance to figure out what his objection was.

"Nope. That busted window was a warning. He didn't pay his *pizzo*. I'm sure of it. I know how these guys work. *Mafia.*" She may have sworn off cussing, but the way she spoke that one word left no doubt as to her intent.

Morrie groaned again, audibly this time.

"I thought we'd be safe here, but it was just a matter of time." Her eyes grew dark. "You know exactly what I mean. Last week it was Olga's Bakery, but at least she didn't live upstairs. It'll be one a week now until everybody caves and pays for protection. Every morning I'm going to wake up, wondering if that's the day I get the visit here at the ballet studio, advising me that I need insurance to be able to keep operating. I'll tell them I have insurance, and they'll apologize so nicely and explain so very patiently that I need the insurance they're offering or bad things will happen. Then they'll shake their heads at how sad it all is. Like they got nothing to do with it. If I don't pay what they want, they'll destroy the studio." She sniffed and fumbled in her pocket for a tissue and blew her nose, then she took a sheet of poster paper to begin her *Lost Dog* notices. "They're responsible for Pierre getting lost." She stuck her chin out, a gesture of defiance and determination, her temper barely contained.

"You can't fight the Mob alone, Carla, and the police are stretched so thin they're not even responding to property crime."

"What about murder? Do they bother with murder? Do they? Huh?" She paused in her description of the little black poodle. "He's a little black poodle. I don't know what else to say." She made circular motions with her black marker. "He's gentle and loving and housebroken and likes to ride in the car. There. Done."

Morrie, back at the apartment search, heard the last part of her description. "He is a good dog. I hope you find him."

"Me too." She looked at the poster and sighed. "But getting back to the problem. It ain't right, Morrie. People got to live and work safe. If we don't stop the Mob now, they're gonna be like a pig that gets fatter and fatter until he blows up. I need a good photo." She picked up her phone and flipped through the several hundred pictures she'd taken of Pierre.

"Pigs don't blow up, Carla, but you're right on the other things. I was really hoping we'd left it all behind, but they just won't let it go. They've burned us out, and they will come here to collect, sooner than later, now that they've made their point." Morrie was fighting an internal battle, torn between protecting Carla at all costs and knowing it wouldn't be possible without fighting back. "All right," he said, closing his computer. "We'll stay here at the studio for a bit. We didn't choose this war, but if we're being forced to fight it, then we will."

"How?" Carla said.

"We start by figuring out what territory the Mob wants and why they want it."

"Two places ain't a whole lot to go on," Carla said, still searching for the right picture. "Here's a good one. Pierre's at the park, surveying his domain." She touched the photo and sighed. She scanned it, loaded the printer, and printed off a dozen sheets.

Morrie reached for the rest of his cookie, then realized he'd already finished it. "I'm hungry. I'll make some stops and see what I can find out. Two fires is a start, and we've got to start somewhere." He checked Carla's poster. "Better add your cell number if you want people to be able to call you."

"Oh crap. I didn't want to give out too much information, but I need that. Thanks." She added the number and gathered up her posters. "I'll be back later this afternoon. Maybe I'll find out something."

"Just be careful. You know how you get."

"I want my dog back."

"I want *you* back. Don't go doing some side-investigating without me." He took his keys from the hook near the door. "Why don't you call Gino and Francesca, while you're on your mission, and invite us over for dinner. We need some brainstorming." He cracked his knuckles. "Feels like old times."

"Feels like trouble."

***

The morning fog that had blanketed San Francisco had burned off, and for the next few hours, until it rolled in again from the Pacific, the skies would be clear and the air warm. It wouldn't last, though, Carla was thinking as she schlepped her *Lost Dog* posters down Union Street. Nothing lasts. Especially the good stuff. She shook off the feeling and continued her trek.

Yellow police tape cordoned off the area where the fire had raged last night. The shops on both sides were closed. Signs on the doors said they'd reopen soon, but with all the heat and smoke damage, *soon* was going to turn into *later*, if ever. She peeked through the window of *Wholly Cow*, the ice cream shop that made the best sundaes in the world, and wondered how much damage they'd taken. The whole area was a black, sodden mess and a team of investigators were sifting through the ashes looking for whatever they could find to either chalk the fire up to an accident or determine it was arson. It didn't seem possible the site could possibly yield anything. There was nothing left. She took a deep breath and moved on, the posters clenched in her hand.

# CHAPTER TWO

*Castel del Mare, Sardinia*

"Do they even make double beds anymore?" Gino was standing in the doorway, eyeing his childhood bed with a critical eye and going through some mental calculations. He concluded it was going to be a tight fit. Confirmation of that would require some hands-on experimentation.

Francesca, already snuggled down under the covers, patted the mattress. "We'll just have to stay close, then. You planning on spending the night on the threshold?" She gave him a come-hither look that signaled the conversation was over.

This time, everything was different. The last time Gino'd made the trip back to his grandfather's estate on the island of Sardinia, nothing had been certain. He'd been dead broke—worse than dead broke. He'd owed the casino an obscene amount of money. It was almost laughable. He'd never be able to pay it off, and he'd steeled himself for the expected lecture, but it never came. What he'd gotten instead was his grandfather's dying request to begin a vendetta against the Mafia, locate a missing diary, and ensure that the old man's legacy as a master forger remained unsullied through eternity. It seemed a fair enough exchange, given that Gino would probably not have lived another week, the way things were going. And, all things considered, it also bolstered his sense of self-worth.

Yes, he was skilled at cards, but he had a gambling problem. He'd come to terms with that. It was a moral weakness. His grandfather, on the other hand, was an international art forger who had become a multimillionaire in the course of plying his trade. That stretched the definition of moral weakness way past the breaking point. His grandfather was a world-class criminal. Truth be known, he'd even stolen the name of Angelo DeMontana's estate and made it his own: *Castel del Mare.* It was a case of the student outshining the teacher. DeMontana had taught him well.

The scales were definitely weighted in Gino's favor on that account, but there was never any question that he'd follow through on his promise. And he did. His grandfather died a happy man, if there could be such a thing, and Gino inherited everything. Every single thing. The art. The estate. The fortune. Plus, he'd met Francesca Kim, along the way, and none of the rest would have meant much without her. She hadn't cared that he was short and insecure and pledged to carry out a vendetta. And she lit a spark that grew until it consumed him. She was slender with short black hair that framed her face, dark eyes that held a promise of love, and a smile that found its way into his heart. And now, tonight, he and Francesca were back where it had all begun, very much in love, married the past three months, and using the bed in a way it had never been used before. Turned out there was more than enough room.

***

With the two hour and fifty-five minute layover at Charles DeGaulle added to the actual flight time, Gino and Francesca were three hours shy of an entire day spent traveling. That, combined with the total lack of sleep due to matters of their own device, meant they'd required serious amounts of high-octane coffee at breakfast.

"You are awake," was Celestina's greeting. She patted Gino's cheek with one hand while setting the coffee pot on the dining room table with the other. Then it was Francesca's turn, and Celestina kissed her on the cheek. There was bread and jam and fruit on the table, and she hovered, encouraging them to eat as if they'd needed any encouragement.

"Sit, Celestina," Gino said, and she obliged, her knees creaking as she lowered herself into her chair—the one closest to the kitchen. Housekeeper and cook, but most importantly, the one who'd raised him, Celestina was a small woman but she ran the estate with an iron hand. The black dress she wore seemed to hang more loosely on her spare frame this year, and she was moving more slowly. How old was she now? Probably close to eighty. He caught her staring at him, reading his mind as she always could.

"Eat. Drink," was all she said.

"This coffee pot holds enough for the Vatican." Gino hefted the container and filled their cups.

"Funny you should say that," Francesca said, reaching for her cup. "Vatican, I mean. I read an interesting fact on the flight. Did you know that Vatican City consumes more wine per capita per year than the entire rest of the world? Seventy-four bottles. Seventy-four! Per person!"

"Religion must make them thirsty," Gino said, "or else they need to drink to get religion off their minds."

"Gino!" Celestina's disapproving look was a bolt of lightning dispatched from heaven.

Gino busied himself with the cereal. "Sorry, Celestina."

While Gino tried to regain Celestina's favor, Francesca took a swallow of coffee, still considering the import of what she'd come across. "Where does all that wine come from? I'm serious, Gino. Don't say grapes. I mean who are the suppliers?" She set the cup down and leaned back in her chair. "I've spent the last year learning everything I can about *Castel del Mare*. It's one of the suppliers, but it's not a major one. Why not? That's the first question, but it's not the most important one. How do we get to be one of them? That's what we need to find out. I think we're looking at some possibilities for expansion here."

"And Communion," Gino said and grinned at Francesca's confusion. "How much wine does the Vatican use during Communion on an annual basis? Could be some possibilities for getting a market share."

With the conversation shifting to business, and with her charges well supplied with food, Celestina took her coffee cup and retired to her room, giving Gino one last pat on the cheek, her gesture of forgiveness.

***

"What do you want to do?" Gino asked.

Francesca studied his face over the rim of her coffee cup. She tilted her head, trying to decipher his meaning and come up with the right answer. She set the cup down, cradling it with both hands, and took the safe option. "What do *you* want to do?"

Gino didn't answer immediately. He pushed his chair back, walked to the window, and stood, hands clasped behind his back. "I don't know. It's like I'm two different people. I'm one person here, and I'm somebody else back home in California." He turned to her and shrugged. "But this is also my home. It's not possible to be in two places at once and live two different lives. This past year, settling all that had to be done with Papa's estate has been tough. You know it as well as I do." He ran his hands through his hair, finally returning to the table and falling heavily into his chair. "Now, all this is ours. What the hell do we do with it?"

"You can't go home again," Francesca said. "That's not my line. It's a universal truth. You left *Castel del Mare* once. It hasn't changed, Gino. *You* have. You repaid Papa. Don't forget that. You get to make your own life wherever you want. This was Papa's dream. If it's yours too, I'm fine with that. But if it's just a responsibility, then the choice gets easier. If *Dark Mountain* is your dream, then that's where we belong." She filled her bowl with orange wedges and grapes. "We don't have to make a final decision now. Set up the caretakers and estate management team. There's plenty of money for that. Maybe five or ten years down the road—maybe longer— who knows? Meanwhile, we can flit back and forth as the fancy or need takes us. It's what the wealthy do. And we're wealthy. Really, really wealthy. I still can't believe it." She laughed and pulled a face that brought him out of the dark place his mind had been. In the silence that followed, Francesca could almost sense the weight of indecision falling away from his shoulders.

"I love you. God knows why you settled on me, but I will love you as long as I have breath. You could have had anybody. Why did you choose me?"

Francesca's eyes danced. "I love you. I've always loved Italian men. You are such romantics. It's that, among other things. You're handsome. That black, curly hair, those dark eyes. Anyway, I loved you when you were poor. Actually, you were far beyond poor, but that's part of your charm. Loving you now that you're a gazillionaire just makes it more interesting."

"I'm short."

"So was Sinatra. You're proportional. You're compact and you move with the grace of an athlete."

"Carla's the athlete of the family. She's the dancer. Plus, she's tall."

Francesca nodded. "She almost looks Irish, with that fair skin. You wouldn't know she was Italian to look at her."

"You would as soon as she opened her mouth," Gino said, and Francesca gave him a look.

Francesca reached for the last roll and slathered jam on top of it. "And who knows? Maybe our children will want to work the *Dark Mountain* vineyard when we've decided it's time to pack up and move back to Italy. We won't need to go house-hunting. We'll already have our home waiting for us. You see, it's perfect."

This time, the silence lasted a bit longer, and Gino's expression was difficult to read. "Celestina won't be here. Our children won't know her," he said, considering what this meant. "It's going to take twenty years at least for any children to be old enough to take over. Maybe even twenty-five." He shook his head. "We should have gotten started on that already if it's ever going to happen."

Francesca took a nibble of her roll. She added a bit more jam. "Gino, we've been married three months. These things take time, but don't worry. You've forgotten that you married an event planner. It's already in the works." She popped the rest of the roll into her mouth, brushing the crumbs from her lips. "We're here all week. Should be just enough time to get the wheels in motion to meet that twenty-year goal. And we don't have to wait twenty years to bring the children here for Celestina to spoil. They can come as *bambinos.*" She gave Gino a lascivious wink.

The future beckoned. The sun was streaming through the open windows, and the air smelled like autumn—spicy and mellow and heavy with the aroma of ripened grapes on the vines, waiting for the harvest that would happen this week. But then, a cloud passed in front of the sun at the exact moment the doorbell rang. It was only a moment later when Celestina burst into the kitchen.

"They're here! Gino! Come, please. They won't wait long before they..."

Gino set down his coffee cup and stared at her. Nothing fazed Celestina. Nothing. But it was obvious that something was out of whack. "Who is here?"

She spat on the floor, then frowned, realizing she'd need to clean it up. "*Them.*"

Gino's memory recall was a weakness he'd been trying to address through his latest online course, *Put Your Mind to Work,* and it only took a moment until something from his childhood surfaced. The autumn collection. The *pizzo.* The annual visit from the Mafia to claim their protection money that ensured the vineyards wouldn't be burned and the bottles smashed in the storeroom. He felt sick. Nothing had changed. Nothing ever changed in Italy. It just went underground, emerging from time to time like a hungry wolf from its lair. He hauled himself out of his chair and motioned for Celestina to sit down. "I'll see to it, Celestina. You stay here with Francesca. If I'm not back in five minutes, take her out the back door and find Aldo. Stay with him."

***

The two men at the front door were polite, even deferential as they expressed their condolences on the passing of Gino's grandfather. The spokesman was clear in his instructions. As a sign of respect, given that the period of mourning would end on the 30th of the month, a courier would be dispatched to collect the annual payment of 25,000 Euros on that day. No checks. No American currency. And no receipt would be forthcoming. The entire visit lasted less than five minutes, and when Gino closed the door firmly behind the callers and returned to the kitchen, he found Francesca and Celestina seated at the kitchen table, holding hands.

"What do we do, Gino?" Francesca asked.

"This is Italy. We do the only thing we can do. In one week, we pay them," he said. "It's just another cost of doing business. Once we pay, we're safe for another year."

Francesca's face reddened and her breathing quickened. She threw her arms into the air. "There's got to be something we can do about it, Gino."

"What? You want to call the police?" He laughed, but there was no mirth in it. "They run the police here. It's an old and venerable institution, extortion. But the Vincento Family has its own set of skewed ethics. Nobody, and I mean nobody who wants to keep on living is going to do as much as throw a piece of litter on the road in front of the estate. We are, for want of a better word, *protected*."

"You're serious."

"Dead serious. And now, I'm going to go and inspect our *protected* vineyards and take some inventory. If we're going to increase production and our market share, we'll need to make some improvements."

Francesca released her grip on Celestina's hand. "All right. But won't that increase our bill to them?"

"Without a doubt. We'll just need to make enough profit to make the venture worthwhile."

***

The estate of *Castel del Mare* encompassed over three hundred and sixty hectares, spreading across the terraced hillsides and extending down to the shoreline of the Tyrrhenian Sea. Thirty of those hectares were dedicated to vineyards producing some of the finest Cannonau wines in the world. This morning, Gino walked along the path in the shade of olive trees planted over half a century ago to his meeting with Aldo Borghese, Celestina's son and manager of the vineyards, along with the rest of the estate. The topic under consideration was a proposed vineyard in a different 10 hectare section on the hillside, where the soils were chalkier. The grapes to be grown there would produce a different wine, although the variety would remain the same. It all came down to *terroir*, the all-encompassing determiner of a wine's quality.

Terroir is soil, topography, elevation, microclimate—working separately and in combination to impart a unique character and complexity to the wines made from the grapes grown in a particular area. Cannonau has hints of plum, ripe berries—including cranberry—and spice. Terroir has the final say when the bottle is uncorked and the wine is tasted.

Gino was weighing the considerable expense involved against the possibility of success, along with the risk. But, he reasoned, there is risk in every venture. Aldo had sent a soil sample to the lab, and the analysis was on the paper Gino was now studying.

To describe Aldo as a man of few words would be doing the man a disservice. Aldo kept a private council and spoke only as a last resort, a decidedly non-Italian trait, but then, there was something of the Roma about him. His mere presence was intimidating to anyone threatening harm and reassuring to those he trusted and who turned to him for help. At a good three inches over six feet in height and weighing in the vicinity of three hundred pounds, two hundred of which were solid muscle, he really didn't have to say much to get his point across. While Gino read the report, Aldo waited.

"What do you think?" Gino finally asked, folding the paper and stuffing it in his pocket. "Should we proceed?"

Aldo obliged with his usual economy of words. *"Si, signore."*

"Then, we shall. Pay the usual wages to the workmen. Keep me updated. I'll be leaving next week. I'll stop by before I go."

Aldo's lips separated in what Gino took for a smile, and then he left. There was nothing more to say, and there was much work to be done.

# CHAPTER THREE

*San Francisco*

There are over 4,500 restaurants in San Francisco, and Morrie Landow had eaten at his share of them over the last several years. They came and went, and only the best managed to beat the odds and settle in for the long haul. *Seoul Food* down in Cow Hollow was one of those that had prospered. Owned by Chan Young Boucher, who was also the chef, *Seoul Food* was Asian/European fusion taken to the limit. The menu changed according to Boucher's mood. Today, he appeared conflicted. The lunch special was fish served over angel hair pasta. It was spicy, Morrie noted. One nod to the Korean side of Boucher, but the rest of him was French, so even if pasta had its origins in the Orient, Italy had claimed it a long time ago. Still, it was good. Better than good, actually. Chan Boucher was an artist whose medium was food. Didn't matter what he started out with. The result was always something exceptional.

"You having some kind of identity crisis?" Morrie's chopsticks circled over the pasta, searching for the best landing spot.

"Nah. I'm a hybrid. That takes the pressure off." Chan untied his apron and tossed it over the back of the counter. He'd inherited his father's height, but the body was all his own. Determined to defy stereotypes, he'd lifted, worked out, done the supplement route, and generally become the poster child for body building. The only thing that hadn't come along for the ride was his hair. He was bald as a baby's behind. He was all muscle and generally all business, but when he smiled, you got a glimpse of somebody you knew you'd like. If you didn't cross him. At the moment, however, Chan was studying Morrie's plate with a critical eye. "You know, not all Korean food is hot."

Morrie looked up, having managed to snag a fair amount of pasta with his chopsticks. "Yes, it is. If it isn't, it should be."

"Perhaps. What brings you to my humble establishment this time? Carla lock you out of the house? No. That can't be it. Your house burned down. Making any headway with the insurance people? Where are you living, by the way?" Chan pulled out a chair and sat. The lunch crowd was done, and it would be a good three hours until the next wave hit. Still, if there were matters to be discussed that didn't need to be overheard by anyone either late for lunch or early for dinner, precautions would be in order. He got up and flipped the *Open* sign around to *Closed*, set the sign back in place, and lowered the shades. "Anyone who wants food will have to pick it up at the mobile order window," he said, returning to Morrie who was still struggling with his lunch.

"It is not possible to have both pasta and fish on chopsticks at the same time," Morrie said, dropping the wooden sticks back on his plate with some force.

"Is that a dare?" Chan picked up the chopsticks, twirled them through the pasta, and stabbed a piece of fish that somehow floated above the pasta and came to rest snug and secure. "Here. Try this. The fork doesn't become you."

"All right. What's the trick?"

"No trick. You must believe it is possible. Then it will be."

Morrie shook his head. "You are full of shit, Chan. You know that?"

Chan laughed. "I got lucky. You're right. The fork is probably your best bet. Hold on. I'll get myself some lunch and join you. I've been running on caffeine all morning. Then you can tell me what's going on."

Morrie paused in his chewing. "Bring two plates. I asked RP to join us."

Chan nodded. "Another meeting of the Bald-Headed League? All right. I'll bring three. RP's got an appetite to match yours."

"And forks!" Morrie called after him.

***

It usually took upwards of six months to get new construction through P&Z, but it was only a day shy of two weeks from the fire until the lot that held both *Harry Lai's Superior Dry Cleaning* and Carla and Morrie's apartment was cleaned up and construction materials stacked at the rear. It had raised a few eyebrows and more than a few questions, but the answers were buried deep in the paperwork, and one could only hazard a guess as to how this miracle had come about.

"As a further item of interest," Morrie said, "the same scenario is playing out on Russian Hill at the burn site of *Olga's Bakery*."

"Somebody's got a shitload of influence and two shitloads of money," RP said, having arrived with his legendary appetite and who was now attacking his second lunch plate. "Any wagers on who it is?"

"Unlike most Asians, I do not gamble," Chan said, "except when it's a sure thing. Then it's no gamble at all. But it's the old man—Enzo Puglisi. He and another suit were there this morning checking things out. Looks like I'm getting new neighbors and there's going to be more trouble. The permit is for a shoe store. It's going to be the same type they've got on Santana Row in San Jose. You know what I mean. A minimalist operation. There's one pair of obscenely priced shoes in the window. The interior consists of nothing but one botoxed woman in a designer suit sitting at a desk, looking bored, waiting for the customers that don't come. If they do brave entry, she informs them everything is on back order and thanks them for coming in. The one in Russian Hill will be a hat store. Same deal."

Morrie set his fork down and pushed his empty plate aside. "So, it's a front for money laundering. Puglisi charges himself rent, makes the deposit in the bank, and the tax man looks away. It's also a good setup to keep an eye on the shopkeepers and make sure everybody toes the line and there's no trouble," Morrie said. "There *is* going to be trouble, but this time we're going to be the ones initiating it. Puglisi and his Mafia goons are not welcome here, and if things fall into place, we'll get them gone for good."

"Covert Ops again," RP said. "I miss the old days."

"Speak for yourself, amigo," Chan said. "I was on the other side of that operation, remember?"

Morrie grinned. "All in the past. Besides, you made an impressive escape. A pity you couldn't take the jewels with you."

"Who says I didn't?"

"Stop!" RP threw his hands in the air. "When you two get started, there's no end to it. You can reminisce when you're racing your golf carts at some senior living facility if I haven't killed the both of you beforehand."

"Point taken," Morrie said. He winked at Chan. "Our Black Brother has taken us to school."

"Mocha," RP said, continuing to eat and not looking up from his plate. "Mocha Man. Just because I'm not a behemoth like you two, don't discount my abilities." He tapped the side of his head. "Brain power is my forte. Basketball is highly overrated as a skill set."

"Can we get back on track here?" Morrie said. "Puglisi or someone in the family is sending soldiers around to enroll each Cow Hollow business in this new protection racket. Harry and Olga opted out. They didn't understand opting out wasn't an option. So, they became object lessons for the other business owners." He picked up his water glass and set it back down. "You got any decent liquor? Plotting always gives me a thirst."

Chan set off for the back room, returning with a bottle of Jack and three glasses. "Private stock," he said.

"Ice?" Morrie asked.

"No way. You some sort of barbarian? You'd never make it in Europe or Asia. Shit. All right. All right. Ice." Chan turned on his heel and returned with a bowl of cubes in hand and a look of utter disgust on his face. After pouring the drinks and raising a toast to fallen comrades, the work began. After the second round, the plan began to coalesce.

"Any shopkeeper who wants to make a living and keep on living will be forced to ante up when the collectors come around," Morrie said. "Carla and I were hashing out some possibilities, but nothing seemed viable. I said it was going to be difficult, but she said, 'Nope. Piece of cake. They got soldiers. We get soldiers. If we can get the shopkeepers to let us know as soon as those goons step inside the door, we can have our soldiers take them out. It's all about timing. We just gotta be there before the goons leave. You figure out that part. So, go collect some of your SEAL buddies and let's get this done.' Then, she sat back and waited for me to make it happen."

"Their soldiers never return to base," Chan said, mulling over the idea. "Interesting. Somewhere along the way, they disappear. Over and over again. Huh."

"But as far as the *you figure it out* part goes," Morrie said, taking a drink of his satisfactorily cold Jack, "I haven't."

"We'll need to be close enough to take them out," RP said. "That's easy. Puglisi has plans for a base of operations across the street. We've already got one." He waved his fork around the restaurant. "Here would be good. We're centrally located. That's a plus. People come and go, which is an additional benefit. Nobody is going to look twice at somebody entering or leaving a restaurant. We'll have our command center upstairs." He returned the fork to attend to the last few morsels on his plate.

Morrie leaned forward, poured one last round, and toasted Chan. "Thanks for the loan of your office, my friend."

"I never loaned you my office. You commandeered it," Chan said, accepting the refill.

"Same thing." Morrie picked up his glass. The ice cubes clinked and Chan winced.

There was silence while they drank, thought, and drank some more. Finally, RP said, "Bracelets."

"You want to expand on that, friend?" Chan said.

"Yeah. We were talking command center. The function of a command center is coordination. Right?" RP shrugged. "The shopkeepers need to be able to tell the command center when they get a visit from Puglisi's soldiers. So, we give them plastic wristlets like you get as proof of admission to concerts and the like." He pointed at his wrist. "The bracelets will have a computer chip embedded that's activated by a button that will transmit a signal with their precise location back to headquarters. We dispatch our soldiers, and," he drained the contents of his glass, "that's all there is to it."

Morrie and Chan exchanged looks. "Soon as RP gets the bracelets made up, we're in business," Morrie said.

RP nodded. "Give me twenty-four hours. The wireless setup won't take long. Whoever gets the pleasure of the Mafia's next visit won't have to do anything but push a little button."

"What about cleanup?" Morrie said. "We don't know how many we're going to be dealing with, but I suspect somewhere in the neighborhood of a dozen before they back off to regroup. The operative word here is *disappear.* So, how do you want to handle disposal?"

A smile spread across Chan's face. "I'll handle it," he said. "Trust me. That's not going to be the tough part. These folks in the neighborhood are scared. They're scared of what will happen if they don't pay. They're scared of what will happen if they don't make enough money to pay. They're just flat out scared shitless and don't see any way out of this. Convincing them to trust us is going to be the biggest obstacle."

Morrie agreed. "All very true. But you're forgetting the key element to this whole operation, and the one reason why they're going to trust us and why the plan is going to work."

It only took a few seconds for the answer to pop into their collective brain. With nods all around, they uttered the magic word: *Carla.*

***

"Come again? I'm walking up and down the main drag in Cow Hollow handing out magic decoder bracelets and convincing everybody they should wear them twenty-four-seven?" Carla stared at Morrie as if he'd lost the last operating marble in his brain. "This time. Slow. This better not go a whole ten rounds," Carla said. "I ain't gonna live that long."

"Actually, technically, they're more like magic *transmitter* bracelets, but yeah. That's it! It's going to work, Carla. But we need you. People listen to you. You've got the gift."

Carla did one of those long, slow head shakes—the kind that says much more than words. "If I remember right, my idea was for you to get soldiers—your Navy Seal buddies—to whack their soldiers until there weren't any more of them, and we won. What does that have to do with peddling bracelets?"

"First, you're not peddling anything. They're free," Morrie said.

"That don't matter. People get suspicious. *Especially*, if something's free." Carla sat, elbows on the table, chin resting on her clenched fists. "Start at the beginning."

"All right." He cleared his throat. "We've got soldiers. We've got me and RP for starters and can put the call out to the rest of the Unit, if necessary. We've got Boucher and his *associates*, as he calls them. So," Morrie did some mental calculations, "safely in the neighborhood of fifteen-twenty guys if we need them." He studied Carla's eyes, gauging how this was going. Her eyes were closed. No help there, so he moved on.

"Chan's office above the restaurant will be our headquarters. RP's installing whatever wireless equipment we'll need to receive the signals transmitted from these bracelets." Morrie picked one up for demonstration purposes. Fortunately, Carla had opened her eyes, so it was a good move. She took the bracelet from his hand and gave it the onceover.

"This is like those things they give you when you go to the hospital or whatever. I don't get it."

"Look closely. See that little dot on the band? It's the transmitter, and each bracelet is coded differently. When that dot is pressed, a signal is transmitted to Chan's office. The receiver tells us the exact location where the signal is coming from. It's simple, and simple is always best. Immediately, Chan dispatches two of his associates to the location to neutralize the goons and dispose of them." Morrie, done with sitting on the undersized chair, pushed it back and stood.

"I get it," Carla said, "but what about the disposal part? We gonna whack them and then what?"

Morrie's expression could only be described as cryptic. With his lips pressed together and his eyes twinkling, he dared Carla to figure out the rest.

"The goons ain't dead?"

"Nope."

"They ain't gonna whack 'em?"

"Nope."

"Then what the hell good is that? What the hell they gonna do with them? Throw them in the bay?"

"Kind of."

When Carla's brain got to working, it went into overdrive on a regular basis. Now, with a few puzzle pieces to work on, she pursed her lips and frowned. "One clue," she said.

"HCB."

"Huh? That ain't much of a clue. What does Chan's other business have to do with it? I thought his brother handled the shipping company?"

"Technically, yes. That's just for the paperwork. Chan is the senior partner of Him Chan Boucher, HCB, according to the logo, and world leader in the container shipping industry. Funny thing about most businesses these days, though. It's so difficult to recruit and keep good employees. Or bad employees, for that matter. I like to think of us as running a profitable sideline—you know, outsourcing employees to the maritime industry." Morrie held up another bracelet. "Those container ships take weeks, maybe months to get where they're going. Plenty of time to learn an honest trade or die trying. Although fluency in Korean would be an asset. Anyway, that's not our concern. Puglisi's soldiers are gone for good."

Carla burst out laughing. "You are a genius."

"Is that why you married me?"

Carla just shook her head. "I love you, Morrie."

"And I love you, Miss Marie. Now, will you schlepp these bracelets? Time is the enemy and we need to get moving on this."

"Understood. I'll go talk to Triz tomorrow morning. She'll come with me. A familiar face will help sell the product." Carla paused, thoughtful. "But not to Cesar. I don't trust him. There's something wrong about him."

If Morrie knew one thing, he knew Carla's read on people was to be taken seriously. If she said Cesar's shop was off the list, it was off the list. "You're the boss of bracelets," he said.

Carla slipped a bracelet on her wrist. "I'm giving one to everybody I meet who might need one, and I'm going to be my own first customer. Once we get this hornet's nest cleaned out and we find a new home, all our troubles will be over."

# CHAPTER FOUR

*New Haven and Environs*

*The Pussycat Club*, one of Dixwell Avenue's less-than-legit establishments, had undergone gentrification since Sally "The Pipe" Puglisi's unsolved disappearance last fall. It had an upscale new name—*The Pleasure Valley Gentlemen's Club*—a fresh coat of lavender paint that covered up the faded pink, and proudly displayed its dress code. For the dancers, it didn't mean much. The Family had efficiently dealt with the necessary personnel changes during the transition phase. Police investigations had come and gone with no damage, and business was picking up—so much so that Joey "Iceman" Vincento, husband of Fiona Puglisi Vincento, was considering expansion opportunities while he waited at the traffic light at the corner of Norton and Whalley. For Joey, however, the red light never changed to green. It just blacked out.

***

"There ain't no continuity anymore," Nanette grumbled, applying some concealer to a zit that had appeared overnight on her chin. She leaned back and studied the effect in the cracked mirror, then she turned her attention to the leather belt that, along with the G-string, comprised her entire costume.

"Yeah. Well, we've got nothing to do with anything. Just be glad you've got a job," Ginger said. "Besides, tips are way better now since the new dress code."

Nanette eyed her friend. "Honey, we don't have a dress code. To have a dress code, you first have to have a dress. This belt is an accessory."

Ginger drummed her fingers on the plastic counter top. "I got a bad feeling. Don't go out there tonight."

"What are you talking? Don't go out there? How am I gonna make any money sitting in here? You're losing it, Ginger. Get a grip. We got the VIP room tonight, and that means a shitload of money. You need to put your book down and stop studying that real estate stuff. We're late."

"All right. Just give me a minute. The exam is next week and I'm not ready."

"Get ready!" Nanette twisted to get a side view and then pushed through the frayed curtain that served as the door to the girl's dressing room. She was gone all of five seconds before she bolted back through the curtain, panic in her eyes. "Oh my God! Oh my God! Dear Jesus! Sweet Mother Mary!"

"What? What?" Ginger spun around on the stool. "What happened?"

"Don't go out there! We gotta get out of here. Now!" She grabbed her robe from the hook on the wall by her station and pulled Ginger to her feet. They grabbed their pocketbooks, sprinted from the dressing room, through the curtain, down the hall, through the manager's open door, across the office, and out the back door that opened onto the alley that ran parallel to Dixwell Avenue and joined Webster a third of the way down the block.

Pausing for breath, Ginger shot a look back in the direction they'd come and then whipped around to face Nanette. "What the hell was that all about?" she gasped.

All Nanette could manage were a few gasps and sputters before bending over and waving her arms about like a human windmill. She held that position for a brief minute, then straightened. "Come on, we got to go!" She grabbed Ginger's hand and they ducked under a broken chain link fence guarding a back yard filled with junk cars and scrap metal. Crouching beside a rusted Cadillac chassis, they scoped out their surroundings, searching for an escape route, while Nanette filled in the details.

"You know, it don't hardly take any time at all to whack somebody. You'd think that going from being alive to being dead would take longer. Anyhow, before I even got to the floor to put my music on, in comes Eddie 'The Weasel' and three other goons. He raises a piece at Prospero and two other guys I didn't recognize at the back table. Then, next thing, they're on the floor and there's blood everywhere."

Ginger's eyes were fixed on the alley beyond the fence. "That's what you said. There's just no continuity. Did they see you?"

"No. Maybe. Dunno. Yeah, pretty sure. Not taking any chances. Don't matter. I saw them. Eddie's hard to miss. He got those beady eyes and that red nose like a drunk Santa. He was looking around, but I ducked back. I don't know where they are now." Nanette startled as a shadow appeared in the circle of light cast by the streetlight. Straining to make out the shape, she sucked in a breath when she recognized who it was. She slipped over to the hole in the fence. "Psst! Tommy!"

Tommaso Puglisi, newly appointed business manager of *The Pleasure Valley Gentleman's Club* and Nanette's current man of interest, stopped at the sound of his name.

"Psst!" Nanette repeated in a hoarse whisper. "Over here!"

"What the hell are you doing there?" Tommy said, having located the source of the sound. "You're supposed to be on stage."

"Uh," Nanette said. "There'd have to be somebody alive first who'd be able to watch my set. Nobody back there fits that description. We got to get out of here. That private party we were entertaining tonight? The whole place is a bloodbath," she said. "Your uncle Prospero is dead. And the guys with him, too. Don't go in! Eddie could still be there."

Tommy's eyes narrowed. "Eddie?"

Ginger had joined Nanette at the fence and was scanning the alley. "Silencers. They must have used them. Didn't want a lot of noise, just a shitload of corpses." She turned back to her companions. "Looks clear to me. Where you parked, Tommy?"

"Sonny's lot." He looked from Nanette to Ginger and then back again. "You sure about all this?"

"Is the Pope Italian?" Nanette said. "Tommy, don't go in there. They're gonna kill us too."

"Uh, Nan, the Pope...Never mind," Ginger said. "Let's go." She tightened the belt on her fluffy pink robe and pushed through the fence. It was three blocks to Sonny's lot on Webster. Tommy set a fast pace and the girls struggled to keep up—Nanette, because she was pint-size and her legs couldn't cover the same amount of ground as fast as the others, and Ginger, because the four-inch heels she was wearing were doing a number on her feet.

"Now what?" Ginger asked, falling into the back seat on the driver's side. She kicked off the black stilettos and massaged her sore feet. "We can't go anywhere dressed like this."

"I should have been there," Tommaso said, his voice grim. "If I hadn't stopped to get gas, I would have been there."

Nanette reached over and rested her hand on his. "You weren't. That's all that matters."

"It matters, but it's not all that matters," he said. "We need a plan. If the family is splintering, there's no telling who's going to come out on top and who's going to be out of the picture. Right now, I don't know where I stand, and I'm not hanging around to find out." He glanced at the briefcase he'd jammed between Nanette's seat and the console. "Everything I need to know is in there."

"Why can't you people have normal arguments?" Ginger asked. "You know, yell, punch. No. You got to whack each other and make a hell of a mess."

"She doesn't mean you personally," Nanette said, glaring at Ginger.

"Yes, I do," Ginger shot back.

"Enough!" Tommaso clapped his hands over his ears. "I've got to stop at the house, call Gennaro, and get a couple of things. There's a place out in Woodbridge we can go to sort this out." He turned to Nanette. "We'll be safe there."

It was a short, silent ride to West Haven. Nanette shifted her weight frequently and winced with each pothole they encountered. Ginger, seated behind Tommaso, regretted her outburst and leaned forward to rest her hand on Nanette's shoulder. It had been a case of fight or flight, and they'd fled. But now what? If they couldn't get out of this situation, nobody would come looking for them. Nobody would miss them. Ginger felt a stab of regret. Hell, she was so alone, she didn't even own a cat. She fought back a sob.

Ignoring his driveway, Tommy pulled up to the curb. "I'll be quick," he promised and raced up the walk to his front door, but quick turned into not so quick.

"What's taking him so long?" Nanette stared at the house. Tommy hadn't turned on the lights, so she couldn't see a thing. "I gotta pee. I mean I *really* gotta pee." She squirmed in her seat, emphasizing her distress.

Ginger, scrolling through her cell for messages, ignored her friend's not so subtle hints. "Here's something to cap a delightful evening," she said. "One more hit. We don't got a boss no more. Joey got whacked tonight, too." She skimmed the headline. "On Whalley. Cameras got both vehicles."

"I just want to go home. But I gotta *go.*"

"Home is not a good option if you enjoy living. Get out and take a leak behind the neighbor's hydrangea bush if you're that desperate. It's as big as a maple tree. Tommy's yard's so bare. Not a shrub or tree or anything. It's like a wasteland. Sure is taking him forever." Ginger leaned forward and then frowned. "*Why* is it taking him so long?"

"Don't know and don't care. I got other things on my mind at the moment."

Ginger sighed. "Here, I'll join you. Never pass up an opportunity, they say." She unfastened her seatbelt and was about to make a beeline for the vegetation when something clicked. Tommaso was never late to work. Except for tonight. It was always business as usual at the Club. Except for tonight. He had conveniently been absent, only showing up after the hit. She and Nan should have been doing lap dances for Prospero and his *goombahs.* Except for tonight. She'd had that feeling, and Nan had spent just enough time trying to talk her out of it. They were supposed to be out there. She gave herself a mental head slap, and her eyes lit on the briefcase. "Nan, move it. Now! Grab your pocketbook and the briefcase. There's no time!"

Nanette didn't ask questions. The two girls made a beeline for the hydrangea bush, throwing themselves on the ground just as a black Jeep Cherokee with tinted windows and no plates turned the corner and pulled up behind Tommaso's Toyota.

Nanette raised her head to see what was happening, and Ginger pulled her back by her hair. "Lie still," she said and did a sharp intake of breath when she saw the driver get out. Eddie. She didn't recognize the two other men. Approaching the Toyota from the rear, his companions fanned out and yanked the doors open, while Eddie checked the trunk. Nanette whimpered, and the sound carried in the still night air. Eddie turned and looked across the street, but all he saw was a cat emerging from a garbage can laying on its side at the curb. The men engaged in a heated discussion, and finally, Eddie pulled out his cell and made a call. The three men returned to their own vehicle and sped away into the night.

"You have got to do something about your taste in men," Ginger mumbled to Nanette through clenched teeth. The ground was hard, sticks and small pebbles and the larger rocks that formed the border for the bush were grinding into her. Nanette, for once, had fallen silent.

Tommaso emerged from the house and stood on the sidewalk, his eyes sweeping the street. He turned to go back inside but then stopped abruptly and walked to the car. The next thing the girls heard was the sound of the driver's door slamming followed shortly by the roar of the engine as Tommaso took off down the street.

"Let's go," Nanette said. "He's gone, the bastard. We can't stay here all night." She started to lift herself into a sitting position but Ginger pushed her back down.

"Not yet."

"What do you mean, 'not yet'? We got to get out of here, and do...something."

"Shh. Not yet." As if on cue, the Toyota came around the corner and crept down the street.

"Don't move a muscle. Don't even breathe," Ginger said.

It took half of forever for Tommaso to pass by their hiding place and continue on down the street.

"He remembered about the briefcase. His one mistake. He's looking for us, and he's not going to give up any time soon. He knows we're here somewhere. Those other two are also probably searching for us."

"We're screwed," Nanette sniffled.

Ginger's attention was no longer on Nanette but fixed on a new vehicle making its laborious way down the street, stopping here and there before resuming its scheduled route. She smiled at Nanette. "Showtime," she said.

"You're not serious." Nanette's eyes flashed from Ginger to their target. "Oh hell, what have we got to lose?"

*Waste Collection and Recycling*, owned and operated by the Mob, has all sizes of collection vehicles that mostly do pickups at night. This specimen was a compact version of the behemoths that regularly serviced the main drags. As it inched its way towards them, Ginger and Nanette rose and shook out the twigs from their robes. Ginger selected a medium-sized rock while Nanette untied the belt on her robe. They made their move towards the driver who now stood on the sidewalk, his mouth hanging open, not believing his good fortune.

"Hi!" Nanette said, removing her robe.

Ginger approached, rock positioned to do its work. In a moment, the garbage man lay on the ground, out for the count. Ginger confiscated his cell from his jacket pocket. "Just in case he wakes up before we're far enough away," she said, "he won't be able to call anyone." She took his wallet for good measure. A few extra bucks never hurt. Nanette retied her robe, and the girls took off in their new wheels, garbage can dangling out the back.

"We need a plan," Ginger said, turning left onto Campbell Avenue. "Where are we going? We can't just drive around West Haven in a stolen garbage truck for the rest of our lives."

"At least we've got the rest of our lives," Nanette said. "So far. I can't believe my Tommy was gonna get us offed."

"Yeah. Well, don't beat yourself up about it. He's not worth it. I've made my share of rotten choices in that department. He just didn't want any witnesses, but he was so focused on finishing us off he got a little distracted. Good for us, though." She shot a quick look at the briefcase, now safely settled in its new surroundings on the floor by Nanette's feet. "That's our insurance policy. Tommaso said everything he knew was in there. Open it up and let's see what he knows."

Nanette slid the briefcase onto her lap and fiddled with the latches. "It's locked." She fished around in her pocketbook and produced a nail file. A little bit of finessing and the clasps sprang open. "Laptop. File folders filled with papers." She rifled through the case. "No money." She closed the case. "What's so important about papers?"

"Could be anything. It's going to have to wait, though. Right now, it's decision time. Where do you want to go?"

"I don't know. Some place safe. Some place warm." Then, inspiration hit. "Disneyland."

"Disneyland." Ginger pondered the choice. "Why not? It's as good a place as any. It's about as far away from New Haven as we can get, and it's warm in LA. All right. Disneyland it is. What time is it?"

Nanette checked her phone. "10 o'clock. Why?"

"There's only one place we can go shopping dressed like this and nobody will give us a second look. It closes at 11. We'll stop at the one in Stratford, get some clothes, a couple of backpacks, and some food. We should be at La Guardia before traffic picks up. We can dump the truck in long-term parking and get a flight. Check the schedules."

"On it."

***

Flying standby can be a hit or miss situation, but Ginger and Nanette snagged two tickets—one window, one aisle—in coach on Alaska's first flight out of La Guardia the next morning. The adrenaline rush was long gone, replaced by exhaustion, and they'd managed to get a few hours of shuteye in the waiting area. Now, aloft at 32,000 feet, their troubles seemed far, far away.

"You ever been to Disneyland?" Nanette asked.

"Nope. Always wanted to. Never thought this is how I'd get there." Ginger turned and grinned at Nanette. "I'm going to get a pair of those Mickey Mouse ears."

Nanette nodded. "Then what? I mean, after the ears and everything."

"I don't know. How much money you got?"

"Cash, maybe five hundred." To Ginger's raised eyebrow, she said, "I been keeping my tips in my pocketbook the past week. I meant to put them in the bank, but I didn't." She looked at Ginger. "That's one thing I did right. I got my credit card, but I'm almost maxed out on it. What about you?"

"About a hundred and fifty, give or take. I'm okay on the credit card for now."

"Wait a minute." Nanette rummaged through her bag once again, this time emerging with the garbage truck driver's wallet. Her lips moved as she counted the bills. "Eighty-seven bucks, but we can't use the credit cards. They'll trace 'em."

In the brief silence that ensued, both girls came to the same realization. Nanette voiced it first. "Maybe we better hold off on Disneyland until we get settled. Our money ain't gonna last long in California."

"Yeah. Just until we get settled. Then we'll go." Ginger's uncertain tone didn't mesh with the confidence of her words. Cold, harsh, frightening reality was setting in. "First things first. We'll get a cheap hotel room with a microwave and a fridge. That'll save us some cash. We need money. We need lots of money."

"Why does everything always come down to money?" Nanette said. "You can die without it. We gotta get work, but I ain't going back to dancing at none of those clubs. There's gotta be something else."

"No, you're right, besides, going from one arm of the Mob to another won't help our plans to keep on living. They've got a lock on the *industry*, as they call it." Ginger looked out the window and peered down at the clouds beneath them. "We don't have any wheels. That's all right. We'll find some place where we can get the bus." She unfastened her seatbelt. "Your turn for the window."

"I'm glad we ain't fat," Nanette said, as they made the seat exchange. "You ever notice how fat people are getting? That guy on the aisle up ahead's got two extenders for his seat belt. It ain't healthy." She curled her lip at the sight and shuddered. "Okay. Do they ride the bus in LA? All I've seen are those freeways with a million cars parked on them. Renting a car is going to seriously eat into our reserves. If we're careful, we've still only got enough cash for maybe a week." She frowned. "This is like going to some foreign country where you don't speak the language. They're gonna know we're not from there."

"I don't think anybody there is from there. We'll adapt. We just need to go slow and take notes. It'll be okay," Ginger said, but she couldn't mask the worry that was taking over. What had they gotten themselves into? "We're okay for now. But next time the flight attendant comes by, grab as many of those snacks as you can. We're going to need them."

Nanette nodded, already rearranging the contents of her pocketbook to make room for the groceries. By the time they touched down, her bag had gained a respectable pound and a half. If this would be breakfast, lunch, and dinner for the foreseeable future, finding employment was going to be Job One.

# CHAPTER FIVE

*New Haven*

Tommaso Puglisi, a mathematical genius fresh out of Boston College with an MBA, was grappling with an equation that made no sense. No matter how he arranged and rearranged the day's events, the conclusion remained the same. His brother had tried to kill him. First, Gennaro had texted him that they needed to meet for lunch at the Club. Then, he'd canceled that and said they'd have to meet that evening at 9 o'clock. He gave no explanation for the time change. Gennaro was not the most communicative person, but this was stretching the boundaries. When Tommaso texted him back, Gennaro's only reply had been a terse *Don't be late. And bring my briefcase.*

However, Tommaso had been late. He'd forgotten to get gas the day before, so he'd decided to swing by the gas station first. That would have made a difference of what? Ten minutes? It shouldn't have mattered, but if what Nanette and Ginger had told him were true, and he had no reason to doubt them, had he shown up at nine, instead of ten or quarter after, he'd have been one more body on the floor. It didn't take a mathematical genius to come to the conclusion that his brother had set him up. Right now, however, the girls were first priority. Tommaso shoved the laptop into his briefcase and snapped the locks closed. He didn't know yet why Gennaro wanted him dead, but there was one thing he did know. If anything happened to Nanette, he'd kill Gennaro with his bare hands.

Tommaso locked up the house, knowing it was a futile gesture, and returned to the car only to find it empty. Gennaro's briefcase was gone. Had Eddie taken the girls? Had Gennaro? God, this just got worse and worse. Tommaso called Nanette, but she didn't pick up. He slammed the passenger door shut and walked around the car, checking underneath, but nothing. And no one. He got in the car and drummed his hands on the steering wheel. The girls weren't dressed for traveling. They had to be somewhere nearby, hiding. What had scared them? Who had scared them, and where had they gone? He tried Nan's cell one more time. Nada.

Ten minutes later, after cruising the neighborhood, looking everywhere, he had to admit defeat. His next and last stop would be Nanette's apartment, although she'd most likely have had the sense not to go there. Still, it was all he had.

***

Nanette's walk-up on Wooster Street was an efficiency apartment. *Efficiency* was a realtor's term for not much room. There was a small kitchen, a living room the size of a clothes closet, and a bedroom of similar proportions, although roomy enough when they needed it. There weren't any lights on, but she'd be smart enough not to advertise her presence, if she were there. He walked up the three concrete steps to the front door and listened, but all was quiet. He let himself in with his key and did a quick walk-through. She wasn't there. Everything was neat and tidy. Except for the bathroom, where a towel had slipped off the rack and landed on the floor. Out of habit, he bent to pick it up, and as he returned it to the rack, he saw the pregnancy test on the counter by the sink. Jesus. A plus sign. And he had no doubts at all. The child was his. Of everything that had happened today, this was the only good thing he could dredge out of it. He took a deep breath. She'd been quiet the past few days. For her, that was out of character, but now he knew why. When was she going to tell him? Then, a more troubling thought came to mind—*was* she going to tell him? Where the hell was she? His stomach was in knots. He had to find her.

Back in his car, with nowhere to go, his thoughts ran wild. He should call the police and report the murders at the Club. He should, but he wouldn't. He'd be held for questioning if he did, and when released, he'd be warned not to leave the state. No. This was his brother's mess, and he could deal with it. Somebody would call it in, but it wouldn't be Tommaso.

After the carnage today, Papa would call a family council in San Francisco. Gennaro would have to meet with Papa. If this was a power play, though, Gennaro wasn't acting alone. He had the brains, but brains weren't enough for something of this magnitude. Who was in on it with him? Tommaso clicked off a mental list of who was where. Papa was in San Francisco. Alphonse, their father, was doing time in Leavenworth. Their aunt Fiona and her son, Nicolo, lived in Boston. That left their uncle Dominic and his sons in New Haven. It could be any of them.

The key had to be in the financials. That was Tommaso's only role in the family. He did the books. Both sets. There had to be something in Gennaro's laptop that held the answer to all this. Tommaso knew one thing for sure. He needed to be at least one step ahead of his brother all the way. That meant booking the next flight to San Francisco to meet with Papa before his brother got there. And somewhere, he needed time to find Nanette before she did something they'd both regret.

# CHAPTER SIX

*San Francisco*

Routines give us security and a sense of control, even when we're not secure and not in control of anything. This was what Carla was thinking this afternoon as she went through her warmup exercises before her young students arrived. Her marriage to Morrie Landow had brought the gift of his name, and when combined with the first name of her ballet heroine, Marie Taglioni, she was now Miss Marie, Proprietress of *Miss Marie's School of the Dance* and as safe as she could be from the Mob's retribution.

It was recital day for Miss Marie's four Saturday afternoon classes. The program, *Autumn Magic,* was a play in four acts that followed the journey of a lonely pumpkin, rescued by a princess and transformed into a jack-o'-lantern at the stroke of midnight on Halloween. Each class performed one act, with the entire cast assembled on stage for the grand finale, when the studio lights were dimmed and little Angela Porto turned on the flashlight that showed the glorious transformation of the lonely pumpkin. Then, the dancers formed a semi-circle around Angela, whose finale was a leap and a twirl, ending in a graceful *plié*. All the students bowed and the recital was complete. It was a resounding success. Nobody had fallen down, had a temper tantrum, or forgotten what to do.

The meet and greet followed. The mothers had laid out the punch and cookies on the long table with its festive cloth, and Miss Marie was working the crowd in a way that was a far cry from how she'd done it at *The Pussycat Club* when she'd danced for the Mafiosos.

At six-thirty, everyone had gone and Carla was cleaning up. She'd just wadded up the paper tablecloth and was stuffing it into the garbage can when two large men—almost as big as Morrie but nowhere near as handsome—opened the front door, lowered the blind, and entered the studio.

No. Not now. Not today. She'd been waiting for this visit. Dreading it was more like it, but the timing was the worst. The Mob wouldn't even let her enjoy one small scrap of happiness. That's what they did. Carla sighed heavily. "Can I help you?"

One of the men stood off to the side. The other, probably the one who could speak English, approached, a large envelope in his beefy hand. She almost expected him to be wearing a pair of brass knuckles. His face was expressionless. His words, however, took her totally off guard.

"Mr. Puglisi is most pleased with the attention you are giving his granddaughter," he said. "He also understands that you are looking for a new apartment. He expresses his regrets that you were inconvenienced by the fire and wishes to be of assistance." Mr. Beefy Hands placed the envelope on the table. "Mr. Puglisi would be most disappointed if you were not to accept his generous offer." With that said, he jerked his head towards the door. His companion responded by opening the door, and both men left.

Carla, still by the trash can with the crumpled tablecloth in hand, looked first at the door and then at the envelope. What the freaking hell was that all about ? She dumped the tablecloth in the can, locked the front door, and returned to her temporary apartment at the rear of the studio where she set the envelope down on the counter and stared at it as if she could will it to open without having to touch it. This is how Morrie found her ten minutes later when he'd returned after his own afternoon activities.

"Is it windy out?" were her first words.

"No." Morrie said. If this was another wind episode, they were packing up and moving somewhere far, far away.

"Good. Just checking." She shot a glance at the envelope. "What do you suppose is in it? It's lumpy."

Morrie's eyes matched the concern in his voice. "Maybe if you open it, you'll find out."

"I know, but I'm scared, Morrie. It's from the Mob. And you know as well as I do, that don't mean nothing good." She gave him an account of how the envelope had arrived. "Here." She pushed it towards him. "You open it."

***

Trained in every aspect of warfare the SEALS kept in their arsenal, not much fazed Morrie Landow. So, when his first reaction to opening the envelope was a low whistle and the second an emphatic, *Holy Shit!* Carla knew this was something she wished wasn't happening.

"What is it?" she asked, her hands covering her face as if the letter contained dismembered body parts or a miniature horse head.

Morrie looked up from the paper he was scanning and then reached back into the envelope and extracted a set of keys which he handed to Carla. "It's a five-year paid lease on an apartment in the Presidio District. And these are the keys."

"Why the hell would he do this?"

Morrie laughed, but there was no mirth in it. "It's part of their twisted honor ethic. It's not easy to understand, but it goes something like this. Setting the fire to make an example out of Harry was a business decision. Killing him was unintentional, but an acceptable cost of doing business. No regrets there, and it gave their 'lesson' to the rest of the shopkeepers some extra power. But, you hadn't done anything to piss them off— yet—and he found out you were his granddaughter's ballet teacher. You treated her fairly, encouraged her, and Puglisi rewards that. It's that simple. So, since he burned your home as collateral damage, now he's taking care of another business obligation." Morrie set the lease back down on the counter. "This complicates things."

"I ain't gonna take no charity from him. He burned up my red dress. I got married in that dress, Morrie. I got standards."

Morrie shook his head. "Not a good plan. We're sort of between the old rock and the hard place. If you don't accept, he'll be offended."

"Disappointed. The goons said he'd be disappointed."

"Word games. A disappointed Mafioso is not somebody you want to be the cause of the disappointment for. Or words to that effect." Morrie reached for the top cupboard and pulled out the bottle of Scotch. He held it up to Carla who got the glasses and the ice from the mini-fridge.

It was after he'd poured their drinks and they'd taken them back to the only two seats they owned—a desk chair that needed some major sanding and varnishing—and an upholstered stool with enough tears in the covering to merit the purchase of some duct tape—and set the glasses on the work table that had seen better days, that Carla was ready to admit she'd be willing to make an exception in this case.

"I guess we could go take a look at it," she said. "I got to tell you that I ain't all that comfortable about it, though. I've been trying to avoid these people. What do they want from me?"

"Actually, nothing but acceptance of his offer. Although," Morrie said, "you've got to consider the ramifications of what that means." Seeing Carla's puzzled look, he explained. "Ramifications. Consequences."

"Got it."

"It's a combination of a real gift and a power play. You accept, and he owns your loyalty. You refuse, and you're now ungrateful and likely to have bad things happen to you. It's a no-win situation on our part."

Carla's eyes were fixed on the envelope, and if looks really had the power to kill, Enzo Puglisi at this very moment was cold as the grave. Probably bloodied. Definitely dead. "But he don't know who I am, right?"

"No. Sally 'The Pipe' Puglisi is, if not swimming with the fishes, at least treading mud with the tadpoles, and Bianca and Michael are doing hard time. Carla Catalano is just another missing person who will never be found." Morrie reached for Carla and held her close. "I swear to you. They will never touch you."

"I love you, Morrie," she said.

"And I love you, Miss Marie Landow. You know," Morrie said, this time taking a more leisurely swallow of his drink, "as long as we remember that everything we say is being heard, we might be able to have a bit of fun with our landlord."

Carla raised an eyebrow.

"Well, we can be certain the apartment will be bugged. They never miss an opportunity to gather information. All we have to do is make sure not to let anything slip that they shouldn't know." Morrie tipped the chair back, resting it against the wall. "And if they're interested in pillow talk, let's give them an earful."

# CHAPTER SEVEN

*California Coast*

"Everybody's hiring, but if you don't have any experience, you can't get hired. How are you supposed to get experience if you can't get hired?" Ginger was stretched out on their motel bed, exhausted after a fruitless day of pounding the pavement, or more literally, making endless phone calls that went nowhere. She held up her hand and made a little pincers movement with her thumb and index finger. "I was *that close* to finishing up my course work for the real estate license and saying goodbye to *The Pleasure Valley Gentlemen's Club* on my own terms. Now? Screwed."

Nanette nodded. "I tried the fast food places, but they don't pay enough to even cover the rent on this place. Screwed is right. We gotta do something, but what? Living a respectable life ain't easy. I don't mind that, but I didn't think it was going to cost so much."

"We need to use our brains." Ginger tapped her fingers on the bedside table. "Think hard. Do you know anybody in California? Anybody at all? Any relatives? Old school friends? Ex-boyfriends? There's got to be somebody we could visit. Then we could get restocked and work on the job thing."

"You kidding? All I got is a bunch of bad memories." Nanette ripped open one of the fruity granola bars and scowled at it. "When we can afford real food again, I'm never, ever going to eat another granola bar as long as I live."

"I hear you. I'm not going to think about food. If I do, I get hungry. I want a real meal with a glass of red wine. The good stuff. Not the crap they served at the Club. I..." she paused while the scattered fragments of a memory slowly came together. "Wine."

"Wine what?" Nanette asked, still glaring at the offending piece of nourishment in her hand.

"Carla used to talk a lot about wine," Ginger said. "She had a cousin who made it. He lived in California."

Nanette snorted. "We should have left with her. But, oh no. We stayed behind." She looked at Ginger. "Why the hell did we stay?"

"I stayed because I had two years left on my five-year plan. Real Estate License. A good future. Nice apartment. Everything was okay. Not great, but okay. I was making good money and socking enough away to give me a good nest egg. Why did you stay?"

"Nowhere else to go." Nanette bit her lip. "I aged out of the foster care system. They packed up everything I could claim as my own and stuffed it in a black garbage bag and handed it to me. And just like that," Nanette shrugged, "there weren't a whole lot of tears shed over me. They shut the door behind me, and my next stop was the street corner." She sighed. "I like that plan idea of yours. I need a plan. Maybe I oughta get my GED." She inhaled and let out her breath in a series of puffs. "Anyhow, back to Carla and that wine cousin. That's not a whole lot to go on. Somebody who makes wine and lives in California. That narrows it down to, I dunno, a thousand people, maybe? I liked Carla, though. At least she got out before shit really went down. I don't remember no wine talk, though. I wonder where she is now?"

"Gee, no idea." Ginger smiled and shrugged. "Disneyland? Could be...?" She stopped in mid-sentence. "Gee?" Frustrated, she shook her head. "There's something there, but it's not coming to me."

"Well, that's something, maybe," Nanette said. "Don't think about it. Sometimes if you don't try too hard, you'll remember."

"Easier said than done."

It was three in the morning when not thinking hit paydirt. Ginger sat bolt upright in bed, her mind placing the final piece of the puzzle. "It's *G*," she said softly, almost not believing her own words. "The guy's name began with a *G*."

"I'm awake. I'm awake. *G*. Wine. California," Nanette said, reaching for her phone. "The basics for a Google search. Keep your fingers crossed. This might just work."

"Hope so. I don't think we've got an overabundance of options."

"That was almost too easy," Nanette said, a minute later, smiling proudly as she displayed the results of her search. "We've got five. Five is a much better number than a thousand. You can't hide anywhere, anymore. Anybody can find anybody." As her words sank in, she lost her smile. "Just like us. They can find us. Ginger, I'm scared."

"I'm scared too, Nan, but we've got this. We've got two choices. We can give up and, what, die? Or we can give it our best shot and see how it all plays out. We can't quit now." Ginger took the pen and paper from the nightstand. The room seemed smaller than it had when they'd checked in. More like a prison cell than anything. Definitely not the home she wanted to find. She swallowed hard to get rid of the lump in her throat. "I'm ready."

"First one is *Galloping Horse Winery* in Napa Valley. Don't see no name, though."

"We can research it. Just give me the names first."

"All right. Um, *Gallatin Vineyards* in Almaden Valley." Nanette said. "California is big on valleys. You suppose Gallatin is somebody's name? Third one is *Greyson Vineyards* in Santa Rosa. Then, *Goose River,* also in Santa Rosa. Last one is *Great Grape Estate Label,* in the Saratoga Hills." She sat back, triumphant.

Half an hour later, sleep was a distant memory and they hadn't found what they were looking for. *Gallatin* and *Greyson* were the only vineyards with a *G* either on the label or listed as owner, and neither of them sounded right to Ginger.

"Well, on the good side, at least we've found out it might not be super-easy to get found on the internet without more information." Ginger was adding some hot water to the packet of instant coffee thoughtfully provided by the motel because nobody with any taste buds would buy it at the store. She set the chipped mug down on the counter. "It was a softer sound—his name, I mean. Something Italian. But that makes sense. Can you add *Italian* to your search?"

"Sure." Nanette bent over her phone and typed. "Nope. We're back to a thousand—back where we started." She tossed the phone on the bed. "No, wait," she said, "let's try this." She retrieved the phone. "Carla would have used his first name. She wouldn't have called him by his last name. She wouldn't have said *Giannone* or *Gallino*."

Ginger looked up from her coffee. "Say that again."

"Say what again?"

"Those names. Say them again."

"I don't remember what I said. I think those granola bars are eating my brain cells. I was just thinking of last names. I dunno. Wait. *Giannone* was one. *Gallino*. That's it. Why?"

Ginger held up a hand. "The first one. That's not it, but it sounds almost right." She closed her eyes. "*Gianelli, Giaccomo...*"

"Here. This might help." Nanette handed over her phone with her search results for *Italian first names for men*. "Is it there?"

They sat together on the bed, reading down the list. "That one," said Ginger, stabbing at an entry. "That's it." She looked at the ceiling. "Thank you, Jesus!"

"All right! We're back in business!" Nanette said.

This time, the search produced only one entry, but it was the one they needed: *Dark Mountain Vineyard*, Santa Cruz, California, owned by Gino Esposito. The dark clouds of doom had lifted. Life was looking brighter. The sun would come up in the morning and shine on them. They had a plan.

Nanette stood and stretched. "I'm going to take a shower, put on my makeup, some clean clothes, and stuff this pink robe in the trash. I don't never want to see it again. Let's rent that car and drive up the coast to Santa Cruz. It'll take a couple of days, and we can work on what we're going to say when we find this Gino dude. Anything's better than doing nothing."

Ginger gave her a hug. "That's the spirit," she said. "Tomorrow night, for a real dinner, you want Italian or Mexican?"

"I'm thinking Italian. If we can afford it, let's buy a bottle of wine with a *Dark Mountain Vineyard* label—for luck!"

***

The morning dawned cloudy with rain in the forecast, but it didn't dampen their spirits. They had a destination, a little cash, and hope. Nanette was behind the wheel of their rental car, a semi-late model Ford Escape, and Ginger was sorting through the folders in Tommaso's briefcase as they bid farewell to LA and merged onto Highway 1 and an uncertain future.

"I can't get the laptop to power on," Ginger said, "and there's no cord, but he's got four folders here: NH Cleanup, R&D, SF OP/Expansion, Financials. The first one is self-explanatory and, considering our current circumstances, he's not done with cleanup since we're still breathing. Joey Vincento, the whackee at the traffic light, was Tommaso's uncle, and so was Prospero, the corpse at the Club. The others were Prospero's lieutenants."

"Scratch two names off the Christmas list. They might have been big tippers, too. Damn. Prospero had them sweaty palms, though. All right," Nanette said, changing lanes to avoid a mattress and two chairs. "That looked like a nice rocker."

Ginger looked out the window. "Needs a few repairs. Anyhow, that leaves Enzo, Tommy, Gennaro, Nicolo, Anthony, Anthony, Jr., Dominic and his kids, and Salvatore. And Fiona," she added as an afterthought.

"You think Tommaso'd take out Anthony? His own father? Or Anthony, Jr.? He's a priest, for Godsakes," Nanette said. "A Jesuit. And Fiona?"

"I don't think they make exceptions," Ginger said, reaching to the floormat to retrieve an errant sheet of paper, "and I also think any of them is capable of anything. Priests don't exactly have a good rep these days."

"Good for us, maybe. Tommy's got a split focus now. He can't be two places at once. He's making a power play and he wants us gone, but he's there and we're here."

"Maybe." Ginger shrugged. "If he's intent on finishing what he started, he'll be there. If this briefcase is worth more than the NH operation, he's already searching for us."

Nanette stepped harder on the gas pedal, and the speedometer obliged. "You know, I never saw much of his place, and we only went out for drinks a couple of times. He asked a lot of questions. I thought he was interested in me. Turns out he was interested in what I knew, what I'd heard, everything. He was using me. He sure was a good dresser, though. Great kisser. Smooth talker. Educated, too. He had that business degree framed on his office wall. MBA. He was a liar, and I believed him." She clenched her jaw and a tear ran down her cheek. She brushed it away.

"Everybody lies. Some do it better than others. It's *why* they lie that's important." Ginger returned her attention to the SF Operations folder. "Basic funding appears to be coming from a protection racket. Nothing new there. There's some maps with certain areas circled. They got names. Can't make them out. The print's too small. They're targeting small businesses." She looked up from the folder. "Small businesses can't afford to pay out big bucks. I'll bet it's seed money for some other operation that's in here." She tapped the computer, returned the folder to the briefcase, and rubbed her eyes. "We need to figure out what to do with this."

Nanette's hands tightened on the steering wheel and a bit of color drained from her cheeks as they passed a Waste Collection and Recycling rig.

"Easy, Nan, they're everywhere, but they don't know who we are," Ginger said. "Take a breath and let it out. Relax. We're going to be fine. We'll be in Santa Cruz tomorrow."

# CHAPTER EIGHT

*Boston*

The handkerchief, neatly folded in a plastic bag, lay in the suitcase, the blood stains now as brown as the last few leaves that clung to the maple tree outside the bedroom window. They too would soon relinquish their hold and accept the inevitable. Nothing lasts. *Sposa settembrina, sposa vedovina.* "Wait just another week," her mother had pleaded. "Wait until October." The warning had gone unheeded. The wedding went on as scheduled, and fate had had its way. *September bride, September widow.*

For Fiona Puglisi Vincento, widowhood was an inconvenience that needed to be dealt with immediately. Nothing against Joey. A woman in a testosterone-infused culture needed a husband to be the front man, and the Mafia was as testosterone-heavy as it gets. Joey had been the perfect husband. He didn't care shit about anything except his goombahs, playing golf, and leering at any female body that came within ten feet.

At forty-seven, Fiona was still slim, her body well-toned, her posture correct, and her bearing regal. She wore her ash-blonde hair shoulder length, letting it swing loosely when she walked. She had her mother's heart-shaped face, fair complexion, ice-blue eyes, and manipulative nature. From her father, she'd inherited a keen intelligence and a ruthlessness that came without benefit of conscience. It was a lethal mix.

Fiona paused in her packing. It wasn't supposed to have ended like this. She'd had it all planned. So carefully planned. What had she missed? There should have been signs, but everything had gone without a hitch until last Friday, when everything had gone to hell. In the aftermath, she'd endured the wake, the funeral mass, and the internment without shedding a tear. The priest had known better than to preach about forgiveness, and she'd resisted the impulse to wear a red dress to the church to show the family what she really thought of them. As was customary with these situations, everything was well-attended. The gaudy and overdone floral pieces, each one more elaborate than the previous, filled the funeral home, obscuring the casket in a pissing match of status. The line of limos that had accompanied the hearse to the cemetery was more than impressive. It seemed as if their occupants couldn't rest until they had proof that Joey wasn't going to do the Jesus trick and climb out of the grave, and so they stayed until the last dirt clod was shoveled in and the priest tossed some holy water over the dirt pile.

Fiona sighed. Joey'd cost her a week from her timeline, and before she could continue, she had to focus on finding a replacement. She left the bedroom and the packing and went to the kitchen, pulled out Joey's chair, and sat. She stared at the cup of cold coffee and the stale donut that still waited for his return. It had been a week now, and the scum on the coffee bore testimony to the passage of time. She twisted her wedding band, pulling until it released its grip on her finger. Holding the gold circle between thumb and index finger, she studied its imperfections—the slight scratch from the time she'd stumbled while carrying the cast iron skillet, the tiny nick from the time it had fallen off the washstand onto the marble floor. A symbol of eternal love. In her case, eternity had been just shy of eighteen years. Seventeen. Another number. Another superstition. Was she meant to be cursed? She set the ring aside, took the coffee cup to the sink and dumped the contents down the drain, adding the donut for good measure. The grinding of the garbage disposal as it digested its meal snapped her out of her reverie. Joey wasn't coming back.

Returning to her bedroom, she freshened her lipstick and turned to the mirror to check the fit of her black dress. Snug but not overly so. Just enough. It was best to start slowly. The web needed to be woven tightly and she'd only have one shot at it. She collected her car keys and set off for the airport.

Flying out of Green in Providence was less stressful than dealing with the chaos of Boston, although everyone else seemed to have come to that realization as well. Still, the total flight time was just about the same, and she'd booked a nonstop to SFO. From there, all that was left was the cab ride to the house she'd just closed on in Pacific Heights. *Specific Whites*, according to her son, Nico. Didn't matter. There was enough property to be a buffer against any prying eyes, and the security system that had cost a small fortune ensured her safety. There wouldn't be another mess up.

The flight was turbulent and seemed to go on forever. When they finally touched down at SFO, Fiona was exhausted and not at the top of her game. All she wanted was to get home. She hailed a taxi, climbed into the back seat, and closed her eyes. Two miles from the airport, however, the driver in the stolen white Cadillac exited 101 onto a side road and parked. Her eyes flew open, and there was a brief moment of recognition, but there was nothing to be done. The driver turned around in his seat to face her, and smiling, lifted the Glock and pumped a lethal dose of lead into the sweet spot between her eyes.

# CHAPTER NINE

*San Francisco and the Santa Cruz Mountains above Los Gatos*

"He'll come back, once he's gotten over being scared," Trizbel said, taking one of Carla's posters and taping it to the shop door. "I put a bowl of water by the door in case he shows up and is thirsty. Try not to worry. He can take care of himself. He'll be all right." Trizbel's words didn't match the doubt in her eyes. She refolded a sweater that someone had tried on and then tossed back on the display table. "They found a broken bottle by the entrance." She tilted her head in the direction of the investigators. "And you know what that means."

"Gasoline. As if we needed any proof," Carla said. "Just like Olga's."

"I'm just wondering how much I'm going to have to pay to stay in business. It's not like I'm making a fortune here. I love this shop. *The Clothes Horse* is my dream come true, but boutique businesses struggle. Each day the goal is to pay the rent. Add in what the Mob would take to leave us alone, and it's more than most of us can cough up." She gave the sweater a final pat. "They'll show up probably sooner than later, now that they figure they've scared us half to death. They won't wait."

"We're not going to wait, either." Carla said. "That's the main reason I stopped by." She took a bracelet from the poster bag and handed it to Trizbel. "We have a plan."

"It had better be a good one," her friend said, examining the bracelet. "Because if this is the plan, you need to do some explaining."

***

The condensed version of the plan didn't take long to tell, and by the time Carla had finished, Trizbel was on board. "I've never liked bullies," she said. "They're generally cowards underneath that hard surface."

"Yeah. But that hard surface usually has a holster with a piece in it. This should be safer than a frontal assault."

"True."

Together, they made the circuit of every business along the main drag and the side streets, with the exception of *Cesar's Cigar Shop*. Everyone was frightened and also frustrated with the lack of police response to the arson and the murder. It didn't take a genius to see that if anything were to be done about it, the members of Cow Hollow's business community would have to take matters into their own hands. Vigilante justice had lost its stigma and seemed the only course of action available.

A little practice, and Carla had her spiel down cold. "Don't try to be a hero," she said more than once. "Push the dot one time. It's easy. Like this." She demonstrated a casual brushing of her wrist that masked the quick push of the dot as her fingers moved across her arm. "Then just keep talking. Agree with everything. Our guys will be there in a flash, and you'll just go back to doing whatever you were doing before the shitheads showed up. They won't bother you again."

By the time she'd made her rounds and said goodbye to Triz, she wasn't depressed any longer. She was fighting mad. With Gino and Francesca back from Italy, the family was in fighting form. They'd outsmarted the Mob once before. They could—and would—do it again.

# CHAPTER TEN



*Dark Mountain Vineyard*

Apart from that one moment when the Mafia had shown up on the doorstep to collect their *pizzo,* the time in Italy at *Castel del Mare* had been perfect. The warm days, the starry nights, the walks through the countryside, Celestina's cooking, and the wine... Home once again, Francesca sat on the edge of the bed, unpacking. It was taking days longer than it should have and also taking more energy than she could summon. She was tired, and no amount of sleep helped.

Stealing a moment from the mountain of paperwork that awaited in the office, Francesca took her coffee out onto the back deck to watch the fog that lay low on the mountains. The marine layer had settled in, and it would be several hours before the sun broke through. A sure sign that autumn was coming. There was a chill in the air, and she wished she'd thought to put on a jacket, but once back inside, she'd be spending the morning on the accounts. The next few weeks would be hectic, and until everything was wrapped up from the fall harvest, she'd be a slave to her computer. A few more moments outside was worth a little bit of a shiver, but then the sound of an approaching vehicle interrupted her coffee break. Her first thought was that the driver had gotten the dates confused and was showing up to transport the wine. She set the mug on the deck railing and went inside to deal with the problem.

***

"Nan, are you sure we're at the right address?" Ginger looked out the window with suspicion at the derelict automobiles lining the driveway that seemed to end at a rundown barn that had seen better days. In fact, the whole place looked like it had seen better days and those better days had been a long, long time ago.

"No. I'm most definitely not sure." Nanette took her foot off the gas and braked. "This don't look right."

"It doesn't look any more or less right than the last three places our GPS has led us to. It's no wonder people freeze to death on dirt roads in the winter. You can't trust this shit." Ginger tossed the GPS into the rear seat and unfolded the paper map the rental place had given them. "No help here, either," she said. "This a street map. In order for it to work, you've got to have streets. I haven't seen a street since we turned off Old San Jose Road. How do people who live here find their way around?"

"Don't know. Don't care. But this place is creeping me out." Nanette slammed the car into reverse and backed out to what passed for the main drag, just as an ancient Ford pickup was about to turn in. The driver, an elderly man with an unkempt white beard rolled down the window. The large, black dog sitting in the passenger seat showed his teeth and growled.

"Lost?" the guy said.

"You could say that and you'd be right," Nanette said. "We're trying to find Adams Creek Road. There's a winery there."

"You drunk?" the man asked.

"We certainly are not," Nanette said.

He gave them a look that could have meant a great many things or nothing at all. "Get back on the road and keep going until you get to where Pearl's old place was. It's the third drive on the left after that." He rolled the window back up and motioned for them to get out of his driveway.

Ginger gave a friendly wave that wasn't returned. "Nice guy," she said.

"At least we know where we need to go now," Nanette said, "but just one thing. How do we find out where Pearl's old house *was?* And do we go left or right?"

Ginger shrugged. "Dunno. He did say to keep going, so let's do that. Then, look for a foundation, maybe? Old fence? I don't know."

Nanette banged her head on the steering wheel.

"Like that's going to help," Ginger said. "Look. Let's just drive until we see a nice house with a white picket fence, a friendly dog, and an old lady out in her flower garden."

"You have totally lost your friggin' mind." Nanette raised her head from the wheel. "All right. Why not?"

Exactly six-tenths of a mile down the road, they spotted a white picket fence. Nanette slowed. A young woman was walking across the yard, carrying an armload of firewood, a compact white dog trotting along at her side.

"What the...."

"Don't complain. Don't question. Just stop and ask her," Ginger said. "No house or flower garden, but there's enough here to work with. I'm good."

This time they were greeted with a friendly smile. Betty, the woman with the firewood and the dog, took pity on them and told them to hang on a minute. Turned out she was heading to town and would be driving right past *Dark Mountain.* They could follow her.

And they did. Betty waved goodbye at the entrance to *Dark Mountain Vineyard.* They drove through the open wrought iron gates, up the gravel driveway, and came to a stop in front of a two-story home with expansive decks, a manicured lawn, mature oak trees, and a sleeping basset hound curled up on a doggie bed by the front door. They parked and got out.

"Here we are," Nanette said. "I have to admit I was getting a little nervous."

"I was getting a lot nervous, but we're here now. That's one thing done. I still haven't figured out exactly what to say," Ginger said. *Hi. We're friends of Carla. We've got a stolen laptop from the Mob and they want to kill us. Also, we're pretty much out of money and don't have any place to stay.* She looked at Nanette. "How's that?"

"Brilliant. You'd better come up with something a little less dramatic if we stand a chance of finding Carla, a meal, jobs—you know—that stuff."

Ginger frowned. "I was thinking the direct approach would be the best." She shrugged. "Okay. Maybe not."

"Time's up," Nanette said. "The door just opened."

"All right," Ginger said. "I'll try to tone it down."

"Please do."

The woman who opened the front door stepped over the dog, still sound asleep, then looked past Ginger and Nanette, as if she'd expected to see someone else. With the girls the only people around, her attention turned to them. "Are you lost?"

"Not anymore," Ginger said, "although it's a question we've been asked a lot today and we have been, lost, that is, until now. I'm Ginger Giannone, and this," she said, nodding at her friend, "is Nanette Fabiano." Nanette gave a small wave. Ginger paused to see how she was doing. The woman nodded encouragement, so Ginger continued. "We're friends of Carla." At that moment, Nanette cleared her throat, and Ginger glared at her. "I wasn't going to say it," she said under her breath. She turned back to the woman. "We're trying to find Carla." She paused. "We're in trouble. I'm sorry. I know this sounds crazy, but we're not bad people. Well, we're not actually *good* people, but if you could tell us how to find Carla, you'd be a lifesaver." Ginger had exhausted her hastily composed introduction and now waited to see what would happen next.

The question, "Why have you come here looking for Carla?" was what happened next.

Ginger gave a sigh of relief. That was a question. Questions were good. They meant the woman wasn't going to tell them to leave. At least not yet. "We're dancers," she said. "At *The Pussycat Club*. Well, it's got a new name now. They call it *The Pleasure Valley Gentlemen's Club*, but it's still a dump. We had to leave in a hurry. Some things came up and we—"

Nanette jumped in before Ginger could finish what seemed to be a confession. "Carla danced under the name of *Vixen*, if that helps prove we know her," she said. Nanette drew herself up to her full height of almost five feet. "I was the French Maid," she said, pride stealing into her delivery. "At least until they got that new dress code and all I got to wear was that belt. It didn't leave any room for creative movement, if you get my drift."

"Nanette, you're rambling," Ginger said, turning away from the woman at the door and then turning back. "I'm sorry. We don't want to take more of your time, so could you please tell us if you know where Carla is? She used to talk about her cousin who made wine in California. We, uh, needed to get out of New Haven, and after I remembered that she called him Gino, we made a list of names and figured out that Gino Esposito was her cousin. Then, we looked it up on Google."

"I thought about that part," Nanette added.

"And so we came here to find Carla and get new jobs and stuff." Finishing on a triumphant note, there was little else to add.

The woman gave them a hard, if confused, look. "Well." She cleared her throat. "That's quite a story. Wait here, please. I'll be back shortly." She stepped back over the dog and went inside the house. There was a distinctive click as she locked the door.

"That's that," Nanette said. "She didn't believe us. She didn't tell us her name after we told her ours. She's gonna call the cops. We got to get out of here."

The girls turned and made a beeline for the car, flung themselves inside, and spun gravel as they fled back down the drive to the road. Neither spoke for the next five miles until they'd reached Summit Road.

"Damn and double damn," Ginger said.

"Crap. It was just a longshot, anyway," Nanette said. "Would *you* have believed us? I sure as hell wouldn't. We had to be crazy to think this would work. Problem is, what do we do now?"

Ginger was fighting back the tears. "Maybe we should go to the cops. Tell them our story. Give them the laptop. But, then what? Then we got no leverage. No insurance policy. No nothing. We're dead. Maybe we get arrested for stealing the laptop or the garbage truck or whatever."

Nanette shook her head. "I forgot about the garbage truck. That's a felony. No. We got this far. We don't give up now, and we have to do something. We can't sit here forever. Decision time. Left or right?"

Ginger looked both directions. "Left. Nothing we've done so far has worked out right. Why should this be any different?"

"Left it is." Left led them to Highway 17 which took them away from the mountains and down into the Santa Clara Valley. "This looks promising," Nanette said, when they got their first glimpse of San Jose. "It's a good-sized city. It's got potential. It looks big enough to get lost in. I bet we can get jobs here and replenish our cash."

"Maybe. I hate to say this, but there's only one way we can be sure of getting some fast money."

"What are you saying? I'm not robbing nobody." Nanette gave a serious head shake. "We've got enough problems without getting busted for that. We don't know the lay of the land here. Way too risky. Uh. Nope."

Ginger let out an exasperated breath. "Don't be stupid. I'm not talking stealing. Dancing. I'm talking dancing. There's got to be some clubs here. We change our names. They never care about any of the legit stuff. A few weeks and we'll have enough cash to do something else. We can look for something more respectable during the day, but at least we won't starve."

"I swore I'd never set foot in one of those places again," Nanette said.

"It's temporary. We just got to keep our mouths shut and our eyes open. We'll be all right." Ginger pointed to a motel up ahead on the right. "*Extended Stay*. They'll have good rates. We can cook there and take showers."

"All right," Nanette said, hanging a right into the parking lot. "It's only temporary, you say. I hope you're right, but I ain't turning any tricks. I've got standards."

Ginger patted Nanette on the shoulder. "Sure you do, honey. Sure you do."

***

Settling in at the *Extended Stay Motel* didn't take all that long, considering that it consisted of opening the door to the suite and dumping the backpacks and laptop on the bed.

"Well," Nanette said, "we're here. New day, new city, same old shit."

"Look on the good side. We still have eleven granola bars and three bags of peanuts."

"Right. Let's get down to business. If we get lucky, we'll be working tomorrow—day after, at the latest. And," Nanette added, "the weekend is coming up. That means more money."

"Right. But first things first. We've got to return the car. That'll save us a bundle. They've got buses here, just like New Haven. We won't need to drive anywhere. We can either walk or ride." Ginger was pulling up the names of some clubs on her phone.

"Looks like West San Carlos Street and Santa Clara Streets are our best bets." She looked at Nanette. "Maybe we should split up in case Tommy's put the word out to be watching for two girls looking for jobs."

"Good idea. We need to get some new names and new outfits." Nanette had walked over to the window and was looking down at the street three floors below. Lots of cars, lots of traffic. "I'm thinking policewoman." She nodded. "*Destiny.* That's going to be my new name. It's positive. Not looking back." She rested a hand on her stomach. "From now on we are new people."

Ginger looked at her and smiled. "We're going to be okay. I mean, we've gotten this far. There's bound to be a few setbacks."

"We need to find a costume shop somewhere around here. Cop outfits shouldn't be too hard to find. As long as they come off easy so I can get down to the essentials. You?"

"I need an asp."

"You've got an ass," Nanette said. "What do you need another one for? You need more padding?"

"Not *ass-asp.* I need an asp."

"What the hell is an asp?"

"It's a snake. I'm going for a Cleopatra motif. You know, gold arm bands, gold forehead band, sheer robe. Yeah." Her eyes took on a dreamy quality as the vision floated before her. "And a snake I can pole dance with. I think it'll bring in the bucks."

"You are certifiable, you know that?" Nanette threw up her hands. "Whatever. Just remember you gotta feed a snake, and we're getting low on granola bars."

"I'll see what I can scare up this afternoon. You ready to go shopping?"

Nanette grinned. "Always."

***

Two hours later, after a trip to the *Everything a Buck Store*, the costume shop, the grocery store, and the drug store for makeup, the girls dropped off their parcels and returned the car to the rental agency. Then, Nanette hoofed it over to Santa Clara Street to check out employment opportunities while Ginger sought out options on West San Carlos. Along the way, however, she made one detour, emerging shortly afterwards from *Erotic Exotics* with a cat carrier containing Bruce, a used imperator boa constrictor marked down from fifty to twenty-five dollars, a small bag holding five traumatized mice, and a pamphlet outlining proper care requirements for a healthy pet.

Bruce actually had a history as a dancer's companion, she'd been told, but the dancer had relocated to the state penitentiary and Bruce had had to stay behind. It was a real bargain, the sales clerk said, and she couldn't get Bruce's transfer of ownership completed fast enough. Bruce was a natural, according to the sales clerk's pitch. He'd been taught to cling alternately to the dancer and then to the pole as if he'd been born to the stage. Skeptical, Ginger forked over the money and sent a silent prayer heavenward.

After that, the rest of the afternoon progressed without incident. It's not that difficult to get hired at a club, provided you can dance and understand that you're a private contractor who has to pay for the privilege of working there. Whether or not a dancer lasts depends on how quickly she can build her reputation and a demand for her private dances and trips to the VIP room. Nanette, now *Destiny*, and Ginger, now *Cleo, Queen of the Nile*, knew the drill. After a quick supper, the girls and Bruce headed off to work. For this brief moment, the stars were in alignment.

# CHAPTER ELEVEN

*San Francisco*

Morrie emerged from the shower to find Carla reciting her word of the day, *futile*, along with its definition, three sample sentences using the word, and a sentence of her own construction into the lamp on the nightstand by the bed. Having resumed her self-improvement program, she was taking advantage of the captive audience the bug afforded.

"My study buddy," she said, pointing to the lamp. "Might as well make use of all the perks we've got. It has to be boring, you know, sitting somewhere, waiting for whatever, and it never comes." She patted the lampshade, probably causing a flood of static to temporarily deafen anyone on the receiving end. "It is *futile* for you to continue listening to me," she delivered her original sentence to the bug. "I'm smarter than you," she teased.

Getting up from the bed, her expression changed. "I was depressed," she said, looking at Morrie. "I know that now, but then I got to thinking that I need a positive attitude. I just got this feeling that I'm gonna—*going*—to find Pierre soon. I mean it, Morrie. I think somebody's dognapped him, and he's just waiting for a chance to escape. I put up enough signs. I know I did. Somebody is, like, holding him for ransom or something. As soon as he gets away, he'll go back to our old place, and Triz promised she'd let me know if—*when*—he does. Today, tomorrow, soon. We'll get him back. I'm *going* to go over to the apartment and check."

With a purpose, a plan, and her new positive attitude, Carla went in search of her cell that seemed to have developed a mind of its own. Standing in the middle of the kitchen, hands on hips, her eyes searched every flat surface for the runaway. She was about to ask Morrie to call her so she could find the damn thing when it rang. "I was just getting ready to call you. Weird how that happens," she said to Francesca, answering the call after locating the phone by the coffee pot. "I looked there," she muttered. "Anyhow, hi. What's up?"

Morrie, having dressed, joined Carla in the kitchen, tapped her on the shoulder, and gave the finger to the lips thing.

Carla nodded and grabbed her pocketbook, holding the cell to her ear while she fished around for the car keys. "You home?" she said.

"Yes. Problem?"

"There won't be in a minute. Let me call you right back." Carla disconnected. A few minutes later, safely inside the Subaru parked in the basement garage, she called Francesca.

"It's safe to talk now. I'll explain later. What's up?"

"I've got visitors. Two women who say they need to find you. Their names are Ginger and Nanette. Ring any bells?"

"What!" Carla said. "Really? Yeah, of course I know them. What are they doing there?"

"Trying to track you down. They say they're in trouble. Should I let them in? Can I trust them?"

"Sweet Jesus! Let them in. I'm on my way! Be there as quick as I can!" Carla disconnected and texted Morrie. "You'll never guess what's happened! I've gotta go to Francesca's. The girls from the Club are there. I never thought I'd see them again! I can't believe it! They said they're in trouble. What do you suppose that means?"

"I'd say it means they're in trouble. I'd want to know what kind of trouble, why they came to you, and what you're planning on doing about their trouble."

Before Carla could reply, her phone rang again.

"This is beyond weird. They appear out of the blue and then disappear back into the blue, or wherever people disappear into," Francesca said.

"They must be scared. I don't think they've ever been out of New Haven before. This is one of the strangest days of my life." She paused to think. "What about if Morrie and me come by for dinner? You can do that manicotti. There's a lot that's been happening. We'll bring bread and some really good cheese. I found this cheese factory type store. You can watch them make it. Next time you're here, I'll take you there. They got vats and paddles and the cheese is incredible." She smiled inwardly. *Incredible* was yesterday's word. "Maybe we can figure out something about Nanette and Ginger. Besides, Morrie's got some stuff to run by you. We've got some bad shit going on here."

"Sounds good," Francesca said. "The food, not the bad shit. You can plan on staying the night. We've got a lot to catch up on and you won't have to drive down the mountain and back to San Francisco tonight."

***

The Santa Cruz Mountains of California are part of the Pacific Coastal Range. Rugged and majestic, with stands of still-surviving old-growth redwood, the mountains have been the refuge of loners, outlaws, and rugged pioneers. Not much has changed. If you want privacy, this is your place. If you want a view of Monterey Bay on the three days out of the year the fog isn't putting up a roadblock, this is your place, as well. And if you wish to grow grapes, it's definitely your place. It's home to numerous vineyards, including the former Old Almaden Winery, once the oldest commercial winery in California and now a park. With a climate ideal for grape production, wine has been made here since the nineteenth century, and many vineyards have been in the same family for generations. *Dark Mountain Vineyard*, owned by the Esposito family and managed by Gino and Francesca Esposito, is one of these vineyards.

None of this had come easily for Gino. Repairing the damages of years of not-so-benign neglect after his parents' deaths had been costly in both time and money, but his marriage to Francesca Kim had been the catalyst of change. While Gino's money management skills were nonexistent, Francesca's were excellent. With Gino attending to the physical details and

Francesca in charge of business matters, the vineyards were restored. This year they'd begun construction on the winery. *Dark Mountain* would soon be in control of everything from harvesting to bottling. It had been a major expenditure, but necessary, to make *Dark Mountain* one of the premier wineries in California.

***

Rush hour never ends in the Bay Area, no matter which direction you're driving, and it was close to six-thirty by the time Carla and Morrie turned onto Highway 17, a four-lane death wish that got really interesting before you exited at the Summit and disappeared into the back roads that had been carved out of a roaring wilderness back in the nineteenth century and hadn't had much done to them since. Realtors enjoyed informing potential buyers that the homes are nestled in the woods. Actually, they're hidden there, and if you make a wrong turn, it won't bode well for your journey. On this trip, however, Morrie Landow and his wife, Carla Catalano, aka Vixen, aka Miss Marie Landow, weren't going wine tasting. Not to say that wine wouldn't figure into the evening, but this trip was about expanding their counteroffensive in their ongoing war against the Mafia.

***

"Where's Pierre?" Francesca asked, peering over Carla's shoulder and not seeing the black poodle that usually catapulted himself off the steps and launched himself into her arms each time he visited. The question elicited a burst of tears and sobs from Carla. "I'm sorry, hon. Come on in." She shot a glance at Morrie who just gave a head shake and took Carla's arm, steering her away from the car and up the steps to the house.

"Sorry for the short notice," Morrie said, handing Gino a shopping bag and taking his accustomed seat on the back deck next to the grill. "We brought bread and cheese."

"Yeah. It goes with everything," Carla said. "I ain't thinking all that clear today, but I know that much." She followed Francesca into the kitchen, Jesse following behind at the hope of a snack, and poured the wine. "It's okay, Fran. You couldn't know. Pierre's lost. I've got posters up everywhere with his picture and description. I put my cell number on the posters, but no name or nothing. I'm getting good at keeping a low profile. Anyhow," she resumed her sad tale, "Pierre got scared with all the noise at the fire and ran off." She blew her nose. "Sorry."

"Nothing to be sorry about. He'll come home. I know it. Seems like everybody's not where they belong. Pierre, first. Then you. You lost your apartment. And your friends, Ginger and Nanette. They came all this way, and now they're nowhere." Francesca took a bottle of wine from the rack on the counter. "Too much. Here. Take the wine out to the deck and sit. I'll be out in a minute. I just need to pop the manicotti in the oven. We'll do the salad after we've caught up. And," she gave Carla a serious look, "it appears there's a lot of catching up to do. Go. Sit." She made a shooing motion with her hands, and Carla gave her a hug.

Family was something Carla appreciated now that she had one. Francesca was her cousin-in-law, but actually more like a sister or a best friend. The dark cloud that had settled on her started to lift. Morrie was right. They needed this.

"It started with this feeling I had," Carla said, plunking herself down in the chair next to Morrie.

"Carla," Morrie said, a warning tone to his voice.

"Well, it did. All right. It all started when they burned down Olga's store – the bakery," Carla paused. "No. It started because Olga wouldn't pay her *pizzo*. That's when they burned it. Next, they burned out Harry, killing him in the process. Our apartment was gone too, so Morrie and me had to move into the back rooms of the ballet studio. Then the goons showed up because Enzo Puglisi thinks I'm a good ballet teacher for his granddaughter, so he offered us an apartment in the Presidio district, but it's bugged and we can't talk."

Morrie stepped in. "Our old friends, the Puglisis, are ramping up operations," he said. "I'm thinking they need revenue for a new venture. Protection the way they've been doing it doesn't pay overly much, but it's reliable. Either they've got a new spin on an old racket or something else is in the wind."

Gino kicked absently at a twig that had blown onto the deck from the oak tree that shaded the west side of the house. "It's probably that and more. Prospero and two of his lieutenants got hit in New Haven." He looked at Carla. "Your old club. You did a good thing, getting out of there. Oh," he added, "and for good measure, they also took out Joey Vincento. I don't get the connection. I mean they're family, but Joey's only the brother-in-law. He's never been on the front lines. My money's on Fiona. She's the one with the brains. Now she's the grieving widow getting all the attention."

"Or she's behind it all," Carla joined in. "I seen her once. She's one cold, hard, woman. Wouldn't trust her. She's got that look. You know." Carla raised her head, narrowed her eyes, and smiled through her teeth. "She also got a face job, but she's got a neck like a dead turtle."

Francesca, picturing the neck image, nodded. "Even if she's the brains, she's going to need some muscle to handle the heavy work. It's doable, but not easy for a woman. Protection is all about enforcement. If she's got the backing of the rest of the family, she must think she has enough soldiers to carry it out."

"But what if she don't?" Carla said. "What if she's just kinda feeling her way through like one of them science experiments? She's just getting her feet wet with something tried and true."

Morrie nodded. "She or they or whoever are laying the groundwork now. They've burned out two businesses to show they're serious. Their next step will be to visit each shop along Union Street, lay out their demands, and if the shopkeepers refuse, they'll be reminded of what happens to those who don't sign the insurance policy. Word will spread fast, and there won't be any more refusals." He held the glass of wine at a distance, admiring the color. "We're addressing that issue."

"See?" Carla said, holding up her arm and displaying the tech bracelet on her wrist. "It's like those bracelets old people wear in case they fall down and nobody's there to help them. Only, in this case, if the goons show up at one of the shops on Union, the shopkeeper presses the little button, but instead of the ambulance—"

"We send another type of assistance," Morrie interjected. "Chan's guys. If we need more support, we call in the reserves. In any case, the taser does its job, and the Mafia is down two soldiers. If they send more, we match them. The goal is to have attrition make them turn their attention to less difficult ventures. It's a gamble," he admitted. "We don't know how committed they are to this, but that's the general scope of the operation."

"Impressive," Gino said.

"Inspired," Francesca added, "but why not call the police?"

"That's what Harry and Olga did," Morrie said. "It didn't work out so well for them. Guerilla warfare is effective, though. Hit and run. Once they know we're going to fight back, they've got two choices—either scorched earth or a change of focus. We're gambling on the latter. The Mob doesn't destroy for destruction's sake. They're businessmen, and it's all about profit. If this venture doesn't turn a profit soon, they'll take another tack."

***

Having moved inside as the night grew chilly, the family regrouped at the dinner table, where the manicotti was pronounced to be perfection, and they returned to the business at hand.

"I wasn't all that eager to share this," Gino said, "but it's relevant. Your shopkeepers aren't going to be forking over huge amounts of money. They can't. And the Mob knows it. They know just how much to take without destroying the business. They're in it for the long haul. Excuse me. I'll be right back. This is worth another bottle." He left for the wine cellar and Francesca looked after him, a sadness in her eyes.

Carla's glance at Morrie was returned with an eye shrug. Whatever Gino had to say wasn't going to be a mood elevator, and that thought turned out to be the unspoken understatement of the evening. When Gino returned with a fresh bottle, he took his time opening it. Finally, the cork removed, he set the bottle aside to breathe. He cradled his empty glass in his hands as if it held the weight of his worries and he was considering how to drown them so they never resurfaced. Finally, he set the glass down, poured, and passed the bottle to Francesca who passed it along to Morrie, an action not lost on Carla who filed it away for a time when the two of them were alone.

All this had been done in silence, and the suspense and the tension had reached the breaking point. Carla snapped first. "Gino, if you don't spit it out—not the wine, whatever the hell you're trying either to say or not to say—I'm gonna get up and slap it out of you! Spill it! Not the wine." She bit her lower lip. "I already said that, didn't I? Come on, Gino. We can help."

Gino's laugh was bitter. "No, Carla. You can't." He took a deep swallow. Finally, he set the glass down and smiled at her. This time, it was genuine. "All right. Here goes nothing."

"Take your time," Carla said, nodding encouragement.

"Carla," Morrie growled.

"Right. Sorry. You don't need my help. Go ahead."

"I just paid the Vincento Family 25,000 Euros," Gino said. "That made *Castel del Mare's* account current. It comes due every year and has for decades. You see, in Italy, it's just another cost of doing business. You accept it. There's nothing—and I mean nothing—you can do about it. People have tried. And they die. It's ingrained in the system. The authorities? They get their share of it. And yes, it makes my blood boil, but I have Francesca to think about, and I'm rather fond of living, as well."

"Shit!" said Carla, and the heads nodding agreement around the table echoed the sentiment.

"So," Gino continued, "if you think you're going to eradicate this on your own, best of luck to you, but luck won't be enough. They've been at this for a very, very long time. You may wound the snake, but if you don't cut off the head, it's not going to die and you're not going to win." His voice trembled with a mix of rage and shame. Rage at the sheer unmitigated gall of the extortionists and shame that he was powerless to fight them.

There are many types of silence, but the silence that followed Gino's confession screamed out for justice and vengeance. Francesca rested her hand on his and held her head high, almost daring anyone to say a word. Of course, it was only a moment until Carla took the dare.

"For Christ's sake, Gino. Why the hell didn't you tell us before? We got no secrets. Well, we got a few but not from each other." Her brow was furrowed and her cheeks were flaming. "How much have they stolen from you? And stolen is the right word. How much?" She leaned forward, breaking the grip of silence that shattered under the power of her words. "This is not a little battle in a small neighborhood, Gino. This is full out war! And before you cut me off or whatever, you're already involved. You got us. We all got each other. Nobody, and I mean nobody can beat that combination. We're family. They're a family. It's gonna be an even fight. We're not finished. Not by a damn longshot. We're just getting started. You better get a grip or I am gonna come over and slap you one. Lord, Gino!" Out of breath, she fanned her face with her napkin and downed the rest of her wine in one gulp. This time, the silence knew better than to hang around and everyone started talking at once to the point that Gino let out one of those ear-splitting whistles.

"Ouch!" Carla said. "That hurt. But you gotta show me how to do that. Could be useful when my dance students aren't paying attention."

"Sorry. But now what?" Gino wiped his forehead and exhaled heavily. "Anybody got any ideas, I'm all ears, but it's been one hell of a long day. I don't think there's a thought left in my head tonight."

"Agreed," Francesca said. "Let's call it a day or a night or a whatever and get some sleep. We'll start fresh at breakfast. The ideas will come then. I'm sure of it."

And then the phone rang.

# CHAPTER TWELVE

*San Jose*

The rain wasn't due until next week, but it had been threatening for the past few days and finally decided it was time to show the world it meant business. First came the wind. It started as a mild disturbance that quickly ushered in a downpour that soaked everyone unlucky enough to have been caught outside. Among the unlucky was Nanette. Her backpack, water-resistant but not waterproof, was doing its best to keep her performance attire dry, and she picked up her pace for the final three-block push to *Eden's Garden*. Head lowered to keep the rain out of her eyes, she almost didn't see the man standing in the doorway engaged in conversation with Mr. Guiccione, the owner. She had to do a quick sidestep to avoid a collision. The man never gave her a glance, and it was only after she'd squeezed past them to get to the door that she recognized his voice.

Nanette made a beeline for the dressing room, the only semi-safe place available. By the time she collapsed onto one of the stools by the wardrobe hangers, she was shaking uncontrollably. If she'd just completed a marathon, her breathing couldn't have been any more rapid or ragged. Panic was welling up from somewhere deep inside, and it took her last ounce of willpower to keep it from taking over. It wasn't possible. It couldn't be possible. She tried to think. At least she wasn't alone was her first thought. That the girls wouldn't be any help, was her second. She had to get out of there without being seen, and she had to warn Ginger.

"You all right, babe?" The concerned voice belonged to Raven, who was sorting through a pile of hair extensions. "You don't have to do this, you know." Her dark eyes narrowed. "You got somebody calling the shots on you? There's numbers you can call to get out of it."

"No. It's not like that," Nanette said. "It's worse. Worse than you can imagine." She buried her face in her hands, too scared to cry.

"Look. I don't know you, but I know scared. And this is way beyond scared. You need to talk before you either blow up or melt down. Neither one is good." Raven took a stool and sat. "I'm not going anywhere. You just take your time."

Finally, after what seemed like an eternity but was only a minute or so, Nanette raised her head. "I'm all right. Really." And then the tears came, unannounced.

Raven dragged the tissue box out of the corner and set it in front of Nanette. "You're doing fine, babe. Let it all out. Get it gone. You'll feel better."

When the torrent had subsided to a trickle, Nanette blotted her eyes and reached for her third tissue. "Thanks. It's just...No. I'm okay now. Really. I got to get out of here before he comes back."

Raven fixed her with an intent gaze. "Before *who* comes back?"

"*Him.*" She inhaled sharply. "Look. I appreciate what you said. You gotta know the Mob runs these places. They don't give shit about us. I gotta go." Nanette slid off the stool and picked up her backpack. "And you should, too." She directed that warning at Zephyr, another of the dancers. "That makeup job you done is good, but you can't hide the swelling. Your face don't deserve that kind of treatment. One time he's gonna hit you too hard." She touched the girl's hand. "Come with me," she said to Zephyr.

"Thanks. I mean it. But I can't. Not just yet," the girl said.

"Don't wait too long." Nanette threw the words over her shoulder as she nearly ran for the back door.

Zephyr slumped on the stool and stared into the mirror. She touched the bruise by her cheekbone and winced. She blinked hard. "Hold on," she called. "I'm coming."

As the two girls fled the club, Raven touched her left ear. "Don't lose them," she said.

***

If 3,000 miles hadn't been enough to escape, what hope was there for safety within the San Jose city limits? After the initial panic subsided, Nanette was left without a clear plan of action. She had a stitch in her side and breathing was difficult. She slowed her pace, her hands pressed against her stomach, trying to make the discomfort go away, trying to think what to do. *The baby.* Nanette had a momentary stab of panic. No. The baby was all right. She just needed to slow down. Nothing was going to hurt her baby. They'd be all right. She closed her eyes briefly and then continued on her way.

When she and Zephyr parted company at the corner, she felt twice as alone and a hundred times more scared. She called Ginger, but there was no answer. She left a message but now was wondering if that had been a bad idea. Ginger could be anywhere. There weren't a whole lot of options. In the end, she went back to the motel, trying not to look back—trying not to draw attention, reminding herself that she was just another eighteen-year old girl with a backpack and not a terrified pregnant woman, running for her life.

Ginger wasn't in the room when Nanette got back to the hotel. Just the laptop, her backpack, and Bruce, doing what he did best—sleeping in his carrier. Nanette paced the confines of their suite, stopping periodically to steal a glance out the window. Ginger should have been back by now. It was getting close to eight o'clock. Her first set would probably be at nine—nine-thirty at the latest. The newbies didn't rate the more lucrative late spots and they needed every tip they could hustle.

Nanette tried Ginger's cell again, but there was still no answer and now her mailbox was full. Finally, desperation gave no other choice. She looked up the number to *Dark Mountain* and dialed. Another dead end. It was after business hours and the call went directly to voice mail. Nanette hung up and stared at the phone. As a lifeline, it wasn't doing a really good job of it. What the hell. Why not? She called the vineyard back and this time left a message. Maybe the lady, whatever her name was, would check her mail and maybe—just maybe—she'd call back. There was nobody else. This was her last hope.

Ten o'clock came and went. Nanette got up and checked Bruce. She had no clue how to take care of a snake and didn't really want to learn. She settled for taking a mouse out of the fridge hydrator where it was nestled in a bed of lettuce leaves. She opened the carrier and tossed the mouse in the direction of Bruce's head. He might have been glaring at her for the late meal. Or he might have been saying *thanks*. It was hard to tell. She jumped when the phone rang.

"God, where have you been? I have been worried out of my freaking mind," she began but was brought up short when the woman at the other end interrupted.

"This is Francesca. I got your message. Carla's here. Everything is okay. Why did you leave? I came back and you were gone."

From one hundred percent panic to one hundred percent relief in the blink of an eye. Well, fifty percent. There was still Ginger to find. "We didn't know what to do. We heard the door lock and figured you were calling the cops. We've been doing nothing but running for days. But now we've got more trouble."

"Hang tight. Where are you?"

"*The Extended Stay Motel* on South Bascom. Room 324, but—"

"No buts. Stay put. We're on our way." Francesca disconnected.

Nanette put the phone down and ran her fingers through her damp hair. "We may get out of this alive yet, Brucie baby," she said, peering into the carrier. "You want another mouse or something?" Bruce said nothing. He closed those slitted eyes and drifted off to wherever snakes go when they sleep.

Time is a curious thing. It either slows down or speeds up depending on what you're doing. Right now, time was taking its own sweet time. Nanette was at the window, watching, waiting, and hoping Francesca really meant what she'd said. And where was Ginger?

***

It took less than five minutes for Francesca to make a pot of coffee, fill the thermos, grab two cups and meet Carla who was waiting at the front door, bleary-eyed and looking a bit rough around the edges. Two cups of coffee later and they were as good as they were going to get. The drive from *Dark Mountain* to the motel in Francesca's VW Bug was a good forty-five minutes. They made it in just over thirty, and as they were pulling into the motel parking lot, spotted a woman running for all she was worth. She darted across the street, oblivious to traffic, and fled into the motel.

"Here goes nothing," Carla said, exiting the VW in hot pursuit. Seven minutes later, she emerged from the motel with Ginger, who'd been the runner, along with Nanette, Bruce, the backpacks, the computer bag, and the three surviving mice. Francesca's VW, early vintage, kept up an admirable speed as they headed for Highway 17 and the hoped-for safety of the Santa Cruz Mountains.

"You guys want to start at the beginning?" Carla asked. "You sure make a hell of an entrance."

"Everything?" Ginger asked.

"Everything. First though, I'd like to know how you got that shiner and the swollen lip."

"Gennaro." Ginger's hand went to her mouth. "Gennaro Puglisi, the new owner of the Club. We thought we'd left him back in New Haven and he shows up here. He grabbed me as I was crossing the street. I never saw him. All of a sudden, somebody had my arm and the next thing I knew, I was in this car and he was driving like a maniac and cursing. He wanted the laptop, and when I told him I didn't know what he was talking about, he hit me. I kept telling him I didn't have any laptop and he kept hitting me. Finally, I had an idea. I told him my friend had it and I could get it, if he'd let me out of the car. He wouldn't buy it, but he told me to call her and have her bring it to *Eden's Garden*—the club I got a job at. He was so pissed. I figured as soon as he got it, he'd kill me—kill both of us—but I agreed. He turned around and drove back to the club to wait. He thought I was calling

Nanette, but I dialed 911 and pretended to punch a few more numbers so it would look good. When the guy answered, I just started talking like I was talking to Nanette and told him everything Gennaro told me to say, and the guy figured out what was going on. He told me to keep talking, that help was on the way. I acted like Nanette didn't want to come, and I had to convince her it was the only way. Gennaro started getting suspicious and told me to put the phone on speaker, but I told him the battery was too low. He bought it. Honestly, I didn't know if it was going to work, but then the cops showed up, and they busted him. They took me downtown to get my statement, and then they let me go. Then I just ran and ran until I got back to the motel, and there you all were." She stopped for breath. "I was so freakin' scared. What the hell is he doing here? What's going to happen to us?"

Nanette patted her on the shoulder. "He showed up at my club, too. Must be some kinda Mob business. Shit. Can you believe the luck?"

"So, what's the deal with the laptop?" Carla asked.

Nanette filled in the details of the hit that missed them, of thinking that Tommy was behind the hit but now thinking it might be Gennaro. "Do you want to hear about the garbage truck we stole?" she asked. "We didn't keep it."

Francesca, who'd been keeping her eyes on the road, managed a quick look in the rear-view mirror and frowned. "That Land Rover's been behind us since Campbell. You stole a garbage truck?"

"Just a small one. Kind of a compact model. Wouldn't accelerate for shit. I think they had a governor on it. Anyhow, it got us out of New Haven," Nanette said.

Francesca took the Summit Road exit off 17. She checked the rear-view again but there was nothing there. She was starting to see danger where it didn't exist. Ten minutes later they hung a right onto Old San Jose Road and then a left onto Adams Creek. Home was just ahead. The gates opened and they pulled into the drive. Shortly, a white Land Rover cruised past, slowed at the gates, and then continued on down the road.

"Everything's going to be all right," Ginger said as they all climbed out of the car and gathered their things. "It's over with. Now we can get back to starting over. We don't have to go back to the clubs." She turned and looked at Carla. "Can we stay with you until we can find a safe place?"

Carla shook her head. "*I'm* not living in a safe space. Old man Puglisi is paying the rent." She glanced around her. Everything was quiet. Peaceful. But still, there was something she couldn't put her finger on. It was a sense. A foreboding. Damn. There was more shit ahead.

"You can stay here," Francesca said. "This is as safe as you can be while you get things sorted out. Now, I need to fall into bed. And so do all of you. Follow me." She led the way to the guest cottage. "Make yourselves at home. You should find everything you need. Sleep well. Tomorrow's a brand new day."

# CHAPTER THIRTEEN

*Dark Mountain*

Last night's storm had been one of nature's more impressive events. The combination of wind and rain had caused downed trees, power outages, and mudslides that had closed roads, including Highway 17. It would be a day or two or three until the damage had been cleaned up and power restored. In the meantime, nobody was going anywhere, except for Jesse, the rescue basset hound, who divided his time and affections between *Dark Mountain* and the neighbors a quarter of a mile down the street. A free soul, he came and went as the spirit moved him, and today the spirit had him at the door, wearing his usual mournful expression, wagging his tail, and waiting to be let out. Francesca opened the door and called the neighbors to let them know Jesse was on the move.

The winds were still up, and Francesca stood in the doorway, watching the tops of the Redwoods swaying, although more gently than they had during the night. Mountain people expect there are going to be times like this. They stock up on essentials and then take whatever nature dishes out, in stride. A gas stove—propane— means that cooking isn't a problem. Only the newbies opt for electric. They soon learn why that's a bad choice. Kerosene lanterns and candles provide light, just as they have for generations. There's a self-sufficiency in the mountains that can ride out just about everything.

*Dark Mountain* had invested in a small gas-powered generator that could pump water from the well to the house. The generator also had the capacity to allow other appliances to be plugged in, and this morning, Francesca had plugged in the coffee grinder. They'd have fresh, hot coffee, courtesy of the ancient Revere Ware coffee maker that required nothing more than gravity to do the job. These simple chores helped with the general mood. Life this morning seemed less complicated—more doable. Until the power came back on, technology had released its hold.

It was nearly ten o'clock, but they'd all needed the sleep. Now, a buffet-style breakfast of scrambled eggs and sausages, along with toast and jam and fruit was waiting on the center island, plates stacked to the side. There was just one empty plate left, waiting for Nanette to make her appearance. When she did arrive, she just took a piece of toast.

"You need to eat," Francesca said.

"I'm not hungry. Maybe a little later," Nanette said. "I'll take some jam, though. Thanks."

With another pot of coffee on the stove, the Esposito Family War Council was ready to convene.

***

"Here it is," Ginger said, swinging the computer bag onto the dining room table. She removed the manila folders and the laptop and shook out the case for good measure. A key fell out. "I didn't know that was in there." She picked up the key and turned it over. "It says *do not duplicate* on it. What do you suppose it opens?"

Morrie took the key from her. "Post office or safety deposit key, most likely." He set it back down on the table. "I'll work on it."

"Now we find out what was worth murder," Gino said, reaching for the folders. He pushed the laptop over to Morrie, who was rubbing his hands together and looking for all the world like a safecracker getting ready to break the bank. "It's all yours," Gino said.

"My pleasure. Nope. Can that. Battery's dead." He looked at Ginger. "No power cord, huh?"

"No," Ginger said.

"All right." Morrie pushed back from the table and went out to his car, returning with a case of instruments and an assortment of cables and plugs. The third cord he tried was the charm. "Could be a while. This baby isn't new. Did you try to turn it on when you found it?"

"Yeah, but it was dead," Nanette said. "You think it's broken? Like maybe it took a bullet or something? I couldn't see any holes or dents."

"Probably just password protected or encrypted if there's anything in here the guy didn't want to share." Morrie grinned. "This is going to be fun." He actually looked like he meant it. He took the laptop and the cord and left for the generator.

Carla did a major eyeroll. "Pass me the *SF OP* folder. I want to know what that slime bag and his goombahs have planned for us. Joey might be dead, but none of those guys work alone." She set the folder down after a quick glance. "What's the Mafia's interest in the protection racket these days?"

"That and the numbers racket have always been a steady source of income," Gino said. "Gives them seed money for their more elaborate plans. Why?"

"With what they did to Olga and then to Harry tells me they're sending a message to the Russian Mafia and the Tong that anybody outside their borders is fair game. They're telling them to back off—that anything outside their jurisdiction belongs to the Mob. The broken window at Harry's and the broken glass at Olga's was a warning to the other shopkeepers. If they didn't ante up, nobody would be able to protect them." She looked down at the folder. "And nobody did. Property crime is at the bottom of any PD's response time. Even if they do respond, what the hell they gonna do? Fill out a report." Carla got up and brought the coffee pot to the table. "Refills?"

"Hang on," Francesca said. "I saw donuts on the counter yesterday. We need nourishment."

"I thought you were into the healthy snack thing," Carla said. "None of that sugar and fat." She gave Francesca a suspicious look.

"I'm hungry," Francesca said, shrugging, and in the feeding frenzy that ensued, managed to snag a cream-filled, chocolate frosted éclair for herself. A gratified smile spread across her face. "Health food never tastes this good."

The other folders focused on wresting control of existing operations from other family members. Joey's plan had been to first establish himself as head of the protection racket in San Francisco and then, over the course of the next year, put his own people in charge of operations. It was an ambitious project.

Ginger had been listening intently, but the donuts were still calling her and her gaze settled on a raspberry jelly donut. "I wish they made crullers here. That is the perfect donut. I mean, this is good. I'm not complaining. At least it's not a granola bar, and that's all that matters."

"Damn straight," Nanette said.

Ginger set her donut on her plate and licked her fingers. "The Mob seem to be moving most of their attention and resources to shoring up and expanding their human trafficking operations. They've got something going down on October 10th. That's day after tomorrow. What is it? And, with Joey dead, will it still happen?"

"Why not?" Nanette, who'd been reading the pages along with Ginger, looked up, a concern in her eyes. "I mean, murder just seems to be part of these guys' daily lives. It never seems to get in the way of business. It *is* business. Whoever offed Joey knows what's in the pipeline. The question is, what can we do about it? I still keep wondering who we can share all this crap with that will believe we're not involved. I mean, you just don't run across essential Mob stuff unless you're connected. Maybe you guys are lily-white, but if we tell the Feds or whoever that we witnessed a hit and then stole this, how are they gonna leave us alone?"

"Honey," Carla said, "someday, once we figure all this out, and once we've got a plan, and once that plan is in motion, and we've all survived, remind me to tell you a story about my family."

"Got it!" While the speculation was raging, Morrie had returned with the fully-charged computer, used his mobile hot spot to connect to the Web, and plugged in the password hacker software. It didn't take long to gain access. "We're in!" The screen had shed its black cloak of secrecy. Wasting no time, he inserted one flash drive after another, capturing the laptop's contents. Backup and then some.

"You can draw a line through Fiona's name," Carla said. "She got hit day before yesterday. They found her in a ditch near SFO."

"Unusual," said Gino. "I mean they've killed women before. Children, too. They don't draw any lines there, but it doesn't happen often." He poured himself a fresh cup of coffee. "And, she's Enzo's daughter. He's the *Don—The Godfather*. Takes balls to whack one of his kids—even more so, Fiona being his only daughter. She and her husband, Joey, must have been up to something. Naughty. Naughty."

"So who's left?" Carla asked. "I mean, if they're gonna... Sorry. If they are *going* to keep killing each other, maybe we should just wait for a lull in the action. It could make our work easier."

Morrie looked up from the computer. "I think it's time to do what they do on all those police shows. We need a wall chart. Names. Relationships. All that shit."

"On it." Francesca took a bite of her éclair and wiped the crumbs from her lap before she got up to fetch the easel, the pad of paper, the markers, and the rest of the equipment from her office. When she'd gotten everything set up, the dining room looked like a corporate planning area.

Morrie took a small notebook from his case, walked to the easel, and did a few neck rotations. The cracks were audible. "Just loosening up," he said, reaching for a marker. "We're dealing with two families: the Puglisis and the Vincentos. When Fiona married Joey, it should have created a merger. That didn't happen. Let's try to figure out why." Moving to the easel, he drew a line down the middle, labeling one side Puglisi and the other Vincento. "So far, so good," he said. "I feel like some kind of professor."

"Just get on with it. Sheesh," Carla said. "What a ham."

"All right. I did a quick look into all the surviving Puglisis, and this is what I found. We start with Enzo Puglisi. Our landlord. He's 74 but still very much a presence. Enzo had five kids: Salvatore, Alphonse, Fiona, Anthony, and Dominic." He wrote each name underneath Enzo and then drew a line through Sally and Fiona.

"Why did you cross out Salvatore?" Ginger asked.

Carla jumped in. "Trust me," she said, and Ginger nodded.

"That leaves Alphonse and Dominic," Morrie continued. "Alphonse is doing time, but a lot of business gets done in prison, and Dominic would appear to have his hands full with the trash and garbage and recycling empire they've created. Then we've got Dominic's two sons, Paolo and Luigi. They work the east coast garbage business. That's too generous. They do what they're told. Collectively, they don't have the brain power to be behind this, but don't sell them short in other areas as enforcers. They're vicious."

Francesca studied the chart. "Enzo's got to be furious."

"Unless he's the one who offed them," Carla said. "Just because he appreciates my being his granddaughter's ballet teacher don't make him any kind of saint."

"True. That takes us to the current generation," Morrie said. "Alphonse was the most productive in that area with three sons: Gennaro, Tommaso, and Anthony."

Carla interrupted. "Whoa. Hold on a freakin' minute. With all that's been going on, it didn't register. Go back a bit to the granddaughter. Angela Porto. She's seven years old. Whose kid is she? She don't fit nowhere."

Ginger huffed. "Granddaughter? That's rich. She's Enzo's kid. Yeah," she said to the surprised looks around her, "he's still out in the world, sowing his seed. Bastard. He brought her to the Club last time he visited New Haven. Sat her down at the bar and Carmine gave her a soda while Daddy was in a meeting. Don't know who the mother is. Or *was*. Poor kid."

"For the love of God," Carla said. "Poor kid is right. This is one messed-up family."

"But as far as who's behind what's going on in the business part of this, from recent personal experience, Gennaro's my bet," Ginger said. "We know he's here and capable of it."

"You can cross off Tommy," Nanette said. "He loves me and I love him." Her tone defied anyone to challenge her.

"How about we just leave his name here so we can remember that?" Morrie said.

"Okay, but—"

"Finally, there's Anthony," Morrie continued, interrupting whatever Nannette was going to say. "Actually, Father Anthony Puglisi, SJ. We'll keep him here too, but he's got his hands full with the Bishop of the Diocese of San Jose. He's the personal assistant to his Excellency." Morrie turned to Carla. "Catholics have more hierarchy than the Italian government." He returned to the easel. "For all practical purposes, we're left with Gennaro or Tommaso." He shot Nanette a look that silenced her before she could figure out what she wanted to say.

"Fiona has—had a son. Nicolo. Goes by Nico. He's a late entry into all of this, but he bears some looking into. He's had numerous run-ins during his teens with the authorities. With his mother and father dead, he may be out for vengeance, unless, of course, he's the one who killed them. It's happened before."

Francesca scanned the remaining names. "That leaves us with, what? Six possibles as the mastermind? Enzo, Alphonse, Dominic, Gennaro, Nicolo, and Tommaso. That's a lot."

Nanette muttered something unintelligible at the mention of Tommaso.

"It makes seven. Add one more to the list. Joey had a brother. He came over from Italy for the funeral and stayed on." Morrie moved to the Vincento side and wrote *Johnny Vincento*. "Johnny's a lone wolf. No children and no other blood relatives now that Joey is no longer among the living."

Carla, looking at the list, considered her response. "We got to reduce this number to a more manageable.....number." She shrugged. "Why isn't there another word for number? Anyway, we know why they're targeting *us*, but why are they turning on each other?"

Setting the marker down, Morrie stepped away from the easel. "The motive for murder always boils down to revenge for a wrong, perceived or real, power desired or denied, profit to be gained or preserved, fear of something or someone, or passion—and that can go either way. The heat of the moment or the built-up heat of denial, and you know, I can't think of anything else. Sometimes, it's a combination of those motives. One thing I'm pretty sure of, though, It's not over."

Gino sat back in his chair, studying his steepled fingers, and had an idea. "We're discounting Father Anthony, but we're only doing that because he's a priest. I say we keep him for the time being." The lightbulb that suddenly exploded in his brain made him sit bolt upright. "Father Anthony." Gino clapped his hands together and let out a whoop.

"You all right, honey?" Francesca gave her husband one of those concerned-wife looks. "You're repeating yourself."

"I know. I know. But it just dawned on me. The bishop. The bishop's personal assistant—Father Anthony Puglisi."

Francesca shook her head. "Okay? What does that mean for us?"

"I have a meeting with the bishop on Wednesday to discuss the expansion of the wine contract," Gino said. "I expect he'll be accompanied by Father Anthony. This is going to be interesting."

"As the token Jew in this enclave of lapsed Catholics, what does SJ mean?" Morrie asked.

"Society of Jesus," Gino said. "He's a Jesuit, and that says a great deal about our priest. He's an intellectual. That's a given. He's also, if he fits the pattern, pious and ambitious. The Jesuits are the kind people who gave us The Inquisition back in the day. I wouldn't put it past them to resurrect it, pardon my pun, if they felt the need."

"So, who's really in charge?" Carla asked. "The bishop or the priest?"

Morrie added Father Anthony to the list. "Eight," he said.

"Shit," Carla said, to murmurs of agreement.

Morrie reclaimed his chair, and Francesca took his place at the easel. "Goals and Objectives. We've done this before. Now that we know who we're dealing with, what's our goal?"

Gino spoke first. "Stopping their protection racket. That one is too close to home."

Francesca flipped to a clean sheet on the easel.

"Put an end to their human trafficking enterprise." The anger in Ginger's voice resonated with the rest of the women.

"Avenge Harry's murder," Carla said.

"Three goals, then. They're all related. Essentially, it all comes down to eliminating the Puglisi crime empire," Francesca said, drawing a circle around all three.

Gino's question, "So, what are we going to do after lunch?" broke the tension.

"Speaking of lunch, Chan's working on the protection racket full bore," Morrie said. "Actually, he's got quite a bit of experience in this area." To the skeptical faces around the table, he explained. "Chan's semi-retired, but the Korean Mafia is not something to disregard. Operating on the principle that *the enemy of my enemy is my friend*, I'm going to leave any involvement at a respectful distance. I trust Chan. He's got a pony in this race, just as we do. He's got his restaurant. Extortion is a good beginning, but our goal is to get the Puglisi family on something that will put them away for keeps."

"Murder," Carla said. "They killed Harry."

Morrie nodded. "That will be the final nail in their coffin. In the meantime, we're going to make them spend all their resources trying to stop whoever is throwing a large assortment of monkey wrenches into their operations." He looked around the table. "That would be us."

"Class dismissed," Francesca said, just as the lights flickered twice and the power came back on. "If the trucks got through to repair the lines, the roads are probably cleared."

"That's an omen," Carla said. "And it's a good one." She looked at Morrie. "Thinking positive."

# CHAPTER FOURTEEN

*San Francisco*

With PG&E at work repairing power lines and CalTrans still moving tons of mud from the roadways, Carla and Morrie's drive back to the City was slow and conversation was limited. The Santa Cruz Mountains were once an ancient seabed, and they're made of clay, limestone, sand, and sandstone, with a sprinkling of shale and granite and schist. When all that gets soaked with the winter rains, gravity takes over. In short, from the moment of their formation, the mountains have been doing their best to slide back down to sea level. In many places, they're having considerable success.

Highway 17 is the main artery connecting Santa Cruz and the coast to Silicon Valley and points north and east, and it winds its way through the Santa Cruz Mountains. A lane closure results in massive backups, suicidal thoughts, and in more than one case, a sincere wish to bail out of California altogether.

Morrie hadn't reached that point, but he had been focused on finding new lodgings that weren't managed by the Mob. The market was tight, but there was a loft south of Market that looked promising, and he and Carla were making a detour on the way home to check it out. "Five minutes earlier, and we might have had it," he said, as they passed the sign announcing the warehouse was now fully leased.

"It was a good idea," Carla said, "and there are bound to be more coming on the market soon. I like the idea of a loft. It's the best of both worlds. You can divide it however you want. If we can find one big enough, we can put the ballet studio on the street side for frontage and have the back for living space. There's a lot of possibilities there." She checked out the empty warehouses on the other side of the street. "It's just a matter of time," she said, "and now that we have Enzo's apartment, the pressure's off."

***

"What's going on? Old Prune Face is blocking the front door of our apartment house." Carla was referring to the manager who looked at them with something between disdain and hatred. "What did we ever to do him? I've hardly spoken three words to him."

"I think we're about to find out," Morrie said. "He's heading towards us with a paper in his hand."

"I regret to inform you that you must vacate the premises within twenty-four hours," was the manager's opening statement. "According to the terms of your lease, the landlord reserves the right to terminate occupancy at will." Prune Face handed Morrie the pertinent page of the lease with the termination clause highlighted in red. "However," he held up a hand to stave off Carla's objections and what appeared to be Morrie making a fist. "However," he repeated, backing up two steps that might or might not have been sufficient to protect him, "Mr. Puglisi understands the difficulty this presents for you and has authorized me to present you with this." He reached into his jacket pocket and produced an envelope which he started to hand to Morrie, but thinking better of it, handed it to Carla instead. He gave a stiff, formal bow and eased past them, disappearing into the garage below from which, shortly, a car emerged and sped away.

"What the friggin' hell was that all about?" Carla sputtered. "I hate these people, Morrie. I really, really do."

Morrie, just as blindsided, threw both arms up in the air, causing the envelope to spiral to the sidewalk.

Carla retrieved the envelope, slit it open, and withdrew a check written on Enzo Puglisi's private account in the amount of ten thousand dollars. They looked down at the check, then at each other, then down at the check again. "You suppose it's good?" Carla asked. "I mean, it ain't gonna bounce, is it?"

"I hardly think so," Morrie said. "Come on, Miss Marie. We have to pack up and move on down the road, and we don't have a whole lot of time. The clock is ticking."

"Okay. Fine. But we're stopping at the bank first to cash this." She waved the check in the air. "I ain't taking any chances."

***

"I feel like one of them nomads," Carla said. "You know, people who never stop moving. Forever. They probably die moving." She looked at Morrie. "Nomad was one of my words last week. I didn't really think I'd ever get a chance to use it. Just goes to show you never know nothing about nothing." She was transferring clothes from the dresser to a black trash bag. She looked around the bedroom. "I am a nomad," she intoned, and Morrie threw a sock at her. She laughed and threw it back. "It's gonna be fine. We've still got the dance studio, but that washer/dryer combo down the hall sure was nice. Beat carting everything to the laundromat every week." She stopped short. "I gave that nice old lady that owns it a poster about Pierre. There." She dragged the trash bag to the door and gave Morrie the look that said, *It's all yours.*

By mid-afternoon, the packing was done and the apartment tidied up. When Morrie said it wasn't necessary to leave the place spotless, Carla waved off his objection. "We're better than they are," she said. Now they were back at the studio from which they'd moved less than a week ago. "At least we can talk now," Carla said. "I felt like a kid at school, passing notes. Wonder who's moving in that's so important?" Balanced on her left leg, she climbed into her leotard. "Maybe it's somebody on our Puglisi-Vincento list? That would be interesting." She finished dressing. "I've got to warm up before the Intermediates get here, and then I've got to sort the piano pieces for the Advanced Adult Class tomorrow night. Maybe you can find out?"

Morrie, laptop already open on the counter, notepad on his lap, and pen grasped between his teeth, ran a hand across the top of his bald head and nodded.

"You know you got a five o'clock shadow on that head," Carla said.

Morrie rubbed his bristly scalp. "Maybe I'll try growing hair again?"

"Change is good," was Carla's reply. "Go for it, but I think that ship has sailed. I like you the way you are. Bald is beautiful. Besides, I can use the top of your head if I forget my mirror. See you later."

***

"Enzo Antonio Puglisi," Morrie began, then stopped to pour the wine while Carla brought the pizza box and napkins over to the counter. "Francesca give you this? It's good."

"She said it's okay. Not as good as this year's will be. Something about a late rain." She took a sip. "Tastes fine to me."

"Hmm. Yeah. It's good." He held out his plate and Carla filled it with three slices.

"They cut it kinda small," she said. "It ain't apizza, New Haven style. Not enough cheese."

"We must adjust," Morrie said, wedging his printout between his plate and the wall. "All right. Here we go. 'Born 1940. Emigrated in 1953 from Sardinia—small town on the coast near Olbia—to the United States. Settled in San Francisco with his parents. Reason for the move is unclear. Father involved somehow in the fishing fleet.'" Morrie looked up from his notes and ripped off a mouthful of pizza. "Another Mob enterprise. Making me think that the old man was somehow connected." He shrugged. "Anyway, Enzo married in 1963. Woman named Giulia. She died two years ago. They had five children. Enzo had at least six. We know all about the family tree from yesterday. Puglisi doted on the daughter, Fiona, according to all accounts. Didn't dote on her husband Joey, also currently deceased. He's besotted with his granddaughter/daughter, Angela Porto," Morrie looked up again, "your star pupil."

"Besotted?" Carla asked.

"Besotted. Means....besotted. Look it up." He continued, ignoring Carla's exasperated look. "Enzo moved into garbage and trash quite easily in his mid-twenties. May have had the way paved for him. Has survived at least three attempts on his life over time. Now spends most of his days in his greenhouse with his orchids. He's won numerous awards with them. And that," Morrie said, "is that."

"That is not *that*," Carla said. "That's the raw material. We need to flesh out his personality profile. He's got a generous streak. Well, sort of. Trying to compensate us for burning down our home—*if* he's the one who burned it. That's kinda twisted, if you ask me. Or, he's making some kind of amends for one of his sons or grandsons. He might still have his hand in as far as the grandsons go. Maybe they just tolerate him. Does he have a temper? If he ordered the fire, he didn't care who got hurt. Just business. That's cold. We know he didn't care for Joey, but he seems to get along well with women. How does he get along with his surviving sons? And those attempts on his life. When? Who? Why? That could be important."

For the next bit, they sat in silence, eating, drinking, and thinking. "We can't be 100% sure, of course," Morrie said, "but Enzo's been pulling back, bit by bit. The last attempt on his life was fifteen years ago. Nothing since then. His sons run the show. I'm going to bed. Care to join me on the cot? The floor?" He looked hopeful.

"Floor. Hold on. I'll get another mat. You're impossible, you know that?"

"Whatever works."

***

Breakfast the next morning was leftover cold pizza and coffee. The microwave was available, but all it did was make the crust soggy. Carla was portioning out the remaining orange juice. It was time to get some more, but space was at a premium in the mini-fridge. Morrie, scanning through files on the laptop while he chewed, suddenly choked and started a coughing fit.

"You okay? Carla asked.

When he could breathe again, Morrie took a swallow of coffee to soothe his ragged throat. "Why do people ask you if you're okay when you can't talk? I know it's just a reflex thing, but shit. It's not like you're going to stop strangling to answer."

"Sorry. You're right. Although, if you could answer, it would mean you were still breathing."

"So does coughing." He got up to go to the bathroom, leaving his half-eaten slice of pizza where it had fallen on the keyboard. Carla lifted it off with both hands, trying not to get sauce in the cracks between the keys. She mostly succeeded but needed a damp paper towel to clean up the rest. As she was working on the space between *J* and *K,* she looked up at the screen to see what Morrie was working on and saw her name big as life in the middle of a list of names, none of which she recognized.

"When were you going to tell me I was in the laptop?" she asked Morrie who'd just returned from the bathroom, all pizza residue washed from his face. "What does it mean?"

Morrie looked at her, then at the screen, then back at her again. He could lie, but she'd know. He shut the laptop and took her hand. Finally, he took a breath and plunged ahead. "It's a hit list," he said. Whatever he'd expected her to say in reply came nowhere near her actual words.

"How come I'm number five?" she asked, her tone almost sulking.

"Honey, this is not the kind of list you want to be number one on. You don't want to be on this list at all! It's a freaking death sentence!"

Somewhat mollified, Carla nodded. "Okay. So what do we do about it?"

"I was making copies of everything so we could turn this over to the Feds, but I do not want your name on it anywhere, and if it's been on there once, it's going to be there forever. They'll find it when they go over it with all their equipment. So now," he released her hand and stared at the computer, "I don't know what the hell to do."

"They never forget," Carla said. "We got a problem."

"Indeed. I'm thinking maybe you should take a short vacation somewhere until we get this issue taken care of." Morrie looked into her eyes, concern and a hint of fear in his. Her answer was what he'd figured it would be. She wasn't going anywhere.

"Get a grip, Morrie. I ain't running any more. One day, you realize the running has to stop. One day, you stop running. I've got you, my life is here, and I got plans to go on living and breathing until God decides it's time for me to die. Not some goon. Not some lowlife scum. *God.*" She raised an index finger and jabbed at the heavens to make sure God got the point. "Besides, I got my magic decoder bracelet." She gave him a warm smile. "Just don't take too long to get to me if I send a secret message."

# CHAPTER FIFTEEN

*San Francisco*

It was getting on towards closing time, and Trizbel was putting everything to rights a few minutes early. People just couldn't resist pawing through the displays. That wasn't so bad, but leaving the stock on the floor when they dropped it was way over the line. She shouldn't complain. Business had actually picked up at the *Clothes Horse* since the fire down the block. Curiosity was driving it, most likely, but this month was shaping up to be the best this year. Foot traffic was key for sales, but parking was at a premium. Much as she hated to admit it, Cow Hollow needed a parking garage. Not one of those concrete monstrosities that would destroy the neighborhood, but something to give folks time for a leisurely stroll and some serious window shopping that would draw them inside. What would it look like? The idea was appealing, and she paused with the heather green sweater half-folded as her mind wandered. She didn't see the men when they entered, and it was only when one of them approached her that she startled. Instantly, she knew. There was no mistaking what was happening. She felt a cold chill but gave the man her best professional smile.

"Good afternoon. What can I help you find?" she asked, finishing the folding and pressing the dot on her bracelet as she returned the sweater to the stack.

The man, mid-twenties, heavy-set, and wearing a cheap knock-off suit that would have fit him better forty pounds ago, sneered. "I'm here to offer you a new insurance program," he said. "It's the only one you'll need. It's a must-have."

She'd rehearsed this a dozen times, but remembering her lines was more difficult than she'd thought it would be. They'd all gone through the training. *Role-playing*, Chan called it. Every possible scenario had been acted out with the appropriate response. Buying time without risk was the goal. She smiled again. "No, thank you. I already have insurance. I've got Workman's Comp, theft, fire, you name it! I'm covered! Oh yes!" she added. "Earthquake, too! Thanks for stopping by, though. If you've got a card, I'd be happy to keep it on file. You can drop it on the counter as you leave." Turning away, she walked slowly towards the front and saw that the other man had taken up his post outside, blocking the entry door. The knock-off suit was right behind her. She could feel his presence and, even if she hadn't, his body odor was more than enough to let her know he was closer than he should be. It was the longest short walk she could remember taking, but just a few more steps and she'd be able to put the counter between them. Instead, his hand grabbed her shoulder and spun her around. He didn't release his grip. Instead he kept tightening it, seeming to get some sort of perverted pleasure out of it.

"Let go of me!" she said, trying to keep the panic out of her voice.

"Not so fast. You need to understand the terms of your new insurance policy."

Trizbel wrenched herself free. Fixated on grabbing her again, the thug at her heels didn't see his associate at the door crumple and fall to the ground, one of Chan's men standing over him, a taser in his hand. "You know why we're here," he continued. "You have twenty-four hours. Five hundred in cash. That's the first installment. Each installment comes due on the first of the month. Don't try anything you'll—"

"I think he was going to say regret," Chan said, kicking the inert body sprawled on the floor.

Heaving a sigh of relief, Trizbel grabbed Chan's arm for support. "I didn't expect *you* to show up. You said you'd be sending some of your men."

"Well, you know. I just wanted to be sure we had everything together." Chan reached for his cell and punched a number. "Two for pickup." He disconnected.

"That's all?"

"Sure." He looked down, then around the room as if he were seeing it for the first time. "No, that's not all. I didn't want anything to happen to you. *That's* all."

"I see."

"Do you?" There was a look in his eyes when he spoke to her that she hadn't seen before. "They'll send the second wave back either tomorrow or the next day," he said. "I expect tonight they'll be wondering where their soldiers disappeared to. The one who sent them won't be suspecting anything on your part. It'll be the other way around."

"They don't trust their own people?"

"No. Not at all. They're really big about giving trust and respect lip service, but that's all it is. They don't know the meaning of the words. They live in fear of each other from the top down. In a weird way, they're all prisoners of it. They live with it morning, noon, and night. So now, in this situation, they're not sure about anything. They don't know whether they've lost the element of surprise or not. Most likely, they'll play it the same way they did tonight. They might send three, but I doubt it. They'll have the word out on these two, though. Excuse me a minute, the van's waiting out back."

With the two insurance agents packed away in their transport to the container ship's hold, and with Chan's associate riding shotgun, the first skirmish in this gang war was over. The adrenaline rush had dissipated, and Trizbel had claimed a chair by the dressing room and collapsed into it.

"You did great," Chan said, returning to the showroom to find Trizbel shaking so hard her teeth were chattering. "Hey, it's all right. It's all right. You did great. You're okay." He stood over her. "Come on. Let's go get a drink and something to eat. I know a good Korean restaurant. I'm a close, personal friend of the chef. Plus, they give me a good deal on the drinks and the food." He laughed. "Tomorrow is time enough to plan for tomorrow."

# CHAPTER SIXTEEN

*Dark Mountain Vineyard*

The storms seemed to come earlier and earlier each year. Francesca stood, coffee mug in hand, at the glass doors that opened onto the back deck. Used to be that you could pretty much count on September and October for some of the best weather. Not too hot, not too cold, but that wasn't necessarily the case any longer. She took a thoughtful sip, watching as a doe with this year's twins, now mostly grown, browsed on the hillside above the meadow. She spied Nanette, walking up the path. The deer noticed her as well and gave her a wary eye but didn't bolt into the forest. Francesca slid the doors open and walked onto the deck. This time, the doe had had enough, and with a snort and stomping of her front foot, led her offspring to a quieter section of the terrain. Looking up, Nanette raised her hand and waved.

Francesca waved back. "Coffee's on," she called.

Nanette nodded, picking up her pace.

"You're up early," Francesca said, refilling her own mug and pouring one for Nanette who'd plunked herself on the stool by the butcher block that occupied the central portion of the kitchen floor.

"Couldn't sleep. My mind just wouldn't stop working. That ever happen to you?"

"All the time. Milk? Sugar?"

Nanette shook her head. "This is fine." She looked around the kitchen. "This is nice. It's comfortable, you know? Not all showy like some people do it up. It's a nice place to be, not just a place you got to work in and can't wait to get away from." She looked down into her coffee, watching the steam spiraling up and disappearing when it met the cooler air outside its porcelain chamber.

"Thanks. It's a lot different from the one where I grew up. I wasn't allowed into it. It was the domain of Cook. It was a fearful place. I learned to avoid it early on." Francesca gave a half-smile, half sadness and half regret. "What about your childhood kitchen?"

"Oh, there were so many kitchens. None of them belonged to me. You got to have a family you belong to first before you can get to the kitchen part." She gripped the coffee mug so tightly her knuckles were white rocks. "I didn't have *Cook*. I didn't have shit. Oh, I had plenty of those, though," she said, pointing to the trash bag filled with yesterday's garbage, waiting by the door. "Thanks for the coffee." She left the mug on the butcher block and disappeared down the hall to her bedroom. She pushed past Ginger who had just emerged from the bathroom shower, her hair wrapped in a towel turban and wearing one of Francesca's robes. The door didn't exactly slam, but it closed with enough of a message to let the world know they weren't welcome.

Francesca took a deep breath. *Well, girlfriend, you put your foot into that just fine. Damn.* Now what? Time. Nanette needed time. She'd come around in time. Everybody had a story. Whatever Nanette's was, she wasn't ready to tell it.

"Looks like you've seen the other side of my friend," Ginger said, reaching into the cupboard for a coffee mug. "Just leave her alone. She'll be back in a bit. No tears, though, and don't expect an apology. For someone who looks like a pixie, she carries an enormous chip on those athletic shoulders." She poured herself some coffee and sat down on the stool Nanette had vacated.

"I'm the one who should apologize. She probably thinks I'm some sort of spoiled rich girl who looks down her nose at everybody who doesn't come with a pedigree. Problem is," Francesca said, "my pedigree is nothing she'd want to claim." She pushed the start button on the bread maker and joined Ginger at the butcher block.

"Foster care," Ginger said. "It's an eighteen-year prison sentence for non-offenders. Some placements are better than others, but I wouldn't wish that so-called life on anybody."

"What did she mean about having so many trash bags?"

"Trash bags? Oh. Yeah. That's what the kids get to put their few belongings in when they get moved from one place to the next." She looked up at Francesca. "No shit. What's the message there? Right. Take your garbage with you when you go. Not much of a step to begin wondering if you're not garbage yourself. And then people wonder why so many of those kids never make it." She turned to see if Nanette had decided to come out of her room, but it was still too soon. "I'm the first friend she's ever had. And now Tommy. She's fallen hard. If a guy so much as smiles at her, she's ready to follow him to the ends of the earth." She sighed. "She's a good kid. Just needs a break."

Nanette avoided Francesca for the rest of the morning and on into the afternoon. She skipped breakfast and lunch and the afternoon was making its way towards evening when Francesca decided enough was enough. She fixed a sandwich plate, straightened her shoulders and took a deep breath.

"Truce?" Francesca called, knocking on the bedroom door. For a moment there was no answer, but then the doorknob turned and Nanette stood at the doorway. Her face was pale and there were dark circles under her eyes, but there was no sign of tears.

"Thanks," she said, accepting the plate and the can of soda.

"Eat," Francesca said. "I'm going to run up to the store to get a few things in a bit. If you want to come with me, it should be safe. Just a store on the mountain. Mostly locals use it."

Nanette hesitated, looking at her lunch plate.

"Eat first. Then if you want to come along, I'll be in my office." Francesca headed back to the kitchen, sparing Nanette the problem of an answer.

***

"The last time my mother saw me was in the delivery room," was Francesca's opening gambit as she and Nanette pulled onto Old San Jose Road with their shopping lists. "Obviously, I don't remember that. My father? Never laid eyes on him, or he on me, for that matter. His part in the whole affair was over quickly—about as quickly as the marriage they tried. He was a two-bit actor who never broke into the big time. My mother, on the other hand, was South Korea's leading lady—Claudine Boucher." Francesca paused in her account to let a fox meander across the road. The wildlife was active these days, getting ready for winter and either hibernation or migration. Anyhow, she chanced a look at Nanette who hadn't responded but who seemed more relaxed. Francesca soldiered on. "So, with girls not being all that desirable as offspring, nobody was interested in accepting the unwanted burden of my existence, and my grandmother took me on as a responsibility. I had everything I needed. Clothes, education, an expense account. Yep. Everything except what a kid needs. So, you see, I do understand. I just spent my time alone in one place, not a series of them."

By the time they left the store and stashed the groceries and toiletries in the car, Nanette had thawed and the conversation came more easily. "They didn't have any live mice, but I guess that's not an item in big demand," she said. "We got to get some tomorrow, though. Bruce gets cranky when he's hungry." She craned her neck to check traffic. "You're okay on the right. Go ahead. But you got Gino now, and he loves you. I can tell. He looks at you the way Tommy looks at me." Her voice softened. "How'd you meet him?"

Francesca laughed and shook her head. "He picked me up on an airplane. I was in trouble with the law. My ex-boss had me framed for embezzlement, and I was crawling back home to my grandmother, hoping to buy some time while I tried to figure out what to do next. Things got even more complicated though, and it wasn't long before I realized Gino was The One." She chuckled. "There's more, but that's for another day."

"But what happened with that boss creep?"

"He's currently in the state penitentiary." She chanced a quick look at Nanette. "Things have a way of working out. You'll see. You just have to believe."

***

Meanwhile, Gino was in his own office, tackling two facets of the same problem. The problem was Father Anthony Puglisi, SJ. The last two discussions of the wine contracts had been handled at the diocesan offices in San Jose, but this time, Gino was thinking, perhaps an invitation for his Excellency, the bishop, to tour the vineyards at *Dark Mountain* and enjoy a complimentary VIP wine tasting would be a better venue for securing an order. If the opportunity presented itself, he might also be able to have a heart to heart with the priest. Gino picked up his cell to place the call. As it played out, however, the bishop was unable to get away due to prior commitments but would send his personal assistant in his stead if that would be acceptable. Gino disconnected. Acceptable? It was perfect.

Each parish in the diocese of San Jose uses numerous cases of wine yearly for Holy Communion. Gino's plan was to encourage the bishop to recommend *Dark Mountain* to the nearly fifty parishes overseen by the diocese. It would mean a tremendous increase in revenue for the vineyard. In recent years, tastes had changed, and the drier wines, such as those grown at *Dark Mountain*, were a good fit for those tastes. It was an ambitious undertaking and Gino's first attempt at breaking free from the old mold. He was hoping for a miracle, but then, the Catholic Church dealt in miracles on a daily basis. Gino frowned. When was the last time he'd stepped inside a church? He hoped that wouldn't be a dealbreaker. His mind traveled back to his childhood before his parents died. Mass, Confession, Holy Communion, the whole nine yards, but then the world shifted on its axis, and even in Sardinia, life was different. His grandfather wasn't devout, even though Celestina did her best. *Bless me Father, for I have sinned...* That's the way Confession started. For a moment, Gino felt a pang of something that might have been a stirring of some long-forgotten religious feeling. Regardless, Father Anthony Puglisi was a Jesuit, and Jesuits are pragmatists. It was worth a shot.

***

If Gino'd had a picture in his mind of what Father Anthony Puglisi, SJ would look like, the reality either came up way short or was way beyond expectations, depending on how he looked at it. The man standing at the front door was dressed in tan slacks, a navy polo shirt, and was wearing tan Italian loafers—no socks. He was young. Gino was not a good judge of age, but the priest was definitely no more than thirty. Clean-shaven. Tall. Father Anthony was a shade over six feet, dwarfing Gino at his five foot six. His broad shoulders suggested he was a swimmer, and he didn't appear to carry any extra weight. There was a power cord in his left hand, a black Tesla parked in the drive under the portico, a question in his brown eyes, and a hopeful smile on his face. The connection wasn't difficult to make.

"Good afternoon," the visitor said, extending his right hand. "I'm Father Puglisi."

"Good afternoon," Gino replied, accepting the offer of a handshake. "I'm Gino Esposito, as you've probably already figured out. Welcome to *Dark Mountain*, the home of excellent varietals as well as a source of moderately dependable electricity." Gino pointed to the outlet just to the left of the entryway. "Plug in," he said. "You're not the first."

"Thanks. The bishop leaves this part to me. He doesn't drive unless there's no other choice. It's a leap of faith setting off from home base and seeing if you can get where you're going on one charge. And it gets tricky on these mountain roads. I'm checking the battery level, trying not to go over the edge into some ravine, and listening to the GPS all at once. It's a workout." He pulled a tissue from his pants pocket and wiped his forehead.

With Father Puglisi decompressing and the car docked at the charging station, Gino began the tour of the vineyards, the bottling facility under construction, and the wine cellar. The last stop was the back deck of his home where a black oak charcuterie board laden with meats, cheeses, and crackers along with a selection of wines awaited, courtesy of Francesca.

There is that moment when strangers sit down at a communal table, and decisions are made. If the company is congenial, the first thing that happens is a general settling in. Packages and other belongings are dealt with, and there's a sense of anticipation of good conversation to be shared and plans made. It's a comfortable feeling. Everyone is relaxed. When the company is unfamiliar with each other, however, there's a different protocol. There are smiles all around, of course. They're polite smiles, sometimes a bit nervous, given the circumstances of the meeting, and they're not necessarily sincere, although they may be, for those looking for a possible future sexual assignation. For the most part, though, it's a feeling-out process, weighing the pros and cons of potential future associations, and it all happens in the instant. By the time the parties have seated themselves and moved their chairs closer to the table, decisions have been made. It's instinctive, merely a watered-down version of fight or flight. For this afternoon's meeting at *Dark Mountain*, the possibility of an assignation was not in the cards, given the sexual preference of Gino, the avowed celibacy of the guest, and the committed disinterest of the only woman present. So, what remained was a business transaction from which all participants hoped to profit. And the business at hand, as far as Gino and Francesca were concerned, went far beyond the potential sales of the Communion wine from *Dark Mountain Vineyard*, although that would have been a nice perk.

"Are you religious?" was Father Puglisi's opener.

"No," Gino replied, leaning forward, "I'm not. Are you?"

Father Puglisi hesitated only briefly. "I guess it all depends on what you consider the definition of *religious* to be." He sat back, his eyes focused on the charcuterie board as if he were in a chess match and his king suddenly in danger. "I believe this visit is about more than the Communion wine," he said. "It's a business meeting of a different focus, and you have me at a bit of a disadvantage. I assume you wish to find new markets for your wine, and if our conversation goes according to the way you hope, that may indeed happen. Every vintner does that. It's how you survive in a cutthroat business, but that will come a ways down the road, and only after you tell me why you really extended the invitation for me to inspect your winery." He lowered his hands and then raised them, palms up, waiting.

The last thing Father Anthony Puglisi expected to hear was Francesca's simple statement, "I'm a Buddhist, Father. You're a Jesuit. You already know what I'm about to tell you." She looked up from the food spread, where she'd been stabbing a few cubes of cheese to add to her plate. "The Buddha teaches that all human life is suffering, and then we die. Once you wrap your mind around that, life isn't quite as uncertain. It's pretty straightforward. We cope. We live. We die. Although, if I may interject something relevant to our situation here, the Buddha never said we shouldn't try to lessen our suffering while we're negotiating life. Arson, murder, and extortion cause a great deal of human suffering. And we've experienced and witnessed all of it. We," she tilted her head towards Gino, "and also our friends and neighbors. If the law can't or won't help, we're going to have to act on our own."

Father Puglisi, having listened attentively, came to the only logical conclusion available to him. "*Omerta*. It's as old as Italy. Don't trust the government. Don't cooperate in anything they ask, and pursue justice with your comrades." He winked at Francesca. I think I'd like to try a glass of that," he said, pointing to the Merlot. "Normally, I prefer an Irish whiskey, but image is everything, and if my family were to find out, I'd be in some serious trouble. They already get nervous enough around me as it is."

About to pour, Gino set the bottle down. "I'll join you," he said. "Man does not live by wine alone. Be right back."

"Your husband is an attentive host," Father Puglisi said to Francesca.

"He is. We need your help, Father." She poured herself a glass of water. "While Gino is fetching the spirits, I'd like to plant a seed, if you will permit me."

"Mrs. Esposito, you have a way of saying a great deal without saying much at all. It's quite a gift, and my curiosity requires I say yes." He eyed her quizzically.

"Francesca, please. Woman doesn't necessarily live by wine alone either." She inclined her head at the bottle before them. "I'm rather fond of that Merlot. I hope you enjoy it." She took a sip of water and stabbed another cube of cheese, adding it to her plate. "The Communion wine. We can meet your price point," she said, "along with whatever quantities you request. I've been looking at the orders from several parishes, and St. Boniface generally orders about fifty cases a year. That would go a long way towards easing us into the bigger markets. If we could pick up that one or one of a similar budget this year, well, we're hoping one satisfied customer will lead to others and allow us to grow our brand." She lifted Gino's glass to let the light reflect on the rich burgundy color. "Lovely, isn't it? And it tastes as good as it looks. Even ecclesiastical tastes have been shifting away from the fruity, sweeter wines to something a bit drier." She set the glass of wine back on the table. "I'll send a couple of bottles with you for you to sample at your leisure. Or, if we can interest you in a bit of marketing, I can make that a case." She gave him an appraising look.

***

With the Irish in hand, Gino and Father Puglisi clinked glasses, filled their plates, and sat back in their chairs. "Twenty-two years ago, almost to the day," Gino began, "my mother and father left me in the care of our housekeeper, Celestina, and went to town. They never got there. They were run off the road and killed. The driver of the car didn't stop. But why would he? It was all in a day's work." Gino studied the whiskey in his glass. "The week before, the collectors had come to my grandfather's home in Sardinia. It was time for the annual payment. The *pizzo*. My grandfather decided he'd paid enough and sent the men away. It was an unfortunate decision he would regret the rest of his life." Gino set the glass down. "With no other living relatives, this estate," he waved his arm around the expanse of *Dark Mountain*, "where my parents had decided to settle, was closed up—boarded up, actually, and the vineyards left to the whims of nature. I remained in Sardinia with my grandfather, a daily reminder that he'd brought about the death of his own son and his daughter-in-law and now bore the responsibility for raising me."

"The *pizzo*," Father Puglisi said. "It is a mortal sin."

"Johnny Vincento." Gino replied. "His name is Johnny Vincento. He killed my mother and my father. And for what? To inflate his bank account!" Gino slammed his fist on the table and his glass fell to the deck floor and shattered. "It stops now!" Hands covering his face, he sat in silence, physically and emotionally drained.

Father Puglisi set his own glass back down on the table. "Johnny Vincento. He's here. And you're right. He has killed. It doesn't matter if it's done second or third or fourth hand or whatever. He issued the orders for others to follow." Father Puglisi took the purple stole from his pocket. "If you will permit me," he said. He kissed the stole and draped it around his neck. Placing his hand on Gino's head, he prayed.

"I always carry it with me," he said. "Especially in California. The way people drive, it's a wonder I don't need it more often than I do." He smiled. "To right a wrong is a noble undertaking. I don't know what I can do to advance your cause, but I will pray for you and beyond that, offer whatever material assistance I am capable of giving. I can tell you this." He folded the stole and returned it to his pocket. "Johnny Vincento is in contact with someone in my family. Honestly, I don't know who. I am not a part of that. Never have been. I serve a different Master. They come to me when they fear the consequences of their actions, and I hear their confessions. What happens there remains in the Confessional. I give them absolution. The rest," he shrugged, "is between them and God. I am just the mediator." He checked his watch and stood. "I do know Johnny's taken up residence in San Francisco in an apartment house owned by my grandfather. That would not have happened by accident. Thanks for the Irish, the food, and the tour. I'll be in touch after I make some calls on both accounts. And yes," he said to Francesca. "I'll take a case with me. God's blessing on you," he said to Francesca, and she knew that he knew. Once she was certain, she would tell Gino.

# CHAPTER SEVENTEEN

*San Francisco and Dark Mountain*

Keeping track of Nanette and Ginger hadn't been difficult. Well, Nanette for sure, and Tommaso figured the girls would stick together. The tracking app he'd installed had kept tabs on Nanette ever since she'd left San Jose. He was more worried about what he'd say when he finally caught up with her. The fact that Nanette hadn't tried to contact him had to mean something. Somehow, she must think he was behind everything. Or maybe she was trying to protect him. Or...he was running out of scenarios, except for the one he feared the most. The one that concerned their baby. Convincing her of the truth wasn't going to be easy if she thought he'd been involved in the massacre. Once her mind started going in one direction, reining it in and turning it around was almost impossible. He clenched his jaw. He had to try and he had to succeed. Their future depended on it.

No matter how many different ways he mentally started the conversation they were going to have, it all just boiled down to one thing. If she somehow believed he was involved in the hits, he had to convince her she was wrong. He wasn't a cold-blooded killer. That was the downside of being born into a Mafia family. The scales were never going to be tipped in his favor, and nobody was ever going to give him the benefit of the doubt. Regardless, he had to try. There wouldn't be another chance. He parked and walked up the drive to the front door, but just as he was about to raise the brass door knocker, a car drove through the gates and sped to the entrance, trapping him on the porch. The woman who got out of the car was holding a paper bag as far from her as she could, scowling at it as if it contained poison.

At first, Carla's face registered a blank. Then, recognition and finally, horror. She turned to flee, but Tommaso caught her arm and drew her into him, placing a hand across her mouth as she struggled to break free.

"Please, Carla. It's not what you think. Please, let me explain. I promise you. I mean no harm. Please." The pleading in his eyes echoed the throbbing in his voice. Finally, she relaxed. He took his hand away and waited. "If you scream, I wouldn't blame you, but I have done nothing to you or to anyone. All I want is a chance to talk with Nanette. She has this wrong idea about me. Look at me, Carla. Am I a killer? Shit. I can't help who my family is any more than you can help who yours is. My own brother is trying to kill me. Please, Carla. Give me a chance. You're the only hope I have. She'll listen to you. Just five minutes. I swear. If she won't listen to me, I'll leave and you'll never see me again."

"Promises. Promises," she said. Call it women's intuition, a hunch, or simply curiosity, but she raised the doorknocker and let it fall against the oak door.

"Thank you," he said and took a deep breath while they waited. "What's in the bag?"

"Mice." The look she gave him dared him to say anything more. "Twelve disgusting mice."

***

"Get Gino," was Carla's greeting to Francesca when she opened the door. "Better make it quick. We don't have much of a window of time here."

Francesca's eyes moved from Carla to the guy standing next to her and then back again to Carla. "You want to come in?" she asked.

"Do we?" Tommaso asked Carla.

"I don't think that's a good idea," she said. "We'll wait here while we work this out."

"Never a dull moment," Francesca said as she set off to get Gino who was in the study watching Sunday Night Football and feeding potato chips to Jesse, curled up on the hassock and making a pile of crumbs on the rug. "Gino, we've got another Puglisi on the front porch, and he wants to come in." She made it sound as if they had a major roach infestation. "Can you come help? Carla's with him."

"Is she all right?"

"Appears to be."

"Where the hell are they all coming from?" Gino hauled himself out of the recliner and took the .38 from the desk drawer. He had a momentary thought of the old dog trotting by his side, doing something heroic, but Jesse was retired from the watchdog business and was doing what he did these days. Nothing. And so, alone, Gino went to greet their unwelcome visitor. "Of the six of us, there's only three the Mob doesn't want dead," Gino said.

"Yet," Francesca corrected him.

***

"I'm not armed," Tommaso said, staring down the barrel of the revolver pointed at him.

"That's a good start," Gino said. "Want to tell me why you're here?"

Tommaso turned to Carla who nodded encouragement. He plunged ahead. "My family, or someone in my family, is trying to kill me. Nanette and Ginger as well. I don't know why. I love Nanette and she's going to have my baby. She doesn't know it. I mean, of course she knows it. She just doesn't know that I know it." He wiped the beads of perspiration from his forehead. "Please. I just need to talk with her. She's got to keep the baby. I promise I'll take good care of her. I've got to talk to her." He'd finished his speech and seemed about to fall backwards. Carla reached out her arm to support him.

Gino let the revolver fall to his side. He looked first at Francesca, who nodded, then at Carla, who also nodded. Resigned to whatever was going to happen, he motioned for Tommaso and Carla to come inside. "Let's go to the dining room. You sit down. I'll get Nanette." Gino's eyes narrowed and he gave Tommaso a quizzical look. "You look like the priest."

"Yeah. I know."

Before they'd had a chance to do much more than close the front door behind them, all hell broke loose in the form of Nanette who had heard Tommaso's voice and had burst out of the dining room, through the kitchen, and down the hall to her lover, murder in her eyes.

"Honey," Tommaso began, but that was as far as he got.

"Don't you honey me, you backstabbing, two-timing, murdering son of a bitch. I'll honey you!"

"*Silencio!*" Gino thundered. "I swear, if it wouldn't put a hole in the ceiling, I'd fire a warning shot. Shut up!"

Carla squeaked and took a step backwards, Francesca rolled her eyes, and Ginger, who had heard the commotion and had ventured out into the fray, looked set to launch herself at Tommaso, fingernails ready to scratch his eyes out.

"Everyone! To the dining room. Take a seat and shut up!" Gino bellowed.

"He's come a long ways," Carla said to Francesca, nodding in Gino's direction.

"Don't I know it."

"I'll call Morrie and have him come down for supper," Carla said, hitting the speed dial on her cell. "We may need him."

As if the director in a low-budget film had given the cue, there came a pounding at the front door, and a voice yelled, "Police! Open up!"

"What the hell?" Gino's head spun like one of those pinwheels on a stick. "Everybody to the dining room. Francesca get the glasses and the wine. Carla—you pour. Everyone sit. Look happy!" he hissed.

Thirty seconds is not a long piece of time, but it is truly amazing what you can accomplish in it when necessary. When the police announced their presence the second time, Gino opened the door for them, his face registering his total confusion.

"Yes?" he asked, projecting an aura of innocent bewilderment at what seemed like a battalion of officers ready to bash down his hand-carved oak doors with something that looked like a piece of pipe with a bolster on the end.

"We have a warrant," the female officer informed him.

"A warrant for what?" Gino didn't have to feign innocence.

"To search the premises," her male counterpart said. "We have reason to believe this is a waypoint for human trafficking." The two male officers behind him looked appropriately dangerous.

"Wait? What? Say that again. What the hell are you talking about? This is my home. This is my family. You are welcome to come into my home, but put that thing down." He pointed at the battering ram. "What the hell? Come in. And don't break anything. You are guests in my home. Show some respect for Christ's sake." He stepped aside while the officers rearranged themselves for a peaceful entry.

"You will find everyone in the dining room. You can make your apologies to them after you have satisfied yourselves we don't have anyone in the basement. We don't have a basement. Or the attic. We don't have an attic. Or the closets. We have closets. Or the garage. We have a garage. In it you will find my 1989 Ford F250 pickup with dump bed and a 1969 Volkswagen Beetle. Two doors. No power steering. No bodies on the floor. Jesus." He wanted to spit at their feet, but that would only have been effective in Italy. "If you wish to enter the wine cellar, I will come with you." He gave the officers a hard look. "It is not that I don't trust you. It's that I don't trust you."

***

Half an hour later, after a search of the interior and exterior that included all the outbuildings on the estate, the four exhausted officers regrouped at the front door where the whole mess had begun. "There's nothing here. Nothing at all. All we've got is a hunch or a bad feeling from an overwrought dancer at some cheap club who was pissed at some guy. You can't build any kind of a case on female hysterics," said Officer Rodriguez to Officer DeLuna. "The other girl is a better prospect."

The female officer—DeLuna according to her name badge—ignored her male counterpart. "We take them aside," she said. "See if their stories mesh. You know the drill." And with that, the contingent of the not-so-finest attempted the second wave of their assault.

Unfortunately for the police, Gino's online course, *Basic Legal Principles: Know Your Rights*, had covered such an eventuality. He raised his right hand as he stood in their path. "If you have satisfied yourself and the parameters of your warrant," he said, "my family would gratefully receive your apologies for disturbing their evening. If you wish to ask any questions, you are welcome to do so, but they will be asked of us in the dining room where we will all remain seated. If you are not so inclined, you may show yourselves out. You know where the door is. And take that pole thing with you."

Officer DeLuna's face was set in a most unbecoming frown that highlighted the creases on her forehead. "We wish to speak with your family members. Separately." She waved at the backup to begin, but Gino held up a hand, once again.

"That will not be possible. Perhaps you did not hear me. You may speak with us as we are, and unless you are prepared to arrest any or all of us at his time, you must leave. Our attorneys will answer any questions you may have."

***

The impasse suddenly ended when Nanette called out, "Raven? What are you doing here? Why are you with the cops?" She paused, studying the woman's face. I know it's you, though. I want to say thanks again for the nose wipes. Boy, you were a lifesaver. I was scared out of my mind and angry, and it all kinda came tumbling out of nowhere. I was running for my life. Well, when the Mob is trying to kill you, it's not easy to cope, you know? We had Tommy's laptop and we thought he was after us to get it back."

Tommy joined in. "No, honey. It's not my laptop. It's Gennaro's. I think he left it in the car so I'd take it to the Club to give it back and he'd kill me there along with Prospero and his lieutenants. You have to believe me. It wasn't me, honey. I should have been at the Club—just like you." Tommy got down on his knee. "Honey, marry me. I know about the baby. It's all right. It's wonderful, but I don't want you dancing anymore." He looked at Raven. "It's not good for the baby, is it?"

Raven's jaw was hanging about as far down as it could go. "Uh..."

Tommy took the response, such as it was, as affirmation. "Marry, me? I love you, Nanette."

"And I love you, Tommy," she said. "I'm glad you're not Gennaro. Oh yes, I'll marry you." And they kissed as everyone on the Esposito side of the aisle cheered. The unplanned deviation from the search and rescue protocol had cost the police the advantage of the upper hand, and now they were stalled without any clear direction while the scene played out around them.

"Who's Gennaro and why is he trying to kill anybody? Everybody?" Francesca asked.

"Gennaro's Tommy's brother," Nanette explained. "He's kinda shifty. Never did trust him all that much. I bet he's in it with Eddie. Eddie's not that smart, but he's mean."

"Stop!" Officer DeLuna yelled. "What the hell is going on here? Are you people all nuts?"

At this point, Ginger entered the discussion. "We most certainly are not nuts as you say. We're just trying to stay alive, and it's got nothing to do with human trafficking, although I suppose the Mob is involved in that too, if it pays well. We were trying to find Carla. She's the only one we knew who might help us."

"Who's Carla?" DeLuna asked.

"I am," Carla said, raising her hand. I'm married to Morrie, of course, but Miss Marie is my professional name." She straightened her posture and smiled. "I run a ballet studio."

"Good God," DeLuna mumbled more or less to herself.

Ginger picked up where she'd left off. "As I was saying, we're just trying to make a living. I was almost ready to get my real estate license, and now look at this disaster. I've got to get a whole new course for California. Do you know how much that costs? Do you?" She glared at Officer DeLuna. "I'm not exactly rolling in dough. What are you going to do about it? We're not safe."

At that moment, as if the heavens had decided the tension had reached its maximum, a purple towel came crawling into the dining room, and Officer DeLuna took a step back and pointed. What the hell?"

"Dammit!" Ginger said. "Now look what you clowns did. You let Bruce out. If you're going to search something, you should put things back the way you found them. The bedroom door was closed."

"Bruce?" said Officer DeLuna and shrieked as Bruce escaped the towel and began twining his entire twelve-foot-long body around Officer Rodriguez's left leg.

"Oh, calm down. He's my dance partner. You'd think he was some sort of wild beast or something." Ginger got up and walked over to her dance partner, unwound him from the leg, and draped him over her shoulders where Bruce relaxed and flicked a forked tongue in the direction of the offending intruders.

"Oh, that reminds me. I put the bag of mice in the fridge," Carla said.

"Look," Gino said. "As you can clearly see, we have our own problems to deal with."

"Except for the wedding," Nanette said. "That's not a problem."

"Except for the wedding," Gino resumed, nodding at Nanette and Tommy who were holding hands. "And, I've got the Church on my back. It's time to renegotiate the Communion wine and the bishop and the pastor of St. Boniface are about to come to blows over a red blend versus a Merlot. What am I supposed to do? Change all the water into wine and be done with it? If I only could!" He threw his hands in the air. "And now, if you're quite finished, would you please let yourselves out? If you have any further questions, our attorneys will be most happy to speak with you." He pointed to the front door. "Good night!"

"Wait!" Carla called. "Hold on a minute. Would you take this with you? You know, to the police station and put it on your bulletin board. I'd really appreciate it." She handed Officer DeLuna a poster. "It's Pierre. He got lost when the Mafia burned down our apartment house and killed Harry."

Officer DeLuna accepted the poster, the creases in her forehead having multiplied considerably since she'd arrived. Anything in the way of prepared remarks she might have had were long forgotten. Silently, she and her team filed out, the last one through the door closing it securely behind him.

"This isn't over," said Gino.

"It is for tonight," Francesca said. "I'll get another bottle of wine."

"One is nowhere near enough," Gino said, his face buried in his hands. "I don't think there's enough wine in the world."

"I'll throw something together for dinner," Francesca said, pushing her chair back and heading for the kitchen.

"Don't forget. Morrie should be here any moment," Carla said, following Francesca into the kitchen.

***

Somewhere between the first loaf of bread and the second and fourth bottles of an exceptionally good Cabernet, the relaxation level of the group had reached a point where the world had taken on a rosy glow and their problems seemed insignificant.

"You're a Puglisi," Gino said, eying Tommaso and cradling his wine glass in both hands.

"Yes. I am," Tommaso shrugged. "Accident of birth."

Gino nodded. "How are you related to Sally?"

"Uncle. He's missing, you know. In my family, *Missing* means dead, and I don't expect they'll ever find him."

"No. I wouldn't expect so," Gino said. Francesca, Carla, and Morrie— who had arrived just in time for dinner—nodded their solemn agreement.

"If you don't mind, I'll stay here with Nanette tonight and go back to the City to do some snooping around in the morning," Tommaso said. "I can't trust any of them."

"I'm going with you," Nanette said.

"No. You stay here. I'll be back. I promise." He kissed her and then turned to Gino and Francesca. "You've been generous." He took out his wallet but frowned when he opened it and found one lone twenty. "I'll go to the bank tomorrow. I want to pay you for your trouble—you know—the room and the food. You've been great to her." He hesitated. "Would you mind if she stayed a little longer? Just until I can find someplace safe for us?"

"There ain't any safe places to find," Carla said. "I sure as hell found that out. You got to make your own safe place."

"I'm working on it," Tommaso said.

# CHAPTER EIGHTEEN

*Dark Mountain*

If a phrase could describe how a protection racket works, *hostile takeover* comes close. In theory, it's straightforward and fairly simple. A company with more resources swoops in and overpowers a company with fewer resources. In the business world, the smaller company is absorbed. In the crime world, for the smaller company to keep in business, it must pay whatever the larger company demands. It's been a mainstay of Mafia rackets, but its one significant shortcoming is assuming the weaker company won't get some new leadership and decide to fight back. Three nights into their counter-operation, Morrie Landow, Chan Boucher, and RP were at breakfast, going over the body count and strategizing.

"That makes a solid eleven guests aboard the ship that sails this morning," Chan said, stirring his coffee with a chopstick. "I expect they're rethinking their method of approach. I don't mean the guests. I'm talking about management. There's a basic tenet of economics: all goods are scarce. At some point, they're going to run out of enforcers."

Morrie, eyes fixated on the chopstick, handed Chan his spoon. "This works better," he said. "Unless you're making some sort of cultural statement."

"Nah. Just too lazy to get up and get one. Thanks," Chan said, accepting the spoon. "Four of them we collected from Trizbel's store. The first two and then the replacements they sent the following afternoon. After that they made some adjustments, hitting four stores simultaneously. And now," he said, "the hold of the ship is going to need serious fumigating when they reach port. The damn thing reeks of cheap cologne."

***

Tommaso Puglisi wasn't technically on the run, although he was practicing extreme avoidance regarding any encounters with his family. This morning, after leaving *Dark Mountain*, he planned to do some surveillance, looking for signs of activity at any of the family residences. His grandfather's place hadn't produced anything of interest. No visitor cars were parked on the grounds, and the lights on in the greenhouse indicated his grandfather was communing with his orchids. The next stop was the apartment house in Pacific Heights.

The family was transitioning, testing the waters with more lucrative enterprises, and discovering that human trafficking was more profitable than the numbers and protection rackets. Judging by the hits in New Haven and near the airport in San Francisco, however, somebody wasn't on board with modern times. Tommaso considered this. Somebody hanging on to the old ways could mean a couple of things—a traditional mindset or a mind not bright enough to think of alternatives. It was a puzzle he was determined to solve.

One thing that never changed was the tradition of discussing business over meals. It was eleven-thirty and a bit early for lunch, but he'd give this place until two o'clock before he called it a day. He stationed himself where he could watch the comings and goings at the apartment house. Shortly after one o'clock, a black sedan pulled up and discharged two male passengers, then took off. That most likely meant airport transportation. One of the two was his brother, Gennaro. Tommaso couldn't see the other man's face, and the men didn't waste any time in small talk while they waited to be buzzed in. Tommaso patted his pocket trying to locate his cigarettes, then realized he'd quit. He settled for a stick of gum. Something was in the works, and it most definitely involved Gennaro, but Tommaso had already been pretty sure about that. His brother wasn't calling the shots, though. If he had been, the visitors would be coming to him, not the other way around. Same for his associate, whoever he was. His grandfather was accounted for. His uncle Dominic was still back on the east coast, and his father, Big Al, still had five years on the tax dodge, hoping to be out in three. Who was left?

***

"We're putting you in danger each day we stay here," Ginger said. "I'd forgotten there really are people like you two." She'd come into the house from the guest cottage in search of Francesca, two sheets of paper in hand. "I wrote this up this morning," she said. "It's a contract." She locked eyes with Francesca. "It's my first rental contract. I checked out the boilerplates online, and it's got all the essentials." She handed the papers to Francesca. "There's one copy for you and one for me. I made it out for three months. That should be long enough for me to do all the coursework for my California real estate license and get hired on someplace to finish my training. I'll keep track of meals and laundry services, and whatever other expenses you incur on my behalf and will make payments in installments as soon as I land a job." She waited while Francesca read the contract.

"This is important to you," Francesca said, setting the papers on the counter.

"Yes. Nanette's just starting out, but I'm starting over. There's a difference. I know how the world works. At least, how part of it works." She blinked hard. "You two have given me a lot more than a place to stay and food to eat. You've given me time to think, and that is worth more than you can imagine."

Francesca reached into the cupboard for another coffee mug and handed it to Ginger. "Come join me. I've got to get back to the books in a bit—it never ends—but there's time for a chat." She eyed the remaining donuts. "They're probably past stale, but I'm game if you are."

By way of a reply, Ginger took two small plates out of the dishwasher that had just beeped. "Warm plates will soften them up," she said, handing the dishes to Francesca. "Where's Gino?"

"In the office. He's expecting a phone call from Father Puglisi."

Ginger stopped with her raspberry jelly donut halfway to her mouth which was open, ready to be fed. "*Father* Puglisi?"

"Uh huh. You heard that right. They're everywhere. Don't worry. He's actually one of the good ones. At least, I think he is." Francesca shrugged. "He's the personal assistant to the bishop. It's a long story, but it's about wine sales." She gave a sort of half-laugh. "Yeah. Really."

"Everybody's got a story," Ginger said, resuming her attack on the donut.

"I'd like to hear yours," Francesca said, "if you're willing to share it."

"It's not all that interesting. I'm a physical therapist. *Was* a physical therapist. I thought I would save the world. Help heal all those broken bodies." She made a sound that was hard to interpret. "Some I helped, but the rest? Insurance scams. People who wouldn't lift a finger to help themselves. It started to wear me down, and one day, I crashed. Keeping all that stress inside takes a toll." She took a thoughtful sip of her coffee. "This is good," she said. "Anyhow, I knew I needed to do something to get my own body working and, long story short, I started dancing. I became somebody else. Somebody who was free." She smiled. "Truth. And the tips were great. It was like when you were a kid and played make believe. It wasn't real. It was a fantasy, and I could lose myself in it. And I did. At least I did until it ended. Just like that!" She snapped her fingers. "It's hard to live a fantasy when your reality blows it to bits. You just go along living your life, until one day, somebody interrupts it. Then, it's up to you to get it back. You can't prevent the interruption, but you can put a stop to it. And afterwards, you may not have the same life you had before or the life you thought you wanted, but it will be your destiny. So, that's my story." Ginger took her mug and plate and stood. "Will you sign my rental agreement? Please?"

Francesca gathered up her own dishes and joined Ginger at the sink. "Got a pen?"

"Right here." Ginger produced a blue gel pen from her pocket. "You know," she said, "some people think we're trash. We're not, but this line of work is not for everyone. Some of the girls don't want to be there. They don't want to talk to you, and you can see something in their eyes that gives you the chills. It's not fear. It's kind of a dead thing. They come and go. It's like somebody makes them keep moving so they don't make friends. I wonder..."

"Wonder what?"

Ginger folded her copy of the contract and gave Francesca a serious look. "What if that cop was right about the trafficking but just had the wrong house and the wrong girl?"

***

Francesca had set up the easel in the dining room. The lists were still on it, daring everyone to find the secrets hidden there. While the evening's discussion at Dark Mountain was short on information but long on suspicions, the addition of Tommaso in an advisory capacity improved the outlook. He didn't waste any time getting down to business.

"First things first," he said. "I went to the bank." He handed Gino an envelope. "Thank you for everything you've done for Nanette." Gino started to protest, but Tommaso held up a hand. "No. Besides," he said, "yes, it's my money but it came from my father, so you can add it to the War Chest." He turned his attention to the easel. "You've got the basics," he said, scanning the lists. "Let me flesh out the thumbnails for you." He gave a half-smile. "Might as well start with the one I know best," he said, leaning forward and folding his hands on the table. He closed his eyes briefly. "I'm Big Al's youngest. Also the greatest disappointment, since I wasn't enthusiastic about joining the family business. I was supposed to take over the family's accounts, but I declined. Starting out my career juggling two sets of books wasn't what I wanted to do. That, of itself, wouldn't have been enough to cause someone to want me dead, so there has to be something else. What it is, I'm not sure. Yet." He paused while Francesca made a check beside Tommaso's name.

"I've got an MBA from Boston College—the same place Anthony went—although his career path was different. He found a way to keep his family, but at a distance. I figure he decided God was the only One who could compete with Papa."

Another check.

"My grandfather, Enzo, still watches what's going on. You've got a good summary of him. Can't add much to it. But remember, he's lost his only daughter, and he's not going to take that lying down. He's old, yes, but he's sharp and doesn't forget a wrong."

Another check.

"My father, Big Al, is in Leavenworth. That said, he's active. I hear bits and pieces, nothing concrete."

Another check.

"My uncle Dom and his boys have their hands full with the trash and garbage. They're at the bottom of the list. And that takes us to the top, where I'd put my brother, Gennaro."

Francesca added the final check, drew a circle around Gennaro's name, and then sat.

Tommaso continued. "I saw him this morning going into one of the family-owned apartment houses in the City. I was doing a bit of surveillance, going from place to place, and I hit paydirt. Someone was with him. I couldn't make out the face, but my money's on Nico—Nicolo. He's Joey and Fiona's kid, and he's got reason to be either looking to avenge his parents or else he's the one who offed them. Wouldn't put either past him. Or my brother, either. They're two of a kind." Tommaso rubbed his forehead and pinched the bridge of his nose as if trying to ward off a headache. "I just don't know who they were going to meet there."

"I can answer that question," Morrie said. "That's our old apartment and we were evicted to make room for Johnny Vincento."

Tommaso let out a low whistle. "Well, that's it then. That's our unholy trinity, and they may have tacit support from others in the family. Violence is our tradition. What they're planning isn't going to be good for the rest of us. You can take that to the bank."

Gino got up from his chair and walked to the sink for a glass of water. Instead of drinking it, though, he set it down on the counter and turned back to Tommaso. "Nico may not know who killed his parents, but I know who killed mine. Justice or revenge. It doesn't matter what you call it. It's long overdue."

"So, what are you saying?" Carla asked. "We gonna hit Johnny?"

"No," Gino said. "That's too easy a way out for him. I want him to lose everything he owns. I want him broken." He picked up the pencil by the notepad and snapped it in half. It made a most satisfying sound.

"You need to know about Gennaro and Nico," Tommaso said. "Gennaro is a classic narcissist. He's aggressive and he's driven. He has no conscience, no empathy, never feels guilt, and believes he is destined for greatness. He's cruel. Animals fear him, and with good reason. He can also be charming and persuasive. He uses women and then discards them. He uses anyone who can benefit him. I suspect he's using Nico, but Nico doesn't know it. That kid is a train wreck. He's not bright, but he is devious. He was in some residential treatment center for years. Don't know why. The irony is that Nico probably thinks he's using Gennaro to become the *Don*. Yes, he really believes it's in his future." Tommaso tapped Gennaro's name. "We're going to need a foolproof plan and a lot of luck."

# CHAPTER NINETEEN

*Dark Mountain*

Nanette had skipped breakfast but was now nibbling on a saltine and sipping a cup of tea. "I'm feeling better," she said to Francesca. "How long does this last?"

"I think it goes on for the first few months," Francesca said, a bemused expression on her face. "How far along are you?"

"Two months. Sure hope you're right. It ain't a lot of fun." She finished her tea and took her cup to the dishwasher. "I've been talking to Ginger about that cop that came by. I think I may have something she can use." Nanette took a crumpled slip of paper from her pocket and smoothed out the creases on the paper as best she could. "It's Zephyr's cell number. She gave it to me when we ran away from the Club. I don't know where she went, but she'd been worked over hard enough that her makeup wasn't doing all that much good. She was scared, but she was ready to run." Nanette refolded the paper. "I want to give it to that cop. Do you think Carla would come with me? She's got experience."

Francesca nodded. "She does indeed."

***

"Got a minute?" Carla walked over to where Morrie was working on the Mafia laptop, some sort of scan program running.

"Yeah. This is going to take a few. Pull up a comfortable chair. You know. The stool. The only other chair we have. I really need to get busy on the apartment search. Want to go look at a couple of places with me later on this morning?"

Carla dragged the stool from the little table in their makeshift kitchen and scooted close to Morrie. "How about this afternoon? Nanette asked me to go with her to see Detective DeLuna this morning. She's got a name that might help in their investigation."

Morrie held up his left hand. "Hang on. I'm into something here. Might be useful." He beckoned for her to come closer and take a look at the screen. "Here's a list of Mob-owned businesses on the east coast and the revenue they brought in last year." He whistled. "Damn. We're talking billions. What's interesting is the proximity of nightclubs to massage parlors. In many cases they're right next door to each other—sort of a one-stop full service thing."

Carla nodded. "That's what they do. Back in New Haven, the Mob bought up the whole block. You could get from one business to another through inside doors. So, you went into the dry cleaner's and ended up getting a private lap dance at the nightclub three doors down the street." Her eyes narrowed. "Convenient. It also made it easy to take it on the lam if the cops showed up. You think that's what they've got planned for San Jose and San Francisco?"

"That would be my guess." He took off his glasses and set them on the table. "We got any more coffee?" He rubbed his eyes. "I need to get new glasses. Everything gets blurry. What did you say about Nanette?"

Carla went to the coffee pot and sniffed it. "It's kinda stale. I'll make a new pot. She's got a phone number to give the cop. I didn't think it was a good idea, at first, but it is. If we can keep the cops on our side and let them do the heavy lifting, it will make our job easier. It will also keep them off our backs."

"Human trafficking," Morrie said. "It's just another form of extortion. Even when the Mob decides to go modern, they never get far from their roots." He looked at the list. "Let me check something." A few minutes later, he pulled up a list of nightclubs and cross-matched them to massage parlors. "Bingo," he said. "Take this with you and show it to DeLuna."

***

Nanette and Carla had arrived at the SJPD shortly after nine o'clock and were now standing at the counter of the reception area, talking to the sergeant on duty. After a few questions as to the nature of their business, the sergeant left them to cool their heels but returned shortly and escorted them to Detective Virginia DeLuna's office. A bare-bones affair that held just the essentials, there was a desk with a laptop, a printer, and a wooden chair for the occupant of the desk, and not all that comfortable a wooden chair at that. It looked as if it had come straight out of a salvage yard. There were two other chairs of a similar vintage opposite the main chair, a gray metal wastebasket overflowing with crumpled fast food wrappings, and four bare walls. There was nothing to indicate either a love of art or bragging rights from a university. No awards framed anywhere, either. The room screamed *Temporary!*

The initial stare-down was brief. Without preamble, Nanette plunged straight into her story. "I got to thinking after you left and figured you were probably confused."

Detective DeLuna closed her laptop, moved it aside, opened the bottom right-hand desk drawer, cleared the rest of her desk in one swoop of her left arm and slammed the door shut. "Confused? You could say that." The anger in her voice was palpable. "Why are you here? It didn't go all that well for any of us, as I remember. Just another dead end, but please, have a seat." She motioned to the two chairs silently waiting for business.

"No. Well, yes. You were at the wrong place and you were looking for the wrong girl. Aside from that, everything was great." Nanette beamed and handed DeLuna the damaged slip of paper. "This is who you want to talk to."

At this point, Carla stepped in. "Look. Before this goes any farther, we got to set up some ground rules. If we get the Feds involved, none of our lives will ever be the same. For reasons I'm not gonna go into here, we were just in the wrong place at the worst time, and now the Mafia wants us dead. That ever happen to you?"

Detective DeLuna offered a weak smile. "So much has happened to me that, frankly, I wouldn't know where to begin. But I have to be honest with you. I *am* one of the Feds. It's Federal Agent DeLuna, but *Detective* makes things easier here at the station. So does *Officer*, at times."

"Shit." Carla pushed back her chair and motioned for Nanette to follow her. "Nice talking with you. We gotta go. Bye."

"Wait! Sit down. Please."

The desperation in DeLuna's voice made Carla hesitate. Also, the *please*. In Carla's experience, this was not a word they used. Ever. "This gotta be off the record or we're out of here," Carla said, and Nanette nodded her agreement.

Agent/Detective/Officer DeLuna took the first decent breath she'd had in the last week. "Off the record. Talk to me. Please."

"Well, at least that explains the lack of décor," Carla said, looking around the room at the nothing that was everywhere. "I ain't never seen a cop's office so naked."

Nanette pointed at the scrap of paper. "That's Zephyr's cell. She got one of those burners. She hides it. She won't answer if she don't know you, though. So, it's not much good."

"Well," DeLuna's voice reflected her disappointment. "I'll keep it, and thanks for stopping by anyway."

Nanette started to get up, then stopped midway. "Don't you want to know where she lives?"

The momentary silence that followed was like the end of Act One in an off-Broadway play. DeLuna's response was the overture to Act Two. "You know where she lives? Why didn't you say so earlier?"

"You didn't ask me."

"You learn early on not to volunteer anything," Carla said. "Say the right thing, say the wrong thing, say nothing. It don't matter. When you're working for the Mafia, you keep your mouth shut and your eyes on your own business if you want to keep on living. They don't got no sense of humor. It becomes a habit. So, lay off her. This is new territory for both of us. Have a little respect, for Christ's sake."

DeLuna nodded. "Sorry. Won't happen again." She looked at Nanette and took a leap of faith. "Where does Zephyr live?" She glanced at Carla, who was smiling encouragement. "We tried to follow her the night we followed you, but we lost her when she ran across the street against a green light."

"I heard her talking to one of the other girls. She didn't exactly give an address, but it wasn't hard to figure out. You got a piece of paper and a pencil? I can draw it better than I can tell it."

"Here's two sheets. Draw your sketch and then make a list. Try to remember every girl. We need to find all of them. Stage name, real name. Anything. Anything at all."

"Zephyr. Yeah, but there's others. There were..." Nanette stopped to count. "Four the night I was there. But that changes. It always does at the clubs. You know what I mean. They come and go. It's like somebody makes them keep moving so they don't make friends." Shrugs. "Maybe I'm way off."

"No, you're right on," DeLuna said.

Nanette sat up straighter.

DeLuna kept a hopeful eye on her only lead.

"It ain't right," Carla said. "This shouldn't be happening today. It's got to stop."

"We're trying," DeLuna said. "But it's going on worldwide. It's slavery reborn with a new name. Human trafficking, it's called now, but it's still slavery. And with the way technology is moving, it's becoming harder and harder to deal with. They're always one step ahead of us. We keep at it. We get it stopped, and these girls get a chance at life. This is something The Mafia is not going to be able to muscle their way out of." DeLuna paused, thinking. "I'm thirty-five. I could see the way you were studying my face. It takes more and more foundation to achieve the look required for this. I identify as 27, and that's old for what I'm doing at the clubs. That's why this has got to go down now. I won't be able to maintain the illusion much longer. Even now, I worry."

Agent/Detective/Officer Virginia DeLuna, identifying as 27, had an athletic build. She was slim and toned. "I can write off the gym as a tax deduction," she joked. She had shoulder-length black hair that she kept loose so it would partially obscure her face as she danced. At the moment, she was twirling a strand around her index finger and caught herself. "Bad habit. I'll never be a poker player. That's my tell. Unfortunate, that. I need a good one for the next phase of this operation."

"Huh? Come again?" Carla was interested.

"What? Oh, the poker player. Yeah. I need professional grade. And somebody that's got no connections to organized crime. It's turning out to be impossible."

"I might be able to help you with that," Carla said. "I'll need to talk to him first, though."

DeLuna's expression was hard to read, but she said nothing. She sighed and her hand went to her forehead. "More lines." She shifted in her chair. "Age shows first at the neckline, but that's easily concealed with a modification of costuming, the addition of scarf or a collar. The eyes, though. Those are tough. Laugh lines morph into creases and then crevasses seemingly overnight. From a distance, I can pull it off, but up close it's getting harder and harder to maintain the appearance of youth."

There was a quick rap at the door and a Uniform came into the office and handed a sheet of paper to DeLuna. She nodded her dismissal and the officer left. "We're too late," she said, turning the paper around so Carla and Nanette could see it. "This is Zephyr." The photograph of the body was graphic. She'd been shot in the head point blank. Nanette covered her eyes.

"They must have found her phone," Carla said. "Bastards."

Nanette lowered her hands from her face and slammed a fist on the table. "You better get to that house quick before they move the rest of the girls somewhere else." She picked up the pencil and drew a diagram on the paper.

DeLuna nodded, her jaw tight.

***

They say confession is good for the soul, but the part nobody talks about is the potential for retribution and physical harm afterwards. And that was why, after their conversation with DeLuna that had lasted the better part of half an hour, Carla and Nanette were uneasy when they exited the police station. "I don't feel bad about leaving out a few of the more personal details," Carla said, but she didn't fill in any details in response to Nanette's questioning look.

"From now on, everything's going to be different," Nanette said. "How do you live a lie? That's what I'm doing. I'm running away."

"No you're not," Carla said. "You're living your truth. The rest is a shell you've cast off. You can call it running away, but it's a time to buy time and make a plan to live life free and on your own terms."

"So, what do I do?" Nanette asked.

"What you're doing. Don't flinch. Don't apologize. And never, never look back. You are who you are now, and we need to protect it. You need to protect your baby. Evil never gives up. I know that one for real. You may think you're in the clear, but that's the moment they come out of the shadows." Carla fished in her handbag for the car keys. "The Mafia is changing the way they do business. They're more...modern. You know. They've gone legit in a lot of ways. Although," she fastened her seat belt, "much of the legit business is to launder the money they got by being crooks. It's nuts."

"Do you think the detective can use anything we told her?"

"Sure hope so. Time will tell."

***

Morrie, back from a lunch run to the deli, and with some good news on the apartment search, found Carla standing in front of the full-length mirror in the studio, pulling at the skin on her neck. Experience had taught him that asking questions never worked out. Unfortunately, he had trouble remembering that. He paused, two lunch bags in hand, and asked the logical question. "Carla, what are you doing?"

"How old is my neck, Morrie?"

"Same age as the rest of you? Twenty-one?"

"No. That's not what I mean. Does it look older?"

It was at that moment he remembered what he had forgotten and realized he was trapped in a conversation that was not going to end well for him. Still, he couldn't seem to tell that to his mouth. "You have a beautiful neck. You have a beautiful body. But you know what's the most beautiful thing about you?" he asked, slowly backing towards the hall and freedom. "Me!" And he beat a fast retreat to their temporary living quarters.

When Carla joined him, he'd had the good sense to have a mouthful of a pastrami on rye sandwich, thus earning a temporary reprieve.

"I'm serious, Morrie. I ain't...I'm *not* getting younger."

Morrie looked thoughtful. He chewed and swallowed. "Honey, nobody gets younger. Life doesn't work that way. You're going to be beautiful when you're eighty. And I hope I'm still around to tell you how beautiful you are then. Now, eat."

"I love you, Morrie."

"And I love you, Miss Marie. I repeat, eat." He handed her the other lunch bag. "Ham and Swiss on whole wheat. No pickles. Double mustard. And a diet soda."

"You know, Morrie, I got this feeling that we're getting close to the end of our problems," she said, accepting the photo and description of the loft Morrie had found and the receipt for the deposit he'd made to hold it.

"I know I should have waited until you could see it, but it would have been gone before you got there. There were three people in line behind me, so I grabbed it. What do you think?"

Carla reached over and wiped a spot of mustard from his face. "It's perfect. From what I can see, the floor is in great shape. Just needs a good cleaning and waxing and the wood will shine." She sighed happily. "We can make it into the home we want. When do you think we can move in?"

"Soon as we go to the realtor and sign the lease. How long can it take to pack up our clothes and toothbrushes?" He leaned back and rotated his left shoulder. "Talk about getting old. I should have handled that tumble from the window without a hitch. Guess I'm getting slow."

"Sometimes, slow ain't so bad, you know," Carla said. "I'm thinking maybe we should take a short rest before we get to all the packing. You know. Recharge our batteries kind of *Rest.*" She leaned forward and kissed him.

Morrie gathered her into his arms. "I never thought I'd have fond memories of a ballet studio," he said, "but it hasn't been all bad. In fact, sometimes it's been nothing short of wonderful."

***

The photograph lay on the desk, casting silent blame in DeLuna's direction. At least that's the way she interpreted it. If they hadn't lost the girl when she bolted, Zephyr might still be alive. But they had lost her, and this was the result. Now, Zephyr was just one more statistic, one more murder to add to the indictment when they made an arrest. *If* they made an arrest. *Hell.* DeLuna closed her eyes and pressed her fingers against them, trying to get on top of the frustration that was eating at her. They needed a break. Just one break. It was a hope. A wish. Might even have been a prayer that was answered, because just then the phone rang.

"DeLuna."

"Yes. Good Morning. This is Tommaso Puglisi. We met the other night?"

*How could I possibly forget,* DeLuna thought. "Yes. Can I help you?"

"Actually, I was thinking that I might be able to help you. It's not a good idea for me to come to the police station. Could we meet for coffee, say around ten? At *Common Grounds* on Paseo de San Antonio? I want to run something by you."

"Ten o'clock," she said by way of a reply and disconnected.

***

It was a spur of the moment idea. There was risk inherent in any meeting, but Tommaso decided that minimizing whatever risk there was would work in his favor. And that's why he made a slight detour on his way to the coffee shop and bought a gift box, some wrapping paper, and a big red bow at The Cheap Store.

"I think you'll find what's in this of interest," Tommaso said, settling in across from DeLuna at one of the small tables by the side windows. He reached for DeLuna's hand and held it briefly while he gave her the gift box with the USB drive nestled inside. "For reasons that you'll understand, I can't give you the laptop, but this is everything that's on it." There was a hint of a challenge in his gaze. "You'll find details of two operations. The first is the protection racket, but the second concerns trafficking. It doesn't appear to be as sophisticated yet as the protection racket, and I assume from this that it's still early days."

DeLuna accepted the box with a warm smile. "Excuse my curiosity, but why are you giving this to me now?"

"You're asking what's in for me?" He glanced around the coffee shop. Two men, probably mid-twenties, sitting in the corner weren't conversing with each other or doing anything except sitting and watching the goings on. "Laugh. Now."

DeLuna had been a cop long enough to know when to play along, and she responded by letting out a hearty laugh, slapping her leg, and shaking her head. Tommaso continued the apparent joke by constructing an air diagram with both hands, stopping to punctuate each movement with a laugh of his own.

"What the hell are you doing?" De Luna asked through clenched teeth, not taking her eyes from Tommaso and continuing the show of merriment by clapping her hands to the side of her head which she continued to shake.

Having completed his hand movements, Tommaso dropped his arms, sat back, gave a huge grin, and reached for his coffee. "I'm being watched. Or *you* are. Regardless, the two guys in the corner. I don't recognize them, and you'd have to turn around to see them, so you'll have to take my word for it. Be glad you're in the U.S. Back in Sardinia, they lack a certain subtlety. They'd drop us both for good measure, get up, walk out, and nobody would say a word.

"Back to your question. What's in it for me? If this all works out, I get to go on living, and that's not an exaggeration. To that end, I'm going to meet my brother Gennaro tonight. It's traditional, the Mafia discussing business over pasta and wine, and Gennaro fancies himself a *Don* in training. I'll return his laptop that he left in my car back in New Haven, apologize for being so difficult to get in touch with. I'll tell him I was in the middle of some love affair or something." Tommaso finished his coffee. "And now, I'm ready to go to work for the family doing what my father spent a couple of hundred grand at Boston College for me to learn how to do. The Books. Both sets. As I get into it, they should yield some good information for you. In the interim, I'm pretty sure Gennaro's sent those two to check me out. He's the insecure type. He's not sure I know that he tried to kill me." Tommaso laughed again and DeLuna patted the little box. "You won't be able to contact me. I'll contact you when I have anything. But there's one thing I need you to do for me. And I need for you to do it now. Today."

DeLuna raised her coffee in a toast and he reciprocated. "Let me know what it is, and I'll let you know if I can oblige."

"You'll find a hit list on the drive. One of the names on it is somebody you know. Carla Catalano. You know. Carla, the ballet teacher. In fact, that's the reason it took a bit for us to decide to surrender this. There's only one way to save her life, and that's to kill her. We'd appreciate it if you'd take care of that for us."

DeLuna's face lost any humor it had held and she spit out the mouthful of coffee she'd been about to swallow. "What the shit are you talking about?" she said. "I'm not going to kill somebody for you."

"Not for real, dammit. Jesus. Just have the report released to the media that a body was found and later identified as Carla. If they think she's dead, she's fine. Will you do that?"

DeLuna's expression never changed. "All right. Shouldn't be too hard. How did she die?"

"I don't know. I don't care. There won't be a body unless you've got a Jane Doe in the freezer. Work it out. How about a hit and run? And now, if you'll forgive me, I'll take my leave." He took a final sip of his coffee, stood, and then bent to kiss her goodbye. "Hope you don't mind," he said.

"Not at all. Watch your back." DeLuna set the gift box next to her coffee, took a final sip, and put the box into her purse. She waited until the two men at the table had left before returning to her car where she made the call to her contact in New Haven.

# CHAPTER TWENTY

*San Francisco*

"We knew we were just buying time. It was unrealistic to think we'd stopped the extortion racket," Morrie said, examining the vial that Chan had handed him. "Interesting, though, that they've recovered and changed tactics so quickly."

"I've already put the sign on the door that we're closed for the week for a family emergency. And if this doesn't qualify, I don't know what does," Chan said. "This goes beyond a protection racket. This is a murder threat, and it's not just for me. It's for everyone who comes through my doors."

Morrie set the vial back in its box and closed the lid with care. "I believe sending this stuff through the mail is a felony, but considering the threat, a simple felony doesn't bother them in the least. It's what they do. What I'd like to know is where they managed to put their hands on a vial of *clostridium botulinum toxin*."

"It's difficult to believe something like this could be easily checked out of a research lab, although recent world events don't rule it out. Outside of a lab? I don't have a clue." Morrie waited a moment, then asked, "What do we do now?"

Chan's face was unreadable, and this time he wasn't playing the culture card. He'd gone undercover. "We continue with what we're doing, widen the area, and increase the number of men on patrol." He shot a glance at the box. "This is a personal warning for me. For my restaurant. Customers get this in their food and they sicken and maybe die. Botulism is death. They could have done a number of things—poisonous mushrooms in a food shipment would also work, and I can't be sure they won't try that as well. There's no demand made. He's just letting me know he knows who I am and he's warning me off."

"He who?"

"It coincides with the arrival of Johnny Vincento. He arrived from Sardinia for the funerals of his brother and sister-in-law and has stayed on. It appears that the deaths haven't severed the connection between the two families. It also appears he's importing Italian tactics to the ongoing power play and has upped the ante. So, my guess is that his presence has two purposes. Family comes first. He wants to avenge his brother's death. That's paramount. Then, since nature abhors a vacuum, he's going to fill the void. He's a gambler—world class poker player—and he brings that expertise to his criminal activities. My guess is he suspects I'm the one responsible for their lack of success to this point, but he can't prove anything." Chan paused. "He's taking whoever started this racket to school. Lead by example, they say. For the moment, I'm going to let him think I've stepped aside."

The box was beginning to assume a malevolent personality. "So what are you going to do with that?" Morrie nodded at the box.

"For now, it's going in the safe. We've been spending so much time dealing with the Puglisi and Vincento families, it got me thinking about my own. I just found out I've got a cousin who lives not that far away. Want to come with me for moral support? I could use some backup."

"You're on your own, my friend," Morrie said. "How much does he/she know about you?"

"She."

"These are the times I'm glad all I have is a brother. You should bring a gift, though. Candy or something. Flowers. Stop at the flower shop on Quintara. It might soften the blow when she sees your ugly face."

"Funny. Real funny. The flowers are a good idea, though. I don't know how much she knows about the family. It all depends what Grandmama told her."

***

All he had to do now was to keep the door from being slammed in his face. A thousand different scenarios of how he was going to do this played out in Chan's mind as he drove down 280 from the City. He could have gone 101, but that was nothing but traffic, buildings, pollution, and people. This freeway was an attempt to convince everyone that land was still abundant. No houses stacked side by side where neighbors never raised their blinds. No yards the size of a quart of milk. Nothing that took away from the California Dream. And for the brief forty minutes that he saw the forests and the hillsides pass by, he could almost believe the lie.

Cities were creeping closer and closer to each other. Sunnyvale merged into Santa Clara that merged into San Jose, and it went on and on and nothing much in between. Where once there had been farms and orchards, now there were the same store chains repeating themselves over and over like a nun reciting the mysteries of the rosary. Ten decades here, ten decades there, but nothing ever changed. It was a circle and unless you found the right exit, you were doomed to repeat it again and again and again until you went mad. There'd been a song written about that. The one last hope of freedom was to be found along the coast, where the land ended, the mountains rose, and the Pacific Ocean was the boundary that said, *no more.* Not even the developers with their hands in the politicians' pockets could buy it. The ocean was the end of the blight, and those who had carved out a piece of land in the mountains, away from the flatlands of the urban sprawl, could breathe fresh air and have room to live.

It would be a good place to raise a family, Chan thought. He was forty-two now, and that kept gnawing at him. If he were going to have that family, time was beginning to be an issue. He glanced at the bouquet of flowers that lay on the passenger seat. He'd pick up another bouquet when he got back to the City and pay a call to Trizbel. First things first, though. He exited the freeway and shortly pulled into the driveway at *Dark Mountain Vineyard.*

***

Gino, just back from the mailbox, glanced out the window as a late model Ford Escape came down the drive and parked by the front porch. He didn't recognize the man who got out of the car. He was Asian, looked to be in his mid-forties. Tall and muscular, he was bald or he'd shaved his head. Neatly trimmed beard and mustache. He stood by the car, a bouquet of flowers in his hand. He straightened, gave the house one more look, and then proceeded up the steps and knocked on the door.

"We've got company," Gino called to Francesca, who was in the bedroom.

"Please tell me it's not another Puglisi," she said.

"Pretty sure we're okay on that point, but he's got flowers." Gino, relieved on one hand not to have to deal with a new Puglisi, and curious as to who would be bringing his wife flowers, answered the door. It was moments like this he wished he were at least half a foot taller. It was impossible to look imposing when he had to crane his neck to get a look at somebody's face, but he'd learned to cope. A neutral expression, a composed demeanor, and patiently waiting for the other person to speak first were the products of yet another online course he'd taken over the summer: *Compensating—Projecting Authority.* Gino needn't have worried. The visitor was not a threat. In fact, the man straightened his shoulders and took an audible breath before offering a smile and an introduction.

"Mr. Esposito." The man inclined his head. "I hope this is not a bad time. I decided on this at the last moment, before I lost my courage. I am Chan Young Boucher, your wife's sort of long-lost cousin. I don't know if she's ever heard of me. I've only recently heard of her. Our grandmother, Yvette Kim Boucher, kept a great many secrets from all of us."

"Gino, who's there?" Francesca called.

Gino left Francesca's question hanging in the air while he studied Boucher. Finally, he stepped outside the door and closed it behind him. "You will forgive me for being cautious. I don't know you, and from what you say, my wife doesn't know you, either. Is there anyone we might mutually know that would speed up this introduction?"

"I should have thought this out better. You're right, and the way things are currently, I understand your concern. I run a restaurant in San Francisco—*Seoul Food*?"

Gino's face registered a blank.

"My father owns HCB, the transatlantic shipping container business? His name is Hin Chan Boucher? I manage the San Francisco headquarters when I'm not at the restaurant which is now closed for a bit." Boucher's eyes darkened.

A head shake from Gino.

"People." Boucher looked down, then around the yard, seemingly searching for a name to drift down from the treetops. Finally, he brightened. "RP?"

"RP who?" was Gino's reply.

"This is my last try," Boucher said. "Morrie Landow?"

"Yes," Gino said. "All right. We've got a beginning. Tell me about your connection to Morrie Landow."

"That's actually kind of murky, for want of a better word. We go back, though. We met during a Special Ops mission. Unfortunately, I was on the other side. That's probably not going to do my case here much good, although Carla likes to rub it in whenever she gets a chance."

"Carla?"

"Yeah. Carla. Morrie's wife. The ballet dancer. You know her? I should have asked her to come with me. She's going to tell me, pardon my language, that I was a fucking idiot for doing this alone."

Gino turned around and opened the door, motioning for Boucher to follow him. "That's all I need to know. Come on in."

***

The bouquet, now artfully arranged in the crystal vase on the dining room table, presided over the introductions and the first awkward attempts at conversation. Gino had taken the mail, which included a small box labeled *fragile,* back to the office, leaving Francesca and her guest to sort out their family history together.

"I brought a couple of photos with me," Chan said, opening a small envelope and shaking the pictures out onto the table. "Didn't think childhood photos would be much help, so I scrounged around until I found this one." He handed it to Francesca. "That's me and my little brother, Sang Joon. Well, he's not so little, but he's younger by half a dozen years. We both work for HCB, my father's container ship business. Actually, that's not entirely accurate, regarding Sang. It's rather complicated." Chan tapped the photo. "My father took this about two years ago, just before I moved to San Francisco."

Francesca studied the photo then looked up, comparing the image to Chan's face. She nodded. "You're quite a bit taller than your brother." She returned the photo to the table.

"I'm five-ten. I get that from grandfather. The French side of the family. From what I've been told, he was quite tall and thin. My brother got the thin gene." Chan winked. "Thin, I am not."

"You don't get along with each other, do you? I can see it in your body language."

"We've had our differences," Chan said.

"I see."

The second photo showed a woman in her late twenties or possibly early thirties. She was holding a cat that seemed to be watching the camera with a wary eye. "Mi Aera gave me this one of her. She is absolutely nuts about her cats. They don't seem to like anyone but her. I think she's a sorceress, actually, and they're her familiars."

Francesca examined the photo. Mi Aera had long black hair, dark eyes and flawless, porcelain skin. She was slender. She was also tall, nearly as tall as Chan. "I see what you mean about the tall gene." Francesca said.

"She's the bookkeeper for the family. Travels quite a bit. She comes to San Francisco to eat at my restaurant when she's in the States." He tightened his jaw. "At least, she used to. That's another story, though. The restaurant, that is." He straightened the pile of photos and handed them to Francesca. "These are for you. Mi Aera wanted me to get your number so she can call you. Actually, Mi Aera is the one who initiated the family search. She found me. She'd badgered Grandmama Yvette until she finally gave in and laid out the family history. The whole strange, sordid mess."

"All right," Francesca said. "I'm ready as I'll ever be. Dive into the whole strange, sordid mess, as you call it."

"If your story is similar to mine, you were never told anything about where all the money came from. But crime pays, and for our family it has paid quite well. We're talking the Korean Mafia here." He shrugged at Francesca's bug-eyed response. "Yep. It's true."

Francesca's eyes grew even wider. "Mafia is not a word I would have associated with Korea."

"Call it what you wish. It's not a term of endearment, believe me, but we can argue semantics another time. The Korean Mafia is just as ruthless as their Italian counterparts. It's all about the money, after all. It's only the means to acquire it that vary. As it turns out, the Bouchers were and are powerful, devoid of ethics, and deal on a regular basis with international crime syndicates, and yes, that includes the Italian Mafia, although currently they and I are on opposite sides of a local situation."

It was at that moment Gino returned from his office, his arms full of files and the box that had arrived in the morning post balanced on top. He paused at the mention of an all-too-familiar word, set his burden on the table, pulled out a chair, and sat down. "Please continue," he said, his expression one of attentive interest.

"All right," Chan said. "I believed Grandmama Yvette was a widow. That may or may not be true, as it turns out. She *assumed* she was a widow, not having heard from her husband in nearly twenty-five years. Laurent Boucher was a dealer in looted antiquities." Chan tilted his head in the direction of the hand-carved oak mantel above the fireplace in the Great Room. "Like that Etruscan pot there you probably got from Grandmama." He sat back and laced his fingers behind his neck. "My guess is it was a wedding gift. She's cheap, plus it's a good way to move the merchandise around. And now," he returned his hands to the table, palms up, "you're an accessory after the fact." He looked at Francesca. "Just saying you might want to get it authenticated and decide where to go from there if you're interested. But, returning to the saga, Laurent was on an acquisition trip to Italy. He never arrived at his destination and speculation was that he'd found himself in the crosshairs of a jurisdictional dispute between clans or families or whatever you want to call them, and they killed him either accidentally or purposefully. That was a possibility, of course, but the occasional deposits and withdrawals of considerable sums of money from his account at the bank in Paris—an account that Yvette had never closed— didn't mesh with the theory. She didn't need the money, and if Laurent were still alive, there was no point in complicating matters. He was dead to her and she never spoke of him again."

Francesca excused herself and went into the Great Room to have a closer look at the pot in question. It was obviously old. Ancient, even. She'd never thought to question its provenance. "Do you suppose the detective saw this when she was here the other night?" she asked Gino who responded by slamming his head on the table.

"Is there anybody in the entire fucking world that has a normal family?" Gino asked.

"I don't think so," Chan said.

"Not likely," Francesca offered.

Gino had raised his head and was muttering something incoherent. It sounded like a Italian curse. All curses carry the same sounds, regardless of the language employed to deliver them.

Chan cleared his throat and continued. "Yes. Well. Yvette was wealthy in her own right. Her father had been a major player and a shadowy figure in Korean political and financial intrigue. It had paid well. She'd seldom used her birth name, Kim Mi Cha, after her marriage, choosing instead her husband's pet name for her, Yvette, and kept her surname, Kim. She's pushing eighty now and divides her time among her homes in Paris, Seoul, and San Francisco. She's left the day to day business affairs to her two sons, Him Chan and Duri. Her daughter, Claudine, was an actress. A good actress but a lousy mother, and that was why Yvette found herself saddled with raising a granddaughter. That would be you." He tilted his head at Francesca. "So, that's the story. You've got relatives. Two uncles, one aunt, and three cousins. My mother died a while back. We're Korean, we're French, and we've got a long, family tradition of living on the other side of the law. Doesn't matter which country. They're all fair game."

Francesca had been listening with rapt attention. "This can't be true," she said. "Grandmama's so proper. She's a philanthropist. She belongs to a gazillion civic organizations. She's...she's...."

"An actress. And a very good one. Who do you suppose your mother inherited her talent from?" Chan's eyes twinkled. "Give it time. Piece by piece it will all start to come together. Little things she said or did. Or didn't say or didn't do. Unexplained absences. But there was an explanation. You just weren't privy to it. She's a shrewd businesswoman and she's Chairman of the Board of HCB."

Gino had been half-listening as he struggled with the sealing tape that had been doubled up at the seams on the box. "I never knew my grandmother," he said. "But then, I have only the faintest memories of my parents." He looked at Chan. "That was my introduction to the Mafia. Johnny Vincento. He had them killed so my grandfather would pay the *pizzo* on *Castel del Mare*." Gino returned his attention to the box and ripped the tape off with a savage motion. "It's never over. Never." The sender's name on the label was Pierce. There was no return address. He felt uneasy. The reason became clear when he moved the bubble wrap away from the contents and saw a glass vial labeled *Xylella fastidiosa* inside. The color drained from his face. He pushed the box away. Somewhere in the recesses of his memory, a workshop he'd attended on diseases of grapes came to the fore and he made the connection. Shit. Damn.

"Gino?"

Francesca's voice seemed to come from far away, and he couldn't seem to find the source. The second time she called his name, the mist dissipated and he was brought back to reality. It was a reality straight from a horror film.

"Honey, what's wrong?"

Gino's color had marginally improved. He pulled the box back to him and looked down at the glass vial nestled in bubble wrap. He dared not touch it. "This," he said. There was no online course that could deal with the situation, only what he'd learned at the annual meeting of the California Vintners Association. Pierce disease. Destroying vineyards, costing millions, bankrupting vintners, and to date, nothing that could be done about it. Once established, it could not be stopped. "This," he said again, "is a death threat for *Dark Mountain*, and shortly we'll receive the terms that our extortionists will demand to *protect* us from it. God! We can't get away from them." He ran his hands through his hair, his eyes fixed on the vial of death.

"There's got to be something we can do," Francesca said, but her voice was uncertain. There was nothing to be done about it in Sardinia. Why would here be any different? But here *was* different. "No," she said. "This time *they're* going to be the ones to pay. We've got to find a way." She turned to her visitor. "I'm sorry, Chan. Maybe we can have that family reunion another time. For now...."

"Understood and agreed. For now, we've got work to do," Chan said. "When I mentioned that my restaurant was currently closed, I didn't tell you the whole story. I got a vial as well. Mine was botulism toxin. The threat was quite clear, but the reason was different. We—Morrie, RP, and I have been dealing with a protection operation they're running in the City. Same guys as this." He pointed to the box. "Johnny Vincento. He knows who I am and suspects that I'm behind the decrease in the ranks of his soldiers. He's right, of course, but how did you get so lucky?"

"He knows who I am, as well. I pay the *pizzo* for the estate in Italy. It appears Johnny's expanding his territory. That's a healthy piece of real estate he's trying to claim. Is he planning to open a chain of franchises?"

"I, for one, don't much care for his business model," Chan said. "But we can operate in much the same way. The Puglisis/Vincentos have made a fatal error."

"I don't get where you're coming from," Gino said. "The Puglisis and the Vincentos are only related by marriage, and now with Joey and Fiona dead, are they even related at all?"

"I get it," Francesca said. "Our relational situation is similar. And I would venture to say that our resources have multiplied considerably with the arrival of my cousin, and your cousin-in-law. That makes us the Esposito/Boucher crime family. Sounds more like a law firm than a syndicate, but it should work." She grinned. "I'm beginning to see a flicker of hope."

"I'll take it," Gino said. "I'll call Carla and Morrie. We need a family council." He smiled at Chan. "An extended family council. We seem to do these often. Can you stay for dinner?"

"You bet. I'll cook. Just show me what you've got in the freezer and in the fridge and give me an hour."

# CHAPTER TWENTY-ONE

*Mostly San Jose*

Growing up in a Mafia family, some things you just take for granted. Everyone Tommaso knew had a nickname. His uncles, Sally "The Pipe" and "Fat" Joey. His father, "Big"Al. It hadn't seemed unusual when they'd all started calling him Tommy "The Fox" for the way he frequently outsmarted his bully of a brother, Gennaro. The name stuck. But Gennaro never earned a nickname, and it angered him no end. You didn't give yourself one. It was bestowed upon you, for good or bad, by others. It was a mark of belonging. And while belonging was the last thing he wanted, he hoped "The Fox" still had some good moves left.

It was a Wednesday and the tourists were out in force at Fisherman's Wharf. Finding a parking space took a while, but he'd finally squeezed into one the size of a postage stamp, six blocks from the restaurant. That actually wasn't bad. It gave him a few more minutes to consider how he was going to play this. Gennaro would be angry, of course. He did anger really well. The best counter action was to ignore it and get straight to the point. After all, he had something Gennaro wanted, and that meant, at least for the moment, that his brother would not be in the position of power. Tommaso had a five-inch height advantage, but they'd both be seated. No help there. It all boiled down to keeping his cool, ignoring any rants, and acting as if nothing had ever happened to cause this delay in making contact.

The case containing the laptop bumped against Tommaso's left thigh as he negotiated the crowded sidewalks, stepping off to the side at intersections, just in case somebody had an eye on it. He'd wanted a lot of people around for safety, but this was too much of a good thing. He tightened his grip on the handle. He'd be rid of the damn thing shortly.

The restaurant was packed, and the line of those waiting to be seated was out the door and a good third of the way down the block. He pulled out his cell to call Gennaro.

"Where are you?" he asked when his brother answered.

"Where the hell do you think I am?"

"If I knew, I wouldn't be calling you. Are you inside, outside, in line? Where? Just give me a straight answer."

"I'm stuck on 101 just outside San Bruno. I haven't moved an inch in the past forty-five minutes and I don't know if I'll ever move again. Three fire trucks, half a dozen CHP cruisers, and I've lost count of the tow trucks. Where the hell are you?"

"At the restaurant. Look. This isn't going to work. I'm going back to my apartment in San Jose. When you can, get off 101 and come to my place. I'll cook. Call it a peace offering. I'm texting you the address. Come alone. No women." Tommaso disconnected before his brother started in again. There was time enough to run an errand. Maybe two.

***

Gennaro showed up shortly after five o'clock. If possible, his mood was even worse than it had been over the phone three hours earlier. "Where the hell have you been hiding?" was his greeting when Tommaso opened the door. "I'm not playing any of your games. Give me my laptop and I'm out of here."

"Not so fast. Come inside before the neighbors call the cops. You can't just go around yelling at people all the time and expect to get anywhere. You'd think you'd have learned that by now." Tommaso looked at his brother, a mix of disdain and simple hatred in his eyes. "I repeat. Come in, sit, have a drink, and we'll talk. You've got nothing to lose and your laptop to gain. Let's just declare a half-hour's truce so we can get on the same page or at least be reading the same book."

Without further comment, Gennaro pushed past his brother and Tommaso closed the door.

"There's whiskey in the cupboard next to the microwave. And Scotch, if you've changed your drinking preference," Tommaso said, moving two highball glasses to the small center island that doubled as a kitchen table.

"Whiskey's fine."

"We'll see how this goes before I start dinner," Tommaso said. "You've got questions, and so have I. Since I called you for this meeting, I'll go first."

Gennaro filled his glass and sat on one of the stools by the island, glass in hand. "Go ahead."

"You asked where I've been." Tommaso eyed his brother's overfilled glass but said nothing. He took his own drink and sat across from his brother. "I've been trying to decide whether or not you're trying to off me." He studied his drink. "Wouldn't put it past you if you thought it would benefit you." He took a sheet of paper from the case on the counter and pushed it over to Gennaro. "Your custom hit list. I checked. I'm not on it. I took that as a positive sign, although I'm still unclear as to why you wanted me at the Club while you, and I'm assuming it was you, took care of some business." He took a drink.

"My turn? Fine. Yes. I wanted you at the Club. In the office, so we could discuss the ramifications of the matter being attended to in the VIP room. I've learned that a lean body moves faster. I was just eliminating some unnecessary, redundant fat. And you, little fox, you took off like a scared rabbit. Such a brave boy."

"Cain slew Abel. And Prospero and Joey were your uncles. And not so much later, Fiona. Family. Gennaro. They were Family."

"You've been listening to his holiness too much. You're beginning to sound like him."

"Maybe. Doesn't mean Anthony's wrong. Doesn't mean he's right, either. Just making an observation about possibilities on a couple of levels." Tommy waited to see how his brother would react. Gennaro was skilled at flipping the script. He'd end up being the wronged party and Tommaso the one falsely accusing him. Of what? Another murder? Hell, if you counted the lieutenants at the meeting, he'd killed over half a dozen. And he was taken aback for being suspected of plotting one more? Typical. Once, Tommaso would have continued the argument, pleaded his case, trying to show Gennaro he was wrong. He wasn't that confused boy trying to reason with his brother any longer. He knew how narcissists worked, and he knew what they were capable of. Had Gennaro marked him for murder? Tommaso would be a fool to rule it out, no matter how much blame and guilt Gennaro tried to shovel at him to deflect. Tommaso pointed at number five on the hit list. "You can cross that one off. I took care of her before I left New Haven."

"You're shitting me." Gennaro set his glass down on the table and picked up the paper. "This your idea of being humorous?"

"Not at all. I don't like people who steal from the family. Makes us look weak." Tommaso got up and went to the stove. "I found it an interesting exercise, actually. Killing isn't all that difficult, especially if you're slightly removed from the situation. Use someone else, use a car, whatever. It's really quite easy." He smiled. "Easy enough for you to check out. Want to stay for dinner? Steak and pasta. I picked up some decent bread at the bakery on my way back from the City."

"Yeah. Think I will."

Tommaso nodded. "You can do the sauce."

***

"Why didn't you tell me?" Gennaro asked.

"Why should I? What was there to tell? Besides, I just did. Tell you. Pass the parmesan. *Please.*" Tommaso looked up from his plate, the fork in his hand pointed in Gennaro's direction. "Tying up loose ends. Cleaning up. It's what I do. There's one more thing." He pried open the lid on the cheese and looked at the contents with disdain. "They didn't have any fresh at the deli section. This will have to do." He sprinkled the pale cheese product on his pasta. "Oh yes. The other thing. The girls from the Club. Don't cause problems where there aren't any. They didn't see anyone. Just the residue. Leave them alone."

"You can't be sure." Gennaro reached for the bread. "Women talk."

"Men don't? Doesn't matter. They didn't see anything. Nanette's got feelings for me, and besides, she's going to have my kid. I like that idea."

Gennaro shrugged. "It's on you."

"That will make you an uncle. Lately, that hasn't been all that safe. You'd best be on your toes." Tommaso scraped the last of the sauce with a slice of bread and pushed the stool back. "I'm going to Papa's tomorrow to get set up with the books." He gave his brother a hard look. "He's expecting me."

Gennaro got up and grabbed the case. "I'll be in touch."

"I'll be around. You know where to find me." Half an hour later, after Tommaso had finished the cleanup, and then waiting an additional ten minutes to be sure his brother had truly gone, he turned off the lights and left the one-night rental. He drove to Santa Cruz and got a motel room on the coast. Just in case.

# CHAPTER TWENTY-TWO

*Dark Mountain to San Francisco*

"The point is we're no longer dealing with a mega-organization—something nameless, faceless, all powerful. We're dealing with maybe four individual humans with flaws and weaknesses. That would be Enzo, Johnny, Nico, and Gennaro. We've just got to eliminate the nebulous fear factor and pinpoint what their flaws and weaknesses are and go from there. Task number one: We need to target weaknesses in the association. Personal and organizational." Francesca had shifted into Event Planner mode. She'd dragged the easel from her office and positioned it against the wall in the dining room. Each seat at the table was filled and looked like a meeting of the Board of Directors of the Esposito/Boucher Conglomerate. She had a fleeting thought of her grandmother, Yvette, Chairman of the Board. Secrets. Everyone had them.

Morrie had been listening, arms folded across his chest and his chair precariously tipped away from the table. "They're into protection, extortion. That's traditional. But this move into trafficking is new. Their focus has always been on the personal touch. You know, murder, beatings—but the future of crime is high tech. Digital. It's all done online, and it's probably why Johnny Vincento stayed on after the funeral. He's head to head with Enzo, but they're a couple of dinosaurs. They should be back in Italy, drinking wine and telling tall tales of the old days with the other old men. They're probably not current on new developments in technology, let alone what we use on a regular basis. They're used to having other people take care of details and the follow-through. So, the question that evolves from this is, who's getting them up to speed on modern ways and means or, and this is more likely, I think, who's handling this for them?"

"It's Tommaso's generation. That means Gennaro and Nico," Gino said. "And judging from what Tommaso said, the money's on Gennaro with Nico taking the orders."

Carla agreed. "I met Gennaro once, maybe twice. He's cold. That's a strength. He got no conscience. Totally one-track mind, although, come to think of it, that could be a weakness. He gets so busy on something, he don't see the other stuff happening around him."

"After Gino got that box," Francesca said, making the word *box* sound like a curse, "I went looking to see where research was being done on the virus. There aren't that many research labs involved. But something interesting turned up, and it involves three of our Puglisis. Tommaso, Gennaro, and Nico all graduated from Boston College in Massachusetts. Tommaso has a master's in business administration and Gennaro has a bachelor's in organizational management. That has me wondering if he's organizing the family members of the organization into live and let die categories, but that's another topic. Nicolo just graduated with a bachelor's in biology. The interesting thing I mentioned? Boston College has a Virology, Immunology and Microbiology Lab. He'd have access to it. I wonder if they were either working on Pierce disease or he had a way of ordering a sample for research? At first I thought it didn't explain the botulism toxin vial, because that falls under bacteriology, but I read on and discovered that bacteriology is a subset of microbiology." She smiled. "Kind of convenient, don't you think? A full-service lab, in a manner of speaking. Of course, there would be protocols for working with samples, but a criminal mind can get around most university policies."

At that moment, there was the by-now dreaded knock on the front door. Gino took a deep breath and got up to see what fresh hell was on the other side. "It's all right," he shouted over his shoulder. "I should give you a key," he said to Tommaso. "Come on in. We're strategizing. It hasn't been a good day for the good guys, but we'll fill you in."

"I've been trying to get hold of Nanette, but she's not answering," was Tommaso's greeting. "I'd gotten a motel for the night and tried to call her from there, but there was no answer. I got worried, but I don't have your number, so the only thing to do was check out of my room and come over. Hope you don't mind. I figured she'd be here, but the lights aren't on in the guest house, and she's a night owl."

"She's got to be there," Francesca said, "although, come to think of it, I haven't seen her since this morning, and she usually stops by around noon for a chat." Francesca got up. "I'm sure everything is fine. She was probably just tired, but let's go check."

Everything wasn't fine. The only occupant of the guest house was Bruce who had relocated his sleeping quarters to the bottom dresser drawer and seemed irritated when Francesca turned on the lights.

"I don't understand," Francesca said. "Where are they?"

***

If you've ever had something stolen, you know before you know. There's something that hangs in the air. It's heavy and empty at the same time. You keep looking even though you know what you're looking for isn't there, and when you finally accept what has happened, the sense of personal violation overwhelms you. It's bad enough when it's a personal item that's been stolen, but when it's a person, there's disbelief, fear, a sense of total powerlessness, and a wave of cold dread that threatens to consume you.

Francesca knew she would not forget the look in Tommaso's eyes when the realization of what had happened hit him.

"We need to call the police," she said, but he stopped her as she turned to run back to the house.

"No. I'll handle it." And he was gone before she could respond.

***

If she'd left under her own will, why wasn't she picking up? The signal indicated she was stationary at Summit Road where it turned right onto

Highway 17 North. Tommaso slowed as he approached the turn, looking everywhere for a sign of her, and then he spotted the phone in the gutter by a waste water drain. Actually, there were two phones. Hers and Ginger's. He pulled over and retrieved them, ignoring the horns blasting from irritated drivers behind him. The screens were cracked from the impact on the asphalt, but Nan's still had a charge. His heart sank. There was no way to know where she was. Then he cursed himself for his stupidity. Whoever had Nan must have used a program similar to the one he'd used to find her. They'd driven right to the guest house as if they'd had an invitation. Nan thought she was safe. She would have opened the door. From there...he cursed himself again. She could be anywhere. Why? Why had they taken her? He'd told Gennaro she didn't know anything—hadn't seen anything. If Gennaro hadn't believed him, he would have killed her when he found her. So, what was the point of kidnapping her and Ginger? Leverage. But for what? She'd be no use to them as leverage if they killed her. How long they'd wait, he couldn't know without knowing what their plans were. For now, he was pretty sure she was alive. He had to hold onto that or he'd go insane. The police would be no help. Even if they knew where to look they'd go in heavy-handed and would probably kill her by friendly fire. He got back in the car, made a U-turn, and sped back to *Dark Mountain*.

***

"While you were gone, RP called. He got a strange transmission," Morrie said. "Actually, he's gotten two, just about an hour apart. Odd, because they're coming from your grandfather's home in Pacific Heights. And to be even more precise, which RP was able to be with a bit of fine tuning of the equipment, the signal seems to be coming from the third floor in the rear of the house."

Gino was still at the door where he'd let Tommaso in. "Do I close the door or do we get moving now? It's after ten o'clock. Going to take us an hour and a half give or take to get there and get in position. What's your thinking?" he asked Morrie.

"We know where the girls are now, but they may move them out in the morning. Anything's possible, Tommaso said. "I don't know what you're doing, but I'm going now."

"Me too," said Gino.

"I'm in," Chan said.

"I'll text RP to get the necessary supplies and meet us there at midnight," Morrie said. "How are you all fixed in the firearms department?"

"I'm good," Chan said.

"All set," was Morrie's answer. "Never leave home without it."

"I'll need something," Tommaso said. "I know. I know. The only Mafia guy here and I'm not carrying."

"Back in a minute," Gino said, leaving for the gun cabinet in the office. "Anybody else need anything while I'm at the store?"

"Me," said Carla. "My .38 isn't going to cut it. You got a Ruger with a 15 clip? That's a nice piece. I like the grip."

Morrie groaned.

"That's not legal anymore," Gino said.

"Deal with it. It's reliable and we can talk law later when all this shit is done. You're going to need two cars. I'm driving one. You're going to need a driver with the motor running when you come out with Nanette and Ginger. Waiting for you to fumble around for your car keys ain't a bright idea."

"Don't forget me," Francesca said. "I'm driving the other car and I made the Olympics shooting team when I was sixteen. It's not open for discussion. My preference is a Glock if you've got one." She pushed back from the table and got her purse from the hall table. "What are you waiting for? Let's go!"

***

"I got no family. Nobody. I was really feeling sorry for myself. Now, after seeing all of this, I ain't sure family is such a good idea," Nanette said, trying the bedroom door one more time. "Still locked."

"You expected them to leave it unlocked? Don't be stupid," Ginger said. "I haven't heard any sounds at all. Probably not unusual, being up here in heaven." She winced. "Wish I hadn't said that. Anyway, family is a great idea. The execution of that great idea, though, sometimes gets kind of a twisted result. That's how you get the Mafia. Still, you've got Tommy. And soon, you're going to have the baby. That makes you a family. It's all on you how that works out. You have to believe."

"I believe that, since we're on the third floor with a straight drop to the swimming pool, there's no way out of here on our own, and if Tommy doesn't get here soon, there ain't gonna be much of a future for us."

"Hate to say it, but I think you're right on that account. Try and get some sleep. Morning will come soon enough, whatever it brings."

"Is it time to hit the button on the bracelet again?" Nanette asked. "Did Carla tell you what the range is on that thing?"

"No, she didn't. But I'm hoping it's working. It's probably been an hour since I pushed it the last time. Can't tell since those goons tossed our phones. At least they left the light bulb in the ceiling fixture. Only because they didn't think about it, I'm sure. I'm going to push the button again and turn on the light. Fingers crossed."

***

Crime in Pacific Heights is generally of the white-collar variety. It's not what you find in the Tenderloin or the Castro or the mean streets of anywhere else. Everybody's safe inside their multi-million dollar mansions, the doors locked against the world outside and the alarm systems engaged. Morning was still about six hours away. There was a full moon, but it didn't matter. The sky was overcast. RP, in black stocking cap, black t-shirt, black running pants, and a skin tone perfectly coordinated for the mission, patrolled the neighborhood, a shadow searching for anything that might put a snag in the rescue operation. Nothing unusual had surfaced. No cars parked along the street. No fitness nuts taking a late-night run. No extra lights on in any of the houses. Somewhere down the street, a dog barked and a light came on. The dog stopped barking. The light went off again. RP returned to his car to wait for the reinforcements. He didn't have to wait long. It was five after midnight when two cars, headlights off, pulled in behind him and cut the engines.

***

Pacific Heights dates from the 1870s. It's an area consisting of about a hundred and thirty blocks, and the more desirable homes have views of San Francisco Bay and the Golden Gate Bridge. It's got a large Italian population—so much so that the Italian Consulate has its home on Webster Street. It's a wealthy demographic, and the home that was the object of today's mission was standard fare for a Mafioso, at least from a landscaping perspective. Manicured flower beds with no plant taller than a few inches around the house and in a few brick-bordered planters on the front lawn and no shrubs or trees. Anyone showing up on the premises would be in full view and there was no place to hide. The only thing missing was a yappy little dog to alert the owner of a foreign presence.

From an architectural perspective, the Puglisi house was a three-story Italianate mansion built shortly after the 1906 earthquake. It appeared sturdy enough to withstand the next one. A brick path led from the driveway to five brick steps that ended at a covered front porch defined by three arched porticos. It was a study in symmetry with the midpoint being the central portico which was wider and taller than its two side companions. The three-stall garage, to the right and slightly back of the main structure, was connected to the house by an enclosed brick and glass corridor with its own mansard roof. The occupants could simply drive in, park, and enter the house without ever having to breathe the outside air. It was an excellent security feature.

Behind the home were three guest houses, smaller versions of the main structure. The back yard included an Olympic-sized swimming pool, tennis courts, and a putting green. Loud speakers attached to poles at a central stone patio would provide a concert experience for the guests and headaches for the neighbors. It had a crammed, ostentatious, amusement-park vibe. All it lacked were a ticket booth, a roller coaster, and bumper cars. Tonight, it was peacefully unoccupied and silent, but all hell was about to break loose.

# CHAPTER TWENTY-THREE

*San Francisco*

Late-night traffic midweek is about as light as it ever gets in the Bay Area, but the highways never sleep, and the noise never quits. You can't escape it unless you can find an isolated pocket several mountain ridges away from the roads, and those are getting harder and harder to find. Highway 17 can be heard miles away, and if you are a lover of peace and quiet, you're not going to find it. Tonight, two more vehicles would be adding their engine noise to the mix, ramping up the decibel level another notch.

"I'm good with the Subaru," Carla said. "Good acceleration and maneuverability, and, most important for tonight, it's got a full tank."

That last comment brought a groan from Tommaso who'd been extolling the virtues of his e-car with its rapid acceleration feature as the better choice for a jackrabbit start until he remembered it needed charging. Again. He was regretting leaving the Toyota back in New Haven.

"Maybe you can get your family to invest in windmills or something," Carla said, reaching for her keys.

"I just filled up the Volvo yesterday," Francesca said, hoisting her shoulder bag. "We're all set."

With all the firepower the occupants were carrying and the lack of concealed carry permits for the majority, the speed limits were not something to challenge, and Carla and Francesca had set cruise control exactly two miles above the posted limits. Any faster, and there was the possibility of getting the interest of a CHP cruiser that was getting bored with a lack of activity or looking for drivers under the influence of whatever. Go the speed limit or below and you risked getting that same attention for being too careful because you were under the influence, as well. Two over was as safe as they could be and hope they would be flying under the radar. It would be a quick trip down the mountain, and once they reached the interchange, they'd be taking 101 to the City, the faster route, barring any accidents or night roadwork.

"Breathe," Carla said to Tommaso, as they hugged the first of the curves. "You're tight. You gotta regulate your breathing. You focus on that, and you'll have more control. I learned that from dancing. Breathing is everything."

"Let's change focus here," Morrie said, turning to face Tommaso in the rear seat. "You've been in the house. Tell me about the alarm system."

Tommaso nodded. "It's a..." He closed his eyes. "I can see the sign on the front lawn. Dammit. I can't remember—no. Wait. Yes. It's a Bronson. I'm sure. Yeah. The control panel is on the wall, just inside the front door to the left, at eye level. We'll have fifteen seconds to disarm it once we get the door open."

"Shouldn't be a problem. You wouldn't happen to have a key, would you?"

"No. Sorry."

"All right. Never hurts to ask. No problem. Fifteen seconds is as good as an hour."

The navigation program on Carla's phone broke into the conversation. *"Speed trap ahead."*

"Shit. *Don't hit the brakes. Don't hit the brakes. Just cruise on by. You haven't a care in the world,"* Carla whispered to herself. Cruise control was something she didn't generally use. It took all the decision-making away from her, and she'd learned that she needed to be in control after so many years of not having had that option. It took every ounce of her willpower to keep her foot flat on the mat. She hummed a nervous tune, and Morrie turned away from Tommaso and rested his hand on hers. The effect was immediate. She stopped the humming and smiled. She *was* in control. She was the one behind the wheel. "Thanks."

"I didn't see him. Did you?" she asked, after they'd put another seven miles behind them.

"I wasn't looking," Morrie said. "By the time you see them, it's too late anyway. You're doing fine."

"I am," she said. "I'm doing great."

Morrie turned back to Tommaso. "Now, describe the interior. Where do we go once I have the alarm disarmed. Where are the stairs?"

"There's an entryway just inside the front door. It opens onto a short hallway. At the end, the stairs are directly ahead, the dining room is to the left, and the kitchen is to the right. It actually looks like a standard tract house on the inside. They spent all the money for show on the exterior. It's no frills, except for the marble floors. They must have gotten them under the counter. They're nice but slick. They've got an Oriental rug running the length of the hall, and it travels. If you run, you'll go skidding and take a fall. You'd think they'd have spent some cash on the inside, but they go out to entertain. Saves on cleanup for the blood," Tommaso said, with a half-grin.

Carla tightened her grip on the steering wheel. "He ain't kidding," she said. "I still can't figure out why you people got to whack everybody when maybe discussing things would be less...messy. You all got anger issues."

Morrie waited until he was sure she had finished. "Last item. Have you ever been on the second or third floors?"

"No."

"All right. Here's how it's going to go down. As soon as I have the alarm neutralized, you lead the way. We believe the house is unoccupied, but we proceed as if it is. We move quickly. No talking. Hand signals only. If, by chance, we run into someone, I'll deal with it. You keep moving. The girls are in the rear of the house. We enter every bedroom on the second floor, and if the girls aren't there, we go up to the third and repeat the process. If a door is locked, I'll open it."

Carla did an eye roll that went undetected.

"We get the girls and move out. No stopping until we've got them in the car. Then, Carla takes them to the ballet studio, and we call the police and wait. Questions?"

"No." Tommaso sat back and stared out the window, concentrating on his breathing, as the lights of one city after another flew by.

***

"There is absolutely no reason why I shouldn't be here," Tommaso said, trying to convince himself more than anyone else. "This is my grandfather's home. I have every right to be here." Focusing on breathing had helped initially, but control was slipping away, and he was heading for a bad attack of the nerves. The only thing keeping him functioning was knowing that Nanette was waiting for him. Another deep breath and slow exhaling brought a clearer focus. That, and the arrival of the second car with Francesca, Gino, and Chan, and the emergence of RP from his vehicle, with the flashlights.

A briefing session ensued curbside, and the rescue mission was underway. RP would continue monitoring the street. Carla and Francesca would remain in the cars, ready to move out once Nanette and Ginger had been freed. Gino, Morrie, Tommaso, and Chan would take the house.

True to his word, Morrie had the alarm system off in twelve seconds, not his personal best but not his worst, either. Flashlights guided their path down the hallway and up the stairs to the second level where the team split to check bedrooms on both sides of the stairs. They were met with nothing but reassurance that the house was indeed empty. For how long was an unknown.

They repeated the exercise when they reached the third floor with its four bedrooms. A ribbon of light shone in the space between the bottom of the door and the uncarpeted wooden floor of the last bedroom on the left. Tommaso, having been given the honors, tried the doorknob. As expected, the door was locked, but the sound of the attempt got the girls' attention, and when Morrie applied some serious muscle to the door, it flew open and slammed against the side wall. "Mission accomplished," Morrie said, rubbing his shoulder and wincing.

"One day you're going to do some serious damage to yourself," Chan said, shaking his head. "You could have brought one of those battering rams like you said DeLuna had."

"Too cumbersome."

This back and forth might have gone on a while longer, but at the sound of familiar voices, Ginger and Nanette, looking a bit worse for wear, emerged from the small bathroom.

"Are you all right?" Tommaso asked, and they both nodded as Nanette ran to Tommaso, Ginger at her heels. "Who brought you here?"

This time, there were head shakes. "Two men. We didn't know who the guy was that was giving all the orders, but the other one was Eddie," Ginger said. "I tried to reason with them, but they just hustled us into the car and brought us here." She shrugged. "They didn't hurt us, apart from a bit of rough handling. But we're used to that." She gave a sigh of relief that could have been heard back on the first floor.

And it was. Or it might have been the sound of the door hitting the wall when they broke in, but suddenly the lights came on and voices could be heard at the bottom of the stairs.

"I hate to break up the reunion, but we've got trouble," Chan said. "Now what?"

The effects of controlled breathing cannot be underestimated. Case in point was Tommaso who rose to the occasion, repeating the mantra he'd used at the beginning of the operation. "There is no reason why I shouldn't be in my grandfather's house. I let myself in and unfortunately tripped and fell against the door." His voice was triumphant.

"Think it'll work?" Gino whispered.

"Got any better ideas?" Morrie said.

"Break a leg," was Chan's response, and then he checked himself. "Sorry. Bad choice of words."

RP agreed.

"Here goes nothing," Tommaso said, starting down the stairs. "You'll be safe here. Nobody in this house climbs stairs unless they're bedding somebody. And that never involves the third floor, but finding a way down would be a really good idea for you guys." He looked at Morrie and Chan. "From what I've gleaned, you've done this more than once. Should be a piece of cake." He did a regulated inhale and exhale and moved towards the door, barreling down the stairs to the landing on the second floor, where he looked over the railing and called out, "Finally, somebody's home. Where've you all been? I was beginning to think I was in the wrong house."

***

"Baghdad. They didn't have three-story houses in Baghdad." Morrie slipped off the backpack and pulled out a canvas bag, inside of which was a rope ladder that was the twin of the one they'd used to escape the apartment fire. "I was really hoping we wouldn't need this. I also was hoping I wouldn't ever have to use one of these again. You'd all better be all right with this, because it's the only chance we've got." He opened the window. It was going to be a tight fit for him, but he'd been in tighter situations. Once they were out the window, the rest wouldn't be a problem. The girls were athletic. They'd be okay. Gino looked at the ladder without enthusiasm.

"One leg over the windowsill and foot on the top rung. Then the other leg. Get a firm grip on the sides and take your time. Not too much time," Morrie added. "But get a feel for it. Then it's one rung at a time. Don't turn. Don't look down. Look straight ahead. Just keep going. You'll touch ground before you know it. Gino's first."

"*Touch* being the operative word," Gino said. "Not *hit*. You don't want to *hit* the ground."

"Three stories is about thirty feet," Morrie said. "Each rung of the ladder is one foot from the next. Once you get a workable rhythm going, the descent doesn't take more than a few minutes, but those few minutes will seem like an hour. Just keep your mind on what you're doing." He motioned for Gino to get moving. "See you on the ground."

With Gino safely on *terra firma* and steadying the ladder for the rest, the pace picked up, which was a good thing, because the outside lights were on and the grounds were lit up and there were no shadows to hide in.

Keeping close to the side of the house, they ran towards the back yard, searching for a place where they could cross over into the neighbor's yard and get to the street from there.

"You know what I have come to hate," Gino said, spitting out a piece of foliage that had wrapped around his face. "Motion sensors. If this neighbor has them, we are screwed."

"Positive thinking," Ginger reminded him.

"I'm positive I hate motion sensors. Wait. Did you hear that?"

"Hear what?"

"Voices. From over there." Gino stopped and pointed at the guest house farthest from the neighbor's fence. "There aren't any cars. Guests would have cars."

Morrie, in the lead, looked over at the house. "We get the girls to safety. Then, if we're still alive after that, we can circle back and check it out."

***

"Uneventful. That's what I like about an operation. Well, at least this part was uneventful," Morrie said to RP who concurred. Morrie threw his backpack in the car and the girls scrambled in. "We can only hope Tommaso's having a similar reception in the house." Morrie glanced at the mansion, where the lights were still on throughout, but everything was quiet inside.

"I hope it ain't *too* quiet inside," Carla said, "if you get my meaning. I'll take the girls to the loft. We just moved in and nobody knows about it. We'll be as safe there as anywhere. No. Correction. We'll be safer there than anywhere else. You need anything, call me."

With Carla, Nanette, and Ginger safely out of harm's way, at least for the moment, Francesca was left cooling her heels in the other escape vehicle. With RP added to their ranks, the guys returned to check out the source of the voices coming from the guest house. Taking the direct approach, Morrie knocked on the door and was greeted with the sound of numerous fists banging on it from the inside and female voices calling out.

"What the hell is going on here?" Gino said. "Christ. There's bars on the windows. That is not kosher."

"Thanks for the tribute to my people," Morrie said. "And you're right. It's time to get DeLuna up here." He pulled out his cell. "Carla, call DeLuna. Tell her we've hit paydirt. They've got captives in at least one of the guest houses. We'll stand by."

In a heartbeat and a half, DeLuna was on the line. "We're on our way with a SWAT team. Don't do anything until we get there. ETA in thirty, max. I mean it. Do nothing. Am I clear?"

"Yes ma'am." Morrie disconnected.

Meanwhile, Gino seemed to have gotten across to the women that he was one of the good guys and that help was on the way. At least, he hoped that's what was happening. Italian bears some resemblance to Spanish, the language the women were speaking. Screaming was more accurate, but the noise level had decreased, and that was a good thing, since the team didn't want anyone from the house to come out and check on the situation. Withdrawing to the rear of the building, just in case anyone looked out the window, all they could do was wait for reinforcements and hope Tommaso was holding his own.

Which he was. A glass of Scotch in hand, standing by the fireplace, he was deep in conversation with his grandfather who'd decided to come home early from the Orchid Festival in Vegas where he'd cleaned up in the ribbon department. There'd been an evening flight to SFO and Enzo had decided he'd rather sleep in his own bed than at a motel. He'd called Gennaro who'd picked him up at the airport.

Enzo had taken his drink to his recliner, and Gennaro had staked out his own piece of territory, his back against the side wall, directly opposite Tommaso. The brothers looked like a pair of mismatched bookends. The conversation hadn't taken long to move from orchids to family business.

"I want you two to get along. You each have a role to play, and I'm not putting up with sibling rivalry. Either of you messes up, you'll hear about it from *me. Capisce?*

*Si, Papa,* Tommaso said, giving his brother a dark look.

"Gennaro? I'm talking to you."

Taking a slow drink from his glass, Gennaro nodded, the habitual smirk spreading across his face.

"I didn't hear you."

"*Si, Papa.*"

"Good. That's done. There will not be any more trouble. That's my boys." Enzo finished the glass in one swallow. "Where have you been, Tommaso?"

With honesty being the best policy in most situations, but something to be considered heavily when it concerned the family, Tommaso followed his grandfather's lead and tossed back the remainder of his drink. "Where was I? I was trying to find out if Gennaro was trying to have me killed. You'll excuse my tardy arrival, but circumstances were giving that possibility considerable credence. I thought it best to investigate before making a mistake I wouldn't live to regret."

"And now?" Enzo pointed to his empty glass which Gennaro rushed to replenish.

"The jury is still out, but I'm here." Tommaso held up his glass, but Gennaro ignored him and returned the decanter to the sidebar.

"It is not good to have bad blood between brothers," Enzo said. "When Alphonse returns, things will be different. That is a son to be proud of. Your father. He never talked. Not even when faced with ten years did he talk. That is a man to be trusted. That is a man of honor. You want advice? You would both do well to take note and follow the example of your father."

In that moment, Tommaso saw something in his grandfather's eyes that matched Gennaro's. It was something dark and devoid of conscience, and he realized why Anthony had fled to the Church. His had been a legitimate escape, but what of Tommaso? Where was his escape? To remain here was to die, either by his brother's hand or another's. He needed an exit strategy.

***

Say what you want about fast food. But it's fast and it's food and the big chains are open long hours. Neither Ginger nor Nanette had eaten anything all day, and the only water they'd had had come from the bathroom sink.

Nanette didn't say anything, but Carla could sense she was not doing well physically, mentally, or emotionally. They all needed a break. Time to step back and regroup, and most importantly, get a hamburger, fries, and a shake. The burger place on Geary beckoned. They ordered, grabbed the bags, and ten minutes later were safe at Carla's loft, sitting cross-legged on the soon-to-be-a-living room floor, cushions piled around them, munching away.

"It was my fault," Nanette said. "I opened the door. I didn't think."

Ginger, mouth full, shook her head. "No. How could you possibly, for even a second, think they'd find us there? I would have opened it, too. But what's eating at me is why kidnap us and not just kill us? I mean, I'm glad about that part, but I don't get it."

"Me either. Eddie called that other guy *Cesar*." She shrugged. "Didn't know him."

An internal alarm bell rang, and Carla paused as she rolled a fry around in the ketchup. "Cesar? Did you get a last name?"

"No." Nanette said. "But he was definitely in charge. They just made us get out of the car at this huge house and dragged us upstairs, locked the door, and that was it. Never said another word."

Cesar wasn't all that unusual a name, but Carla only knew one man with it. Cesar Torres, and, as she'd said whenever his name came up, there was something about him that was off. He sent out bad vibes. He was the one proprietor of a business in Cow Hollow she refused to give a bracelet to. She looked at her cell, debating if she should call DeLuna with this bit of information. It could probably wait. But then, if it would help the detective dealing with the women they were rescuing, maybe it shouldn't wait. She took a bite of her burger and made her decision somewhere between the third and fourth chews. She washed her food down with a bit of her strawberry shake and dialed. Her call went to voice mail. Made sense. She disconnected and sent a text.

***

When Detective DeLuna and her team of five pulled up in front of the Puglisi mansion, Morrie and RP were waiting. "I thought a brief introduction to be in order," Morrie said, jerking his head in the direction of RP. Pulling himself up to attention, he began. "To add credence to my position here, I'm Commander Morris Landow, United States Navy, retired, and RP was on my team." To DeLuna's uncertain expression, he added, "SEALS."

DeLuna gave an appraising look, then nodded.

Morrie continued. "We have secured the exterior. Francesca is waiting in the Volvo three houses down. Gino and Chan are in the back yard, guarding the target. Tommaso is inside, most likely on the first floor. The occupants, the number is unknown, returned while we were taking care of some business on the third floor. Tommaso provided the necessary distraction. His condition is also unknown."

DeLuna turned her gaze to the house. "What kind of business?"

Morrie cleared his throat. "Nanette and Ginger were being held on the third floor. They're now with Carla in a safe house. There are three guest homes behind the mansion. Target is to the extreme left. It's one-story. Window is barred."

"Thank you...Commander." She took a deep breath. "Remain here. Continue your watch."

"Ma'am."

DeLuna turned to her team. "Two additional friendlies in the back. Our target is the house on the extreme left. Check your weapons." She scanned the surroundings, then signaled to her team. "Go!"

****

*"¡Amigos!"* De Luna shouted. "Friends! *¡Nosotros estamos aquí para ayudarles a todos!* We are here to help you. Move away from the door! *¡Todos se alejan de la puerta!"* The women gave no response, and with time of the essence, DeLuna signaled for the battering ram. The door gave on the first hit. Eleven women had been crammed into the guesthouse. With sleeping accommodations for four, they'd probably been taking turns using the bed, and exhaustion had overcome them. Now, the older women, none of whom

could have been more than twenty, were guarding the younger girls, huddled together on the bed.

DeLuna was the first through the door. "*Todo va a estar bien.* Everything is going to be all right! You are not in trouble! *¡Nadie está en problemas!*"

Thirst, hunger, the promise of a better future and ultimately betrayal and fear had led the women to this place, but the new woman who promised real help opened her arms to the youngest who ran to her and the rest had nothing to lose by trusting her.

DeLuna signaled to one of her backups. "Get a van and blankets. We're taking them to the shelter." She sat down on the floor. "*Los ayudare a todos.* I will help all of you. *Todos ustedes están a salvo ahora.* You are safe now." One of the younger girls began to cry.

***

The sound of the battering ram pierced silence of the night and carried into the house. Gennaro, true to character, bolted from his chair and ran to the front door. His abortive flight came to an abrupt halt when he was greeted by the large presence of RP, effectively blocking that avenue of escape. Before Gennaro could turn and try another exit, RP had him on the ground, a foot pressing on the small of his back and the Ruger pointed at his head. "An intelligent person runs away from trouble, not towards it, asshole."

"You could sit on him," Morrie said. "It would be less tiring than standing."

"The idea is to hold him, not kill him," RP said.

"Good point. Shouldn't be long for backup. If you get tired, let me know."

"I'll get you," Gennaro spat, although the words were muffled since he was mostly talking to the dirt. "You'll all pay for this."

"Whatever." Morrie was intent on watching some motion on the street. A late model Toyota had been about to pull into the drive but then stopped, backed, and continued on down the street. Morrie grabbed his cell. "Francesca. That black Toyota. See where it goes. Give him room. Not too much. Try to get a plate."

"On it." She disconnected just as two SWAT team members ran from the back towards the front door, conveniently left open by Gennaro. There was a brief outburst of shouting followed by an abrupt silence that seemed to echo in the stillness. When Tommaso and Enzo, both in cuffs, exited the house and with the addition of Gennaro, the night's haul was complete. Gino and Chan joined Morrie and RP in the front yard, but it was close to three in the morning before the vans arrived to transport the women to the shelter and DeLuna could call it a wrap.

"Thanks," Morrie said. "You know you've probably saved his life."

"I don't take chances," DeLuna said. "And right now, I don't know jack shit about your man, except that he's a Puglisi, was in the house, and for all I know, fed me a line so that he'd have an alibi for being there. Time will tell. But for now, he's being treated no differently from the other two. No better, no worse."

Morrie nodded. "In your shoes, I'd do exactly the same."

"Good. Thanks for the help. All of you. Tomorrow, I'd like a word or six with Ginger and Nanette. My office. Ten sharp."

"Doesn't give them much time to rest up."

"Ten. Sharp."

"One thing." Morrie pointed at the security camera mounted above the portico. "There are five more of them. One at each corner of the house, and one in the back yard above the pool. They may tell you who brought the women here. And that," he turned to leave, "includes Ginger and Nanette. Don't forget. They're victims, not suspects."

DeLuna said nothing. Just then Morrie's cell rang. DeLuna had turned to go, but Morrie held up a hand, and she paused, questions in her eyes.

"You're on speaker," he said to Francesca. "Detective DeLuna is here."

"Right. You're going to like this. That Toyota made tracks straight to your old digs. It went into the garage just like it owned the place, and I saw the garage door closing, so I'm guessing the driver had arrived home. I didn't have time to look at the license plate when I was driving past, so I snapped a photo with one hand before the car got all the way in. It's blurry, but you can read the numbers if you squint."

By this time, DeLuna's curiosity had won out over her suspicions and her temper. "Where are you now?"

"At the curb. I'm waving at you."

Morrie covered his mouth and coughed.

DeLuna threw her hands in the air. "It just doesn't end with you people, does it? What the hell do you mean, 'your old digs'?"

"Morrie can tell you about that better than I can, but getting back to the problem at hand. You need to know that the cast has increased. My guess is that the driver of the Toyota is the new resident of Morrie and Carla's former apartment. That would be Johnny Vincento. He was on his way to the house for an early morning something or other, saw you all, and beat a hasty retreat. Too bad he didn't show up a little earlier, or you guys a little later, and you would have gotten him, too."

DeLuna, her expression thoughtful, shook her head. "Maybe we have." She looked at Morrie. I'll have those cameras brought to headquarters and the film analyzed. If we can put Vincento here during the time the women were being held captive, we have grounds for at least a visit. We were too late for Zephyr. One of these guys killed her or had her killed."

"The window of opportunity for apprehending the driver has temporarily closed. If he'd been here when you arrested everyone, he'd have a tough time slipping away. You'd have his passport, and you'd know his whereabouts when or if he made bail. But you didn't." Morrie rubbed his eyes. "I need some sleep. Listen. Vincento's here on a visa, and if he gets jumpy, he may decide to head home early, and you won't be able to stop him. Might be better in the end to let him think he's not on the short list."

DeLuna was forced to agree. "I see your point. I can play it that way, but he's going to be under surveillance, in case he rabbits."

# CHAPTER TWENTY-FOUR

*San Jose*

For the convenience of the majority of the parties, everyone was scheduled to report at the SFPD at 10 the next morning. The only ones inconvenienced were Gino and Francesca and Bruce. Gino and Francesca because they had to drive home from Pacific Heights, get virtually no sleep, and then drive back to the City during rush hour, and Bruce because he'd not been fed the previous day and had let Francesca know his displeasure by glaring at her as she dropped a mouse in his dresser drawer. At least he might have been glaring. It could have been the reflection of the sunlight on his eyes, but since Ginger was the only one who ever spoke to him, Francesca just did the mouse drop and left, shutting the bedroom door firmly behind her.

Parking was the first hurdle, but they found the last open slot in the parking lot. Admittance to the station was the second challenge. The sergeant at the window had a copy of DeLuna's guest list and located their names on it. After producing identification, Gino and Francesca were buzzed into the interior where they joined the rest of the group in a large room filled with not much of anything, apart from folding metal chairs.

"This is kinda like the bakery," Carla said. "You got to take a number but there's no donut when it's your turn. And we didn't get any numbers."

Perhaps because of what had transpired when she'd attempted to interrogate the group at Dark Mountain or perhaps in the interest of saving time, Detective DeLuna opted to hold a group session. She was prompt and wasted no time on preliminaries.

"We have video from the security cameras," she said, nodding for an officer to distribute copies of photos of two men. "Quality is less than optimal, but there's a clear head shot of the driver when he exits the vehicle and of the passenger who goes around to the back of the vehicle and opens the hatch. The video continues with the men installing bars on the only window of the guest bungalow. That's the one that held the women. We've talked to them, and they all agree these are the men who brought them to the house. With the name provided by one of your group, we have confirmed the driver's name to be Cesar Torres. He's local, but since the apprehension of the suspects last night, he's gone off the radar. We have a BOLO on him. Does anyone have any additional information on the passenger?" DeLuna's voice had lost its terse, professional quality and was one tone away from begging. "All we've got is Eddie 'The Weasel' and anything you might be able to add to that would be helpful."

"That's him," Carla said, and Nanette and Ginger agreed.

"Any last name?" DeLuna said.

"I'm sure he's got one, but that's the reason these guys use nicknames." Carla gave an encouraging smile. "It's so they can talk to each other about each other without you knowing who they are. Of course, after you know who they are, it's kinda wasted energy. But, like now. It works."

"Eddie 'The Weasel'," Detective DeLuna repeated. "Any other help you can give me?"

"He ain't local," Carla said. "He's out of New Haven. Maybe the cops there can help you. He's got to have a rap sheet. He's a creep. *Testa di merda*," she swore.

DeLuna nodded. "The women rescued from the cottage identified him as the one who killed Zephyr. They said he enjoyed it."

"That's Eddie," Ginger said. "He's a psycho. Nanette and I ain't safe. Again. Still."

Nanette said nothing, but tears rolled down her cheeks.

"You got to help them," Carla said. "For some reason Gennaro wants them dead or worse. The girls you rescued are safe in a shelter. You got to do the same for Ginger and Nanette. Especially since you got Tommaso locked up now."

"I can't leave Bruce," Ginger said. "He needs me."

"I'll take care of Bruce," Francesca said. "I think he's starting to grow on me. Sort of."

Nanette had reached for a tissue and was blotting her eyes. "I want to see Tommy."

DeLuna shook her head. "He's being arraigned this morning. If the judge allows bail, we'll get word to you."

The tears began again. This time Nanette let them. "He got me out of there last night," she said. "You got to let him go."

"It's out of my hands. It's all up to the judge, although in a trafficking case, especially when there's been a murder, bail isn't a given. But I promise as soon as I find out anything, I'll let you know."

Ginger put her arm around Nanette. The tears had become heart-wrenching sobs. "You got to stop that. It's not good for the baby," Ginger said. "Tommy needs you to be tough for him and for the baby."

Nanette reached for a new tissue, blew her nose, and took a ragged breath. "All right." She gave DeLuna a hard look. "As soon as you know anything, you tell me, whatever it is."

"I will," DeLuna said. "And the rest of you, lay off the vigilante justice. Let the police handle this." Her words were met with silence. "In case, you didn't hear me, I said you are to call the police."

Morrie smiled. "We did."

***

Carla and Morrie, heading back home to the loft, had been rehashing the morning's events, trying to find something positive that had come out of it.

"It's like that burger I ate on the way back here last night with Ginger and Nanette," Carla said. "There's a bite out of it, but the rest of the burger's still there."

"I'm guessing that the bite that's gone from your burger is the end of the human trafficking operation," Morrie said. "At least for now, but a good lawyer is going to be able to poke some serious holes in the prosecution's case." To Carla's questioning look, he continued. "First, none of the girls identified any of the Puglisis as involved. Second, Enzo was in Las Vegas the entire weekend for the Orchid Festival, and he can prove it. He says the premises was used without his knowledge or consent, and you can't disprove a negative. It's one of those universal legal loopholes. He also said that Gennaro was there because he called him from the airport to give him a ride home. I know and you know that they know it's not true. So do the police. But that and five or six bucks, maybe more, will get you a coffee at a designer caffeine shop." At that moment, they passed a designer coffee shop, and Morrie stared at it. One of life's weird coincidences. "The outlier in all this is Tommaso," Morrie continued. "He was there with us and got arrested as collateral damage. The arrest will give him credibility with Enzo. The reason Tommaso was there, to rescue his fiancé and her friend, will negate that."

"And me," Carla said. "Don't forget. He killed me. That was thoughtful. Now I live without worrying about getting killed. DeLuna showed me the police report."

"True. That was nice of him, but if Enzo wanted to, he could press charges on Tommaso for B&E. He won't of course, but when he starts going back over last night's sequence of events, Enzo will eventually wonder how Tommaso let himself in without a key and without knowing the code to disarm the alarm system. He'll check that bedroom on the third floor and find it empty. It's going to get dangerous for Tommaso, and if he's thinking about continuing to help the cops as an inside man, he needs to rethink that."

Carla's expression changed from discouraged to hopeful. "You know who else is in deep shit?" She looked at Morrie who stole a glance her direction. "Eddie and Cesar. With them out of the way, ain't nobody gonna rat on Enzo. It's like poetic justice. I bet, right now, there's a hit out for both of them and they ain't gonna last twenty-four hours."

It was Morrie's turn to look thoughtful. "DeLuna's not going to like that. A case of that magnitude would have made her career, but that's her problem, not ours." He swerved to avoid two pedestrians who'd jaywalked from between two parked cars to save all of ten seconds walking to the corner crosswalk. "I've been in that cigar store. Torres has good inventory. He's got the regular stuff, but he's also got premium, and I'll bet there's Cubans in the back room, if you're known. No wonder, catering to the Mafia elite. I wonder..."

"Wonder what? Morrie, I hate it when you start a sentence and don't finish it. It's hard to keep up with you."

"Sorry. I was thinking I might enjoy being a cigar store proprietor. I would get to sample my own inventory. Who knows? There may be a whole new career waiting for me."

"Yeah. You and your SEAL buddies, sitting around, smoking cigars. It ain't a bad idea. You should try it. Better wait until they off Eddie and Cesar though. Might look suspicious otherwise. You know, asking about taking over the lease before Cesar's in the morgue. If they find him."

"Good thinking. Although, I'll wager they will find him. Enzo wants to make a statement. Hard to do that without the visuals."

***

Gino and Francesca, back home at *Dark Mountain*, were on the back deck with a bottle of wine, a pitcher of lemonade, and the charcuterie board piled with cheeses, an assortment of crackers, and some sliced apples with a caramel sauce dip on the side. "Lunch," Francesca pronounced. "I'm going to sit and do absolutely nothing except eat, drink, and focus on us. It's good to be alone again. Just the two of us." She raised her glass and paused midway to her lips and sighed. "And Bruce."

"Agreed. I need a breather," Gino said. "Everything has been moving way too fast. It's like one step forward, twelve steps to the side. Are we making any headway at all?" He filled a plate as he talked. Down in the meadow, the doe and her twins were browsing in the tall grass. "Peaceful. I like peaceful. We need more of it."

Francesca nodded. "There's a tang in the air. Another year almost gone. What are we going to do, Gino?"

"For now? They're making us wait. Their plan is to make us nervous, anxious, ready to pay anything they want to save the vineyard, when they finally show up."

"I repeat, what are you going to do?"

"They'll be armed. If this is all a ploy of Johnny Vincento to get the vineyard, and they give me the slightest excuse," he set his glass down on the table, "I plan on killing them."

****

Francesca made a detour to the back deck on her way to bed. She'd been waiting for the right moment to tell Gino the good news about her pregnancy, and tonight had started out perfectly, but then the conversation took off in a different direction. She rested a hand on her stomach. Best to wait. It might be too early. Anything could still happen, and if something did... She felt the sting of tears and blinked hard to force them away. The harvest moon lit up the sky and it was almost bright as day. The air was still. There would be the perfect time. She just had to be patient.

Sound travels far on water and also in the mountains, and it can be difficult to pinpoint the source, especially at night. The screech owl that lived in the live oak at the top of the driveway was carrying on about something somewhere over the next ridge. There were plenty of mice and rabbits close by, but for reasons known only to the owl, tonight's hunt had taken her far afield. Judging from the yips of the resident coyote pack, her presence was not appreciated. Predators are territorial. That includes animals as well as people, and intruders or interlopers are not welcome. The owl must have taken the hint. She'd returned to her home turf and glided silent as a shadow above the deck, on her way to the meadow.

"Those pups are pretty much full grown now," Gino said, joining Francesca at the railing. "Big appetites. The deer are wary now. This one is sticking close to home."

"You think they'd take down a full grown deer?"

"They could and they would. They're opportunists. But they're smart. They'll do scavenging if they can. Less work. I talked to a hunter on his way over to Mount Madonna. He said the pig farmers over there will dump a dead hog in one of the ravines to save themselves the trouble of digging a hole. In the space of a week, there's no trace. Nothing. No bones, no nothing. Nature's cleanup crew."

"Hmmm." Francesca yawned. "You're a fount of information. On that pleasant note, I'm going to bed."

# CHAPTER TWENTY-FIVE

*San Francisco and Dark Mountain*

The arraignment had gone as expected, although not as DeLuna had hoped. The consigliere had argued that Mr. Enzo Puglisi was unaware his guest homes were being used for illegal purposes and had not been in residence at the time of the alleged incident. With crime a growing concern in even the best neighborhoods, bars had been installed on the window of the guest home for safety, a common precaution in these dangerous times. The circumstantial evidence, however, weighing heavily in the other direction, Enzo, Gennaro, and Tommaso Puglisi were bound over for trial, the date to be set at a later time. Bail was set in the amount of $500,000 for Enzo Puglisi and $200,000 each for Gennaro and Tommaso Puglisi, as none of the men were deemed to be flight risks. Their passports were to be surrendered.

The consigliere returned his papers to his briefcase, shook hands with Enzo, and left the courthouse. The look Enzo gave Detective DeLuna was not difficult to decipher. Gennaro smirked and clapped his grandfather on the back. Tommaso's eyes held fear, and DeLuna made her decision on the spot.

The three Puglisis filed out of the courtroom, but as Tommaso, the last in line, approached the door, DeLuna nodded at one of the officers who responded by stepping in front of Tommaso and blocking his forward progress.

"Tommaso Puglisi," De Luna said, "you are under arrest for the murder of Carla Catalano." She nodded to the officer. "Take him into custody."

***

Detective DeLuna frowned at the paperwork that seemed to have doubled in the two hours since she'd been in court. "Remove the cuffs," she said to the officer who had brought Tommaso to her office. "I'll take responsibility. That will be all for now." The officer complied without comment.

"Thank you," Tommaso said. "I must admit, my prospects weren't looking all that great. Never thought I'd welcome a murder charge. What happens next?"

DeLuna waved away his concerns. "We've just bought a little time, that's all. I'm advising you to lose your cell phone. You can get a burner, but until we can put this case to bed, you're going to need to disappear. Jail is out of the question. You wouldn't last an hour. And you shouldn't return to any place you've been previously." She tapped her pencil on the desk. "Where can we stash you?" she seemed to be asking herself, rather than Tommaso.

Tommaso's mind had been running along the same tracks, and when he noticed the cross that DeLuna wore on a chain around her neck, he had the answer. "I'll move in with my brother Anthony for now. If I'm not safe with him, there's no hope."

"You've got another brother. Of course. You're Italian. You sure he's not going to turn you in or kill you?"

"Sure as I can be. Anthony's a priest. That won't mean anything to Gennaro, of course. He'd kill God if he thought it would profit him. Location is everything. There'll be a spare room at the rectory. Anthony and I look a great deal alike. We're the same height, same build. I'll get a haircut and dye my hair. Anthony's six years older than I am, but from a distance, it's as good a disappearing act as I can think of. Especially when I put on the collar."

DeLuna studied him. "All right. I'll drop charges for insufficient evidence, but once you leave here, you'll be on your own until the trial. You probably don't need my advice, but you'll want to arrange your own legal representation if we don't get all this taken care of before the trial date. "

"Understood. So, we need to get down to business," Tommaso said. "I've been going over the books. At first, I didn't see anything that jumped out at me, but when I separated out expenses for each club and massage parlor, a pattern emerged. It was obvious when I knew what to look for. And that should give you what you're looking for."

"Enlighten me."

"Glad to. You've got the USB drive. If you'll trade places with me, I'll bring up the program we need."

Shortly, DeLuna was staring at the monitor. "I don't see anything. What should I be looking at?"

"The linen service. Towels, specifically."

"Okay." The screen that was up belonged to *Eden's Garden*, a combination club and massage parlor. "It says five bundles."

"Go to the next screen, *Pleasure Massage*."

"Three bundles."

"Keep going. Try one more."

"*Dance Party*. Six. So, the number of towel bundles corresponds to...what?"

"The number of trafficked women at each facility. It's a bookkeeping entry. Talk to the women. They'll tell you how many of them worked at each place. It's a code. You'll need to tread carefully here, but the devil's in the details. All the managers, all the owners of these establishments are involved in this. I don't know if they use names or numbers or pieces of macaroni to identify the women. I'm still looking for those records, but I'll find them."

DeLuna sat back, lacing her fingers behind her neck. "So, when I match the women to the clubs and massage parlors, this is all going to lead back to the Puglisi family."

"Especially since the other set of books—the ones that get shown to the government for tax purposes—don't have these entries, and since this linen service doesn't exist. It's all on paper. Hope this helps."

"It's going to be the key that opens this case wide open." She smiled at him. "Thank you. This is the break we've needed."

"There's still extortion and murder. Enzo is wounded, not dead. It's not over yet."

DeLuna called for the officer to escort Tommaso back to await processing for his release. "The paperwork should take about an hour. Do not leave him unguarded, and let me know when he's been processed and released." She nodded her dismissal.

****

When Morrie's cell chirped, Carla panicked. "Don't answer it, Morrie. It's bad news."

"What? Now you're telling me you know what the call's about before I even answer?" Morrie looked at the love of his life as if she'd finally lost it. After he'd heard the brief message from the caller, though, he disconnected and stared at her. "I'm married to a sorceress."

Carla shook her head. "It's in the vibrations. Evil carries on the air. Who was it?"

"DeLuna. She's charged Tommaso with your murder. Smart move, actually. She's potentially saved his life."

"Damn."

Morrie waited for more, but Carla was uncharacteristically silent. "Don't worry," he said. "My guess is that she's going to drop charges as soon as she's got Eddie either in custody or on a slab and nail him with it instead or do something else to get Tommaso safe. DeLuna's sharp. Quick thinker, too."

"So what do we do now? You know, it's all backwards. All the good people are in hiding or in jail, and the bad guys are running around free. It ain't right."

"For now, yes. But hiding is better than dead." He returned the cell to his pocket. "I'm going out for a bit. Stay inside. And away from the windows. Please."

"Be careful."

"Always."

****

Silent observers in the recent drama, Johnny Vincento and his nephew, Nicolo Puglisi, had been keeping a low profile at the apartment. With no direct ties to the estate in Pacific Heights, they'd avoided the dragnet. Now, however, with Enzo and Gennaro having joined them, the gloves had come off and tempers flared.

"You never bring trouble to your home! Never! What the hell were you thinking?" Johnny didn't give Gennaro a chance to answer but continued his rant. "And it wasn't even *your* home. It was your grandfather's home. Do you even know what you've done? You're looking at twenty to life! For you, I say *good!* But for your grandfather, this is a life sentence. He will never see the light of day again. And why? Because of you! If you were my grandson, you would be a dead man now, just waiting for the moment you took your last breath! Never knowing when it would come. Does it come now? Tomorrow? When? You don't know. But you would die, most certainly. And you would scream for death before I was finished."

"Enough!" Enzo paced the floor, looking out the living room window from time to time at the street below, watching, waiting—for what he didn't know. He was no longer certain of anything. His own flesh and blood. The idiocy was one thing. The consiglieres would deal with that. He, Enzo Puglisi, would serve no time. Of that he was sure. Money took care of everything. No. The issue at hand was betrayal. "I have lost two sons and a daughter! Who has done this? Why have they done it? I have no answers!"

"I have not done it," Johnny said, his face red. "I have lost a brother. The sister-in-law, as well, although I did not know her. Still," he bowed towards Enzo, "my condolences."

"Papa, you did not lose anything. You gained your life. Salvatore is nowhere. Dead? Most likely. But he had nothing to do with today," Gennaro said. "The others, Prospero and Fiona and Joey were conspiring to kill you. And you, an old man tending to his flowers, could not see what was so plain to everyone else. Fiona. Yes. Your daughter Fiona would have put the contract out on you. And why? So Joey Vincento, her husband, would take over when you were dead." Gennaro spat on the floor. "I killed them to save you. That is my confession. Should I run to Anthony to make it official in the eyes of God?"

Enzo, the color drained from his face, collapsed onto the sofa. "What are you saying, Gennaro?"

"Oh Papa, you heard me, and your ears lie to you as much as do your eyes. You refuse to see. You want to kill me now? What would that accomplish? Revenge? Fine. Be vengeful but be grateful to me at the same time. You will find they are an incompatible twosome." Gennaro turned on his heel and left the apartment. The silence in his wake was finally broken by Nico.

"This is pitiful. You are pitiful," he said, disgust dripping from his words like venom. "Are you just going to sit there or are you going to do something?" He ran his hands through his hair. "All right. Do nothing, you weak fool. The blood of my mother and my father cries out to me! " He was gone before his grandfather could respond. When Enzo did open his mouth to speak, his words were slurred, and the left side of his face drooped. He grabbed for the arm of the sofa, but his hand would not obey, and he fell to the floor.

***

The Last Rites of the Roman Catholic Church are Confession, Anointing with Sacred Oil, and Holy Communion. By the time Father Anthony Puglisi arrived, Enzo Puglisi had breathed his last. To all appearances, he was beyond any mortal assistance to ease his introduction to God on the other side of the veil of life. In the interests of *just in case,* however, while the paramedics stood by with the gurney to transport the body, Father Anthony Puglisi went ahead with the anointing. One never knew if the soul might still be present if the body is still warm.

Meanwhile, seizing the moment, Johnny Vincento took the unexpected and serendipitous opportunity to consider his options and do some planning. If all he had to deal with were two inexperienced hotheads, a grandson under a murder charge, one of Enzo's sons still in the slammer, and the remaining son content with running the garbage racket on the east coast, it was a heaven-sent opportunity for absorbing the fractious Puglisis into his own organization. The hotheads just needed management and some fear instilled into them. The same probably went for the one charged with murder. Alphonse was an unknown. Undoubtedly, he been at work while in prison, doing what, remained to be learned. He would be the biggest concern, although removing him wouldn't be difficult. It would require a phone call which Johnny made without delay.

***

Watching the drama unfold from a vantage point across the street and two houses down, Morrie Landow pieced events together the best he could. The conclusions he drew were that, first, there had been a falling out in the family. The abrupt exits would give that idea credence. The arrival of Father Anthony Puglisi, and finally the EMTs made for some interesting speculation. Somebody was ill, had had an accident, or was dead. Murder was a logical possibility, and Johnny Vincento's lingering presence was enough to suggest he was somehow involved.

***

Morrie 's call to Detective Virginia DeLuna was put on hold, but she answered after a short wait.

"DeLuna."

"You said to call the police. Something's gone down at the Puglisi mansion. I've been minding my own business, enjoying a coffee, sitting in my car. Been here a couple of hours. Just as I arrived, Gennaro Puglisi ran out the front door with Nicolo in hot pursuit. I couldn't see where they went, but they weren't playing tag. Then, at a more leisurely pace, Johnny Vincento also made an exit. Subsequently, a priest arrived, and now the EMTs are here, with a gurney. I suspect a death."

"Good to know you're leaving the investigative work to us, Commander, but I'll see what I can find out." She disconnected.

***

Waiting for a return call wasn't something that required he remain glued in place, so Morrie swung by Chan's shuttered restaurant before heading back to the loft. He'd just parked when the phone rang, but it wasn't Detective DeLuna.

Glancing at the number, Morrie smiled. "Hey, Gino."

"Where are you?"

"Just about to stop at Chan's. You need something?"

"Yeah. Remember last year when we needed that tarp for some cleanup here?"

Silence on the phone from Morrie. Then, a cautious, "He can't be back."

"No. No. We're good on that. This would be a new one. I've got the tarp, but I could use some help with it. You can bring Carla. Chan too, if he's available. We need to have a discussion."

"Right. Be there soon as we can." Morrie disconnected and exhaled audibly. Instead of getting out of the car, he texted Chan. It only took a couple of minutes for him to lock up and pile into Morrie's car.

"You're being more cryptic than usual," Chan said. "What's this urgent matter?"

Before Morrie could answer, the phone rang again. This time it was DeLuna with the update. He hesitated but didn't inform her that she was on speaker with an audience.

"All I can confirm is that Enzo Puglisi is dead," she said. "Apparent stroke. And that's all I know. No idea where Gennaro and Nicolo are, and if they don't report when it's their court date, I've got a problem."

"Thanks. Appreciate it. I'll keep my eyes open."

"Please do."

"One of these days, we're going to have to put an end to this Puglisi-Vincento problem. And I mean a final, ultimate, no-coming-back-from-it end," Chan said.

"Working on it," was Morrie's response. "In fact, I think we're going to make a good dent in the execution of that as soon as we get to Gino's."

"I can hardly wait."

With Carla added to the passengers in the Subaru, Morrie turned south and retraced the familiar route to *Dark Mountain*, where they found Gino and Francesca on the deck, three bottles of wine in front of them, one already opened, a glass of iced tea with lemon slices floating amongst the ice cubes, one wine glass filled nearly to the brim, breaking all conventional pouring practices, and three empty glasses waiting for business.

"Drink," was Gino's greeting. "Then, we'll get down to work. It's been another one of those days, and frankly, I'm getting fed up with it. This needs to end."

"Funny you should say that," Morrie said. "We had a similar conversation on the way down here, almost word for word."

For the next twenty minutes or so, they enjoyed the wine, and Francesca the iced tea, speculating as to how they might bring about their goal of freedom from the Mob. Finally, Gino drained his glass and stood. "Shall we?" He turned to Francesca. "This is at least a three-mouse job, wouldn't you think?"

"If you say so. I knew I should have picked up more when I was in town. I'm not sure it's going to work. What if he won't take the bait, in a manner of speaking?"

"Then, we move to Plan B."

"We don't have a Plan B. We don't even have a Plan A." Francesca went to the fridge and went mouse shopping in the hydrator, again. With the mice in the bag, she took a deep breath. "All right. Lead on."

Gino led on from the kitchen, down the hall, and opened the door to the last bedroom on the right where Bruce, no longer cuddled on the purple blanket in the bottom dresser drawer, had moved to the window where he had proven his worth as a guard snake, having interrupted Eddie "The Weasel" in his attempt to enter the room and wreak whatever hell and havoc he had in mind. He must have come in head first, planning perhaps, to slither down the wall and wait until he'd reached the floor before standing. It had not been a good decision. He'd definitely reached the floor. That part had worked just fine. The part that wasn't just fine was that Bruce had taken the opportunity to vent his displeasure at being disturbed by winding himself around Eddie's neck and then doing what boa constrictors do. He constricted. Eddie's attempts to pull the snake from his neck had only ended in his arms being incorporated into another coil. In short, Eddie was quite dead, and Bruce was looking pleased with himself. At least, as pleased as a snake can look. After all, if he could just figure out where to begin digesting this unexpected meal, he'd be set for months.

"So," Gino said, his eyes analyzing the situation. "This is what we came home to. Any ideas?"

"I don't think he's trained to respond to voice commands," Carla said, eyeing Bruce who returned the look with something that approached a threat. "And," she chewed on her lower lip, "he's giving me the stink eye. That ain't good."

"I noticed that too," Francesca said. "But we have to do something. This isn't going to work." She took a mouse from the bag and dangled it by the tail in front of Bruce who merely looked at her as if she had a screw loose. You couldn't blame him. This was the kill of a lifetime. She returned the mouse to the bag.

Chan reached into his pants pockets and pulled out a knife.

"No!" Carla and Francesca's duet stopped Chan as he was about to take the easy way out and turn Bruce into fillets. "You can't hurt Bruce! He saved our lives. Besides, he's Ginger's dance partner," Carla yelled. "Jesus! He's a hero! Bruce, I mean. Jesus too, but you know, in a different way."

Chan looked at the knife, shrugged, and returned it to his pocket. "All right. But I have to tell you that things aren't looking promising. And we can't wait for decomposition to set in. It's going to stink."

Morrie flexed his fingers, cracked his knuckles, and walked over to Bruce, looking for a vulnerable spot in one of the coils. "If I can just get something started, maybe we can find out where the end of his tail is and then work up from there." But Bruce's tail was firmly tucked into one of the larger coils that had compressed Eddie's shoulders until his body looked like somebody had tried to use it for an accordion.

"You know, I really thought one of us would have an idea." Gino sounded defeated, but then, Carla began to hum.

Francesca elbowed Gino, and pointed at a faint undulation in Bruce's midsection. "Hold on," she said. "Sorry. Bad pun. I'll be right back."

And she was, with her phone. A bit of searching and she found the YouTube video she was looking for. She clicked play, turned up the volume, and one of Ginger's performance tunes filled the room. That slight undulation in Bruce's midsection grew until his entire body was caught up in the musical moment. Gradually, he relaxed, and keeping time to the beat, flowed like a serpentine river until he'd left Eddie behind and Francesca could scoop him up and drape him across her shoulders.

With the song on permanent replay, the guys got Eddie out of the room and, with three mice as his reward, Bruce was returned to his drawer to eat and then sleep the sleep of the righteous. With the window and door closed securely, the first phase of the operation was complete.

***

"Now what?" Carla said. "Same as last time?"

"Wait. That's the second time I've heard something to that effect. Is there anything I should know?" Chan's eyes, suspicious, traveled from Carla to Gino to Francesca and finally rested on Morrie.

"I don't think that's a good idea," Francesca said. "Honestly, the less you know, the better."

"I don't know anything."

"That's good," Francesca said, smiling. "Everything will be all right. This really doesn't happen all that often."

"Once a year," Carla muttered.

Morrie hesitated, then gave up. "This is a need-to-know-operation and he needs to know." With no argument forthcoming from the rest, he gave an abbreviated version of the death and disposal of Sally "The Pipe" Puglisi. "So, last time, we used a new septic tank. It was perfect. It'll be years before it's pumped, and even then, the sludge will end up far from here. Unfortunately, the house is occupied now, and there aren't any new ones under construction. So, that's out."

"Septic tank," Chan said. "Now I understand the need for the tarp."

"Yeah," Carla said. "It washed off just fine with the garden hose. I did it over there." She pointed to the bed of asters. Quite tall asters, actually, and blooming heavily. "Fertilizer. He was a piece of shit, after all."

"Yes," Gino said. "But that was then and this is now. Same problem, but we need a different solution. We can't report it to DeLuna. The whole force will show up again, the Puglisis, however many of them are still alive, will find out, and we won't be in a good place." He ran his hands through his hair, rubbed his chin, and finally threw his hands in the air.

"Pigs," said Francesca, joining him at the table. "Not the Puglisis, although they are. I'm talking Mount Madonna swine." She filled her glass and sat back in the deck chair.

"You're right!" The worry left Gino's face. "It's actually coyotes, not pigs, but it's going to work. Easy is always best."

"You want to elaborate a bit more?" Morrie said. "And Mount Madonna is not all that close. Driving any farther than we have to with a corpse in the car or truck or whatever is risky. Not that the whole damn thing isn't risky, but on the sliding scale of risk, let's keep it as low as we can. Okay?"

"How about just two ridges over?" Gino said. "There's a pack of coyotes there. You can hear them at night. The Weasel will make a good-sized feast. Bones break, even the big ones—skull, femur—and the fragments will be scattered across the wilderness by morning. Nobody's going to go looking, and there won't be anything to find. Same drill as last time with the clothes and any other personal effects." He clapped his hands. "I'll go gas up the ATV and hitch up the cart. Don't worry," he said to Morrie and Chan. "Only the locals know their way around these old footpaths and trails. And they want to keep things as private as we do. If these mountain trails could talk, ours wouldn't be the first story they'd tell."

# CHAPTER TWENTY-SIX

*San Jose and the Pacific Coast south of Santa Cruz*

Agent/Detective/Officer Virginia DeLuna examined the parcel that had come in the morning's mail. Addressed to her, it was one of those small flat-rate boxes from the USPS. It weighed practically nothing. There was no return address, but it set off some internal alarm. "Rodriguez," she called. "Take this to the bomb squad. Might be nothing. Could be something. We haven't had any anthrax-laced envelopes in a while. Just label it suspicious and get back to me when you find out."

She put the parcel out of her mind while she dealt with the latest setback in the Puglisi trafficking case. Gennaro Puglisi had been gunned down in the parking lot at the funeral home where he'd been making arrangements for his grandfather's funeral. It would have been a convenient location if not for the autopsy that would need to be done at the hospital. An unnecessary undertaking, DeLuna thought and grimaced at the unintentional play on words. When you've seen one Mob hit, you've seen them all.

This left the investigators with the owners of the clubs and massage parlors that had used the trafficked women. It would take more work to make Tommaso's code something they could use in court. Linking the owners and management to Enzo and Gennaro would have been the best way to go, but you can't try dead men. She tapped a finger on her computer mouse, and when she looked at the screen, saw she'd typed two rows of lower case *j*'s. In frustration, she shoved the mouse away, but she shoved too far and had to pick it up off the floor, and then hit her head on the edge of the desk as she straightened up. She rubbed her head. Things weren't going all that well.

Could there be somebody else in the background making sure he wasn't mentioned in any testimony? Johnny Vincento? A possibility. Nicolo, also. Regardless, the Puglisi ranks were shrinking, and that wouldn't be bad unless Vincento was just cleaning house before moving in with a whole new bunch of relatives.

Her thoughts were interrupted with the return of the box and a report. No anthrax. No bomb. Just a box of strike-everywhere wooden matches. She turned the box over, slid the cover off, fingered through the contents, but it contained nothing unusual. As a message, it was obscure. She set it aside, returning to the trafficking case, but she wasn't able to get the matches out of her head. She went through a mental inventory of other threats she'd received in the past, because this had to be some kind of threat. They'd all been vocal, loud, and usually amounted to the *I'm going to kill you* variety. The most recent had been at the courthouse when Gennaro had given her that look. It was a silent threat.

She placed a call to the SJFD for a check on her condo, but it hadn't been necessary. They were already at the scene working the fire that had been called in by a neighbor. By the time she got to the cross-street, the barricades were up, the fire had gone to three alarms, and she'd needed to show I.D. to watch the rest of the four-plex go up in flames. There had to have been some kind of accelerant used to get that much involvement so quickly.

The anonymity of city living makes difficult work of accounting for everyone in an emergency. She didn't know her neighbors and had only spoken to them in passing, and now she wished she'd taken the time to learn their names. She hadn't seen any of them watching the fire, and that was troubling. She gave the address of the rental agency to the chief to begin tracking down the residents. With any luck, everyone would have been at work. No pets were allowed, and for once, she was glad of it.

The crowd was growing outside the barricade. Pyromaniacs enjoy watching the results of their twisted work, and she panned every face in the crowd with her phone camera, hoping to hit paydirt. Hoping she'd see Nicolo hanging back, but present. When she got back to the office, she'd have the video copied and enlarged. She should have been afraid, but that would come later. *You've done your worst, short of killing me, you son of a bitch. It's not enough, and you've made a big mistake.*

***

"Any word from Tommaso Puglisi?" DeLuna's voice, hoarse as if she'd smoked a dozen packs of cigarettes and then gone without sleep for a week, greeted Morrie as he was juggling the coffee grinder and an unopened bag of coffee while trying to keep his cell from falling into the sink.

"I know where he is," Morrie said. "At least, I know where he's staying. I don't know what he's doing at the moment."

"I need to talk with him, and I don't have his new number."

"Hold on." Morrie swiped through the calls on his phone. "I'll text it to you. Okay. You should have it. What's going on, if I may be so bold?"

"My house was torched last night. Professional job. Nothing left. I'd gotten a package at the station this morning. Had it checked for residue, contents, the works. Just a box of matches. Nicolo was taunting me. That son of a freaking bitch. It's got to be tied to the trafficking case, and with Enzo and Gennaro dead, it's got to be either Vincento or Nicolo."

Morrie stared at his phone as if he'd somehow connected to another universe. "Back up. Gennaro's dead? When did this blessed event occur?"

"Today. At the funeral parlor parking lot. I know. Nice touch. Their numbers are decreasing, but not fast enough. Shit. Look. I know we haven't been all that...I don't even know what the word is, but if you've got anything, anything at all, I need it."

"I may. Back with you in a couple of hours. Got to see some people, and it's going to take some in-person conversation. They don't trust phones."

"Understood." She paused. "Thanks."

"Yeah."

***

Once again, there was the problem of gun disposal. For the moment, the .22 was in a plastic bag on the kitchen counter next to the fruit bowl. Reaching for a banana, Gino eyed the firearm, questions swirling in his brain. They still hadn't addressed the reason Eddie had broken into the house. He might have been looking for Ginger and Nanette, thinking they'd returned after being freed. It was a possibility, but Eddie hadn't entered the guest bungalow. He'd come to the main house. Gino, having lost his appetite, returned the banana to the bowl. Eddie had been sent to either get something from the house, scope it out for something in the future, or kill him and Francesca. Which was it? They'd bought some time with Eddie's death, but how much?

The answers were out there somewhere, but the immediate task was disposal of the firearm.

The banana would have been a snack, and Gino was getting hungry. They could take care of two things at once. They hadn't had seafood for dinner in a while, and water, in the form of the ocean, was their preferred method for disposing of the Mob's used firearms. This would be the multitasking effort of the day. None of them had touched the gun, but Gino rubbed it down, just to be safe.

"Want to go for a ride?" he asked Francesca. "We could pick up some crab for dinner. Stop at the bakery and get a baguette. Ride along the coast for a bit. Throw the gun in the ocean. The usual."

"Sounds good. We need a salad too. And dessert. I've been awfully hungry lately. Can't seem to get enough to eat." She looked wistful. Maybe tonight at dinner. Candles, music...it would be the perfect setting.

***

"I remember the first time I rode in this car," Francesca said, wrestling with her headscarf. "I felt so free." Her face grew serious. "You drove quite fast."

"Speeding is required when you're driving a Maserati," Gino said. "You're conspicuous. Everyone is looking at you. Envious. Wishing they were you." He paused, the garage door halfway open. "Conspicuous. Everyone looking at us." He frowned. "Next time."

"Right." Francesca sighed. "Not the right choice for the task at hand." She considered their inventory. "The Volvo or the old Ford pickup?"

"We don't have to go all the way the other way, either."

"The Volvo it is. Dependable. Modern with a flair. But not overly so. The perfect choice."

Searching for a private location, they pulled off Highway 1 at the third turnout after they'd left Soquel. Deviating from the path that had been made by hikers and those seeking whatever people looked for when they sought access to the ocean, they trudged through the tall grasses and vegetation that took their moisture as much from the air as they did from the sandy ground. Finally they reached land's end. Some fifty feet below, the tide was ebbing, everything being carried out to sea. But probably not the .22. It would sink, embedding itself in the sand and rocks below, hopefully to rust in peace. At least, that was the plan.

"The second time," Francesca said as Gino pulled on the plastic gloves, took the gun from the bag and hurled the weapon as far as his strength would allow.

"The last time," was his answer.

The tides come and go, as they have since the beginning, making ripples on the sand and leaving shells behind. And there is something calming and reassuring about their constancy. That's what Francesca was thinking. "The outgoing tide just seems to bring peace," she said. "It's like..." she paused, thinking of the right words, "it washes away all the troubles of the day, and the incoming tide brings a promise of peace."

"Just so long as it brings peace and not a piece," Gino said. "I never want to see that gun again. May it sink into the abyss forever."

# CHAPTER TWENTY-SEVEN

*San Francisco*

"You know, DeLuna's fire makes the third one that's likely connected to the Puglisis," Carla said, mopping her forehead with a washcloth after her first class of the morning. "Somebody really likes to play with matches." She dropped into the chair by the little table in the workroom at the studio. "Those kind of people are nut cases. There was one when I was a kid. He used to draw pictures of houses burning and people burning. They finally sent him away somewhere. I mean, Eddie was a cold-blooded creep, but at least he worked for a living. He didn't kill people just because. He got paid for it. But arsonists set fires for fun. No. I don't think you can fix that kind of crazy."

Morrie looked at her as if she'd just told him she'd known Jack the Ripper personally. "Of course!" He kissed her. "That's it!"

"What's it?" Carla asked, but Morrie was already dialing DeLuna, and she answered on the first ring, not sounding much better than she had earlier.

"You've got Carla to thank for this," he told DeLuna. "Arson cases. Yours makes the third we can logically tie to the Puglisis. The other two were the ones that burned our apartment house and the bakery. Harry was killed in the fire which involved an accelerant. I don't know about the bakery, but that's your area. I got to thinking. Nicolo Puglisi was sent away to a residential treatment center for teens in San Diego. Maybe you could find out why. I'm wondering about the fires. Just a thought. Anyhow, I promised I'd share what I learned. Good luck." He disconnected and grinned at Carla. "Did I ever tell you that you're brilliant?"

"Not often enough."

***

Detective Virginia DeLuca, recently added to the roster of the homeless, and with a mug of coffee that had been sitting long enough to be somewhere between tepid and cool and that hadn't been all that great to begin with, finally had something to go on.

A call to the rehab facility for juveniles near Boston had hit pay dirt. After a fire at the family home that killed a housekeeper, Nicolo had been dispatched to an intensive care unit for the mentally ill. He'd been released twice, but after two more incidents, was returned to the center until he was pronounced cured and released when he turned eighteen. He was now twenty-three. So. DeLuna sat back in her chair to digest this information. It appeared he segued easily into the family business with a specialty. The lab had enlarged the video she'd taken at her condo fire, and she was intently studying the sea of faces that had gathered to enjoy the spectacle of somebody else's misfortune.

The face she was looking for would be in the back, not too close to the action, but on the edge of the crowd. A loner. He, for most pyromaniacs were male, would be there for the adrenaline fix like some sort of depraved animal feeding on the carcasses of loss. The video quality would never make it in Hollywood, but she'd kept a steady hand as she'd filmed. Initially, many of the faces were partially hidden by the bodies in front of them, but since they'd come to watch, they'd want to be able to see, and that meant they'd move around until they had a clear view. She'd done the panorama going both directions half a dozen times, just for that reason.

On the third pass, she found who she was looking for. The smirk caught her eye. Others were intently watching, their faces almost blank, mouths frequently half open in something that might have been disbelief or wonder. But Nicolo Puglisi's face claimed ownership, and that disgusting smirk was unmistakable. It seemed to be a trait he'd either copied from his brother, Gennaro, or it was part of the Puglisi genetics. Regardless, it sent a chill through her. She marked the time on the video, sat back, and took a sip of coffee, not even noticing it was now stone cold.

She had enough to bring him in. She had his history, his threat, and his presence at the scene. On a hunch, she checked the dates of the fires for the dry cleaner's and the bakery and then called the local news station to see if they'd sent out a crew to film. They hadn't for the bakery, but Cow Hollow was a popular tourist spot, and they'd covered it. She put in a request for a copy of the film. Late this afternoon was the earliest she'd get it, but if she could place Nicolo Puglisi at that fire, she'd have a case that would be as tight as she could make it. Traffic cameras were another possibility, a longshot. Still, nothing ventured...

Matching license plates to video is tedious, mind-numbing work. It's a task usually given to new recruits or used as punishment for minor infractions for veterans. Nobody enjoys it, even though most of it is automated. Today, however, there were no new hires and nobody had screwed up. Detective DeLuna, a fresh mug of coffee and a jelly donut at hand, with a list of vehicles registered to every Puglisi on record, along with license plates, prepared to do battle. It was a brief war. Not being sure how long it would take for the fire to become visible after ignition, she'd set herself a two-hour window back from the arrival of the first engine at the scene. *Olga's Bakery*, mid-block on Polk after the intersection at Francisco, hadn't had a lot of traffic between midnight and two in the morning on a Thursday. In fact, there'd only been fifteen vehicles during the timeslot she'd chosen. The printout of those plates, when matched with the printout of the Puglisi fleet, hit Bingo with car number five, a brand new black Caddy registered to Alphonse Puglisi. But since Alphonse was enjoying the hospitality of the State of California, that meant another of the clan had been driving or someone associated with them. It wasn't the clean fit she'd been hoping for, but it wasn't a misfit, either. It tied a Puglisi vehicle to the scene at the time of the crime. DeLuna scowled into her mug. Police coffee was swill. She needed something legit, and a minor celebration was in order. Caffeine City was just around the corner, and it was serenading her.

The trafficking case was her investigation, but with the lines between it and the protection racket having blurred, jurisdiction with the team handling it would have to be thrashed out. Complicating the situation, she was now one more victim in an ongoing arson investigation that was part of the protection racket. Except in her case, there was no protection to be bought at any price. The smile had vanished, but the need for good coffee hadn't. She cleared her desk and set off on the quest for nourishment.

***

Tommaso Puglisi's accommodations at the rectory of St. Mary Magdalene's were a cross between a monk's cell and the luxury suite at a No Tell Motel. Essentially, adequate but nothing to give a guest the incentive to move in long term. What they did provide, however, was a chance to work in safety without having to make idle chit chat. Anthony did oversee the rations, however, so Tommaso didn't have to risk venturing out. So far, everything was good. Except for the pasta. Anthony had never learned the concept of *al dente.* The pasta either broke your teeth or was mush. Today, it was mush, which Tommaso had turned into a sort of soup by the addition of more sauce and a vigorous stir with the spoon. While he slurped, he continued to work.

The Family owned thirty-three clubs and massage parlors distributed throughout the greater Bay Area, with the majority in San Jose, San Francisco, and San Bruno, and their records were kept in a double set of books which he possessed. The first set, clean, scrupulously honest, and a total fiction, were reserved for the government and of no interest to Tommaso. It was the second set, where everything was set down in meticulous, incriminating detail that he needed to analyze, but there'd been no key to deciphering the entries. It was as if the whole damn thing had been double-encrypted and then translated into a foreign language without a name. He'd tried every program he knew, but after three days he was still stumped. It wasn't on the USB drive, but there had to be a key somewhere. Where? If today hadn't been one of the rectory's quieter days, he would have let out a primal scream. Instead, he simply banged his head on the table, which brought his brother into the room as if summoned.

"What?" Tommaso mumbled, his voice muffled by the desktop.

Anthony waited.

Tommaso rolled his head to the side, glared at his brother, and then rolled back. It was pointless. Anthony was like a rock. The man had the patience of the saint he was named for. It was one of his more annoying characteristics. Tommaso gave up and raised his head.

"What the hell are you doing?" Anthony asked.

"Priests aren't supposed to say hell," Tommaso said, and Anthony gave him one of those beatific smiles that was as phony as the set of books he couldn't decipher. Tommaso inhaled and exhaled with enough force to create a small draft that sent three scraps of paper fluttering to the floor. "This is making me nuts," he said. "There has to be a key somewhere, but it's not here." He shoved the chair back and stood, facing Anthony. "A key. Where would they keep a key?" He stared at the computer, but it kept a silent counsel.

"Someplace safe?"

"Thanks," Tommaso said. "I would never have thought of that."

"Seriously, Tommy. Did you check every inch of the briefcase before you gave it to Gennaro?"

"Yeah. Maybe. I think so. I don't know." He rubbed his face, trying to remember. Then, an idea. "Maybe Nanette and Ginger found something when they had it. Or maybe Morrie or Gino or somebody." He threw his hands in the air. "It's gone through a bunch of hands since Gennaro left it in my car. And I can't ask him. He's dead. Christ."

"But you can ask the rest of them." Anthony said, with a pointed look at Tommaso's cell on the desk by the laptop that held the stubborn USB drive.

"Communicating with the girls goes through more steps than a Pilates class," Tommaso said, "Protective custody, they call it." Thinking more clearly now that his rant was done, he nodded. "The sooner I get what DeLuna needs, the sooner they'll be safe outside. All right. Working backwards, I'll start with Gino."

***

"Remember when Ginger and Nanette first arrived?" Gino asked Francesca.

"I don't think I'll ever forget. Why?"

"Tommaso just called while I was bringing in the groceries and the mice after our outing. He's working on the Puglisi accounting books, and he's stuck. Apparently, they've been done in some sort of code and he was wondering if there might have been anything else in the laptop case that would shed some light on his problem."

Francesca, about to turn the fresh crab into a salad, paused with a monster claw in her right hand. "Papers. There were some papers, but we copied them when we made the USB drives and gave them to him." She set the claw down on the counter and opened the utensil drawer. "You seen the thing that opens this sucker?"

"What thing?"

"The *thing*. I don't know what you call it." She continued to rummage. "I could whack it with the meat tenderizer, I suppose." She looked up, doubtful. "It's kind of like a nutcracker but bigger and it's got a different shape."

"Right. I understand perfectly." He hung the car keys on the peg by the door, the act triggering a memory. "That's it," he said. "Key. There was a key. Remember? Morrie's got it. I hope." Gino hit the speed dial.

"Ask them if they want to come for dinner. We've got enough crab and if they're going to drop off the key at the rectory, they'll already be more than halfway here. Tell them to ask Tommaso if he wants to come too. There's plenty, and he's got to be lonely and worried about Nanette."

***

"It's called a seafood cracker or a crab cracker," Carla said in answer to Francesca's question. "I've been meaning to get one of them. I've been using a hammer. Works great, although the crab kinda goes shooting off the counter and ends up in some weird places."

While the crab salad was a hit, the key Morrie had brought with him was the main item of interest. He'd determined it was a key to a safety deposit box, and that was the extent of anyone's input until Carla posed a seemingly unrelated question. "If you need a code to the books, who did the books before you took over?"

Tommaso, more than eager to get away from his brother's cooking, had jumped at the opportunity Morrie offered to join the family for dinner. "I don't know," he said, then brightened. "But I can find out easily enough. He'll have signed his name as the preparer for the Federal and State Income Tax Returns. It's all done online now. No paper. Everything is saved to the Cloud and backed up on USB drives." The triumphant moment was gone. "I don't have the password to access the Cloud, and those USB drives are in the desk in what used to be my office at my grandfather's house. They're not on the laptop, for obvious reasons." He returned the stares he was getting from the group. "Well, I didn't expect I'd be leaving so soon, and the circumstances weren't all that conducive the last time I was there, if you all remember. We had other objectives."

"It's okay," Carla said. "This time there aren't so many of you to deal with. I mean, I'm sorry about your grandfather. He was nice to me when he didn't know who I was. Your brother, though. Can't say I'm sorry. He was bad news."

"That's true," Morrie said, "but the two we have left, Johnny and Nico, are not going to be all that welcoming to uninvited guests."

"We'll need a distraction," Francesca said.

"No. We don't need to do that this time. The law is on our side."

"That's crazy," Carla said. "You sure? I mean, that ain't never happened before."

"Yes. Call DeLuna. She'll get a court order to get the records from the IRS. We don't need to do anything but wait."

Carla sat back, arms folded. "I could get used to this."

***

"I guess when the Feds get involved, there's a whole different time schedule," Tommaso said. The digital copy of Enzo Puglisi's last filed tax return to the IRS was displayed on his monitor, having arrived within three hours of the request. With a brief glance at income, which was in excess of twenty million dollars, and expenses, not surprisingly itemized at just a shade under sixteen million dollars, the return was a work of art. Actually is was the artwork of David Avrams, of the accounting firm of the same name. "This guy is good," Tommaso said.

"No surprise there," Gino said. "They know the Feds are going to go over these with considerable care."

Francesca did a quick search for the Avrams Accounting Firm, but there was a notice on their website that they had closed their doors permanently, effective the 31st of December the previous year, due to the unexpected death of the founder, David Avrams. "Shit. Well. That's going to complicate matters," she said. "Wait. Let me check something else. Obituary. Maybe Avrams had a wife. Widow. Whatever. We can't have gotten this far to have a dead end." She winced. "Sorry. All right. We're okay. I think." She continued to read. "David Avrams is survived by his wife, Ruth. No mention of children or anybody else." Francesca set her phone down on the table. "All we need now is an address for Mrs. Avrams, and Tommaso can make a house call."

"Flowers," Carla said. "Tommaso should bring her flowers. Kind of a belated funeral gift. Then he can introduce himself as the family's new accountant and tell her how much her husband's work impressed him and all that shit before he gets to the real reason he's there." She pointed a finger at Tommaso. "You got to be sincere, though. People can tell. I bet she's no idiot. And she's probably not even all that old. *Unexpected* when they talk about death is usually a heart attack. Probably the stress of working for the Mob. Anyway, I bet he wasn't fifty yet."

Finding the phone number of Mrs. Avrams wasn't difficult. It turned out to be the firm's contact number on the website. "Before you call her, let's do a practice call," Carla said. "I'll be her."

"Come on, Carla," Morrie said. "This isn't necessary. How complicated could it be?"

"Humor me." She nodded at Tommaso. "Go ahead." She answered on the third imaginary ring. While Morrie gazed heavenward, holding his tongue, Tommaso introduced himself and then asked if he might stop by to pay his respects. She agreed to see him and suggested he stop by at ten the next morning. She could give him fifteen minutes, as she had an appointment at eleven. "All right," she said to Tommaso, "you can stop there." She gave Morrie a triumphant look. "Psychology," she said.

Morrie groaned. When Carla was in her psychology mode, she usually turned out to be right.

"Look," Carla said. "She picks up the phone, and out of the blue you tell her you're her husband's replacement. You know she's suspicious, but she don't know exactly why she's suspicious. What's she gonna do?" Carla spread her arms wide, gathering in her thoughts and her audience. "She's gonna check you out before you show up. That means what? She's gonna call a Puglisi to make sure you're on the up and up. That ain't gonna work out all that good for us." She looked at Morrie. "We need another plan."

Morrie swore under his breath. "Carla's right. Ruth Avrams is not an idiot. She was married to a professional. A professional, I might point out, who was responsible for the financial affairs of a Mafia family. Of course she's going to be suspicious of the visit." He began pacing the length of the dining room, forming and discarding ideas with each step. "I don't know," he said. "And what would make her want to help us out, anyway? Nothing. No Plan B. Again."

"I just thought of something," Francesca said. "Avram's obituary didn't mention any other relatives besides his wife. It didn't mention his schooling. It really didn't say anything at all. Don't you find that a bit odd? And then the firm closing up right after his death. It was a successful outfit, judging by the clients. Why wouldn't the widow hire another accountant or even a full staff? It doesn't make sense. I think we need to find out all we can about David Avrams. The key may be there."

"I think we need to find out all we can about Ruth," Carla said. "She's the one who most likely wrote the obit."

Thanks to the wonders of the internet, it only took a few keystrokes to do the investigations. David Avrams had graduated *summa cum laude* with a law degree from Yale University. He had no living relatives. Ruth Avrams had earned a bachelor's degree in business at Cornell and had been a court reporter in southern California before joining her husband's accounting firm. She was a member of Congregation Beth Israel in San Francisco where she taught Hebrew classes.

"That's good information, but…" Gino said.

"Do you have one of the documents with you that you can't decode?" Francesca asked Tommaso.

"Sure. I've got my laptop. Don't go anywhere without it these days. It's the only insurance policy I own."

"Let me see one," she said, taking a deep breath.

"Okay," Tommaso said, turning the laptop so she could see the screen. "Here's one."

"OK! That's it," she said, triumphant. "Everybody, come here. Take a look. We've got it!!"

"What am I looking at?" Gino said. "All I see are a bunch of wavy lines."

"Yes, that's exactly it! It's shorthand. Think about it. Ruth Avrams taught Hebrew, and she did the books for her husband in Hebrew. "

"I'll be damned!" Morrie said.

"I certainly hope not," Carla replied, making the horn sign with her hands to ward off evil. "Don't talk like that. So. All we have to do now is find someone who knows shorthand and Hebrew." She clicked her tongue against her teeth. "Shouldn't be too hard?"

"It's going to be practically impossible," Francesca said. "Court reporters use shorthand, even though it's not used in everyday business anymore. We need a list of Hebrew-speaking court reporters."

"No, we don't. It's all right," Morrie said. "I'll find out what kind of shorthand Cornell taught when she was a student there. There can't be many different types. Then I can load that shorthand program. After that, I'll get RP to write a translation program for it. Give me twenty-four hours, plus or minus. More plus than minus." He nodded at Tommaso. "We're almost home."

# CHAPTER TWENTY-EIGHT

*Santa Cruz and Dark Mountain*

When you've got money, life is easy. That's what Nicolo Puglisi was thinking while he stirred his coffee and waited for his real order to arrive at *Uncommon Grounds*. To be precise, he was merely the one sent to pick up the order he'd called in for Johnny. Payment had already been taken care of.

On a side street close to the university in downtown Santa Cruz, the coffee shop, *Uncommon Grounds*, dealt in much more than caffeine, and the staff was dedicated to customer service. Today, however, the entrepreneurial grad student who had developed a lucrative side hustle was late. Nico shifted in his chair and strained to look over the heads of the students blocking his view of the window. He'd give Sergei, if that really was his name, five more minutes. Leaving without the test tube would majorly piss off Johnny. That thought was not pleasant. He couldn't go back without the stuff. Five minutes passed. Nico gave it five more, but something had gone wrong. He pushed through the cluster of students at the entrance, stood a moment, looking up and down the street, then gave up. Sergei had stiffed Johnny, and by extension, Nico would be equally suspected. He could feel the sweat running down his back. He'd been the one to vouch for Sergei. Nobody crossed Johnny and lived.

*What if?* The words repeated themselves over and over in his mind. Nico stopped half a block from his car, considering an idea that had just occurred. It should work. Johnny was violent. He was crafty and cunning, and he trusted no one but himself, but he was not an educated man. He paid people for their knowledge, trusting that money, coupled with fear, would buy their silence. It usually did. When it didn't, they were silenced permanently. Nico had witnessed it firsthand, at Johnny's insistence, and he'd made sure the lesson registered. One day, when Nico had learned everything he needed to know, he'd teach Johnny a lesson. For now, playing it safe was the smart thing to do.

Johnny would either buy it or he'd have to kill Johnny before Johnny had a chance to do him.

The vial he ordered would contain the perfect poison: *thallium sulfate.* Colorless, odorless, and tasteless. The unlucky recipient wouldn't even know they were ingesting poison. The smirk spread across Nico's face. Genius. He was a fucking genius. He stopped at the university's science supply store and found the rack of packaged test tubes. He opened a package, took out a tube, and put it in his pocket. He shoved the package back and left the store. When he got to his car, he filled the tube two-thirds of the way with the contents of his water bottle, and sealed it. There was no way Johnny would sample the goods to see if it were the real deal. *Genius.*

***

"Why did the Mafia get started in the first place?" Francesca paused in her efforts to patch the pie crust she was rolling out. She'd positioned the new piece of dough over the hole she'd made and given it a thwack with her fist. The result was a lump that wouldn't stick. She gave up, rerolled the dough, and started over. "I really think the weather has something to do with this," she said.

"Actually, that's true." Carla was watching the baking with mild interest. "The moon, too. I think it's nature's way of telling us we're not in control of anything. But the Mafia? Well, back in the day, you had a bunch of clans. No laws. No nothing. And people needed protection from each other, so some guys saw an opportunity and the results were mixed. The people got protection, but they had to pay for it. If they didn't, they were dead. It's never changed. It's like they're stuck in their past. And now they've got police and courts, but they're just as bad. On the take, or whatever. They turn a blind eye in exchange for power and money, so the people aren't any better off than they were with the Mafia. But now, they're here, and we've got them. Kind of like a bad rash."

The dough was behaving better the second time around. Francesca flipped it into the pie pan and tucked a wayward strand of hair back behind her right ear. All that did was leave a streak of flour on her cheek, and the hair flipped back out.

"Here." Carla leaned over. "Let me help. You need two hands if we're going to have apple pie tonight. Turn around. I'm good with hair."

With her hair neatly braided and the pie filled with apples and ready for the oven, Francesca collapsed onto the stool opposite Carla. "Last year, it was pumpkins. Remember?"

"Hard to forget. That pumpkin saved our lives. I saved the seeds. The junior pumpkins are nearly ready for Halloween. Not sure an apple would be as useful. Sally was a big target."

"There's a fairy tale about a poisoned apple and Snow White or something," Francesca said. "I hope this isn't going to become an annual event. This year, we've got Johnny Vincento, and I wish we could get rid of him once and for all. I never was all that interested in fairy tales or poisons, but I sure would like part of the 'happily ever after', if it's possible."

"We're getting closer. Soon as Tommaso gets the books decoded and DeLuna can prove Nico set the fires, Johnny's never going to see the light of day again, and they'll send Nico to the loony bin. Guy's a creep."

The sound of a car pulling up and the knock at the door that followed interrupted their conversation. Francesca slid off the stool, opened the drawer next to the sink, and took out the .38 revolver, while Carla reached into her purse for the Ruger she'd claimed since the night of the raid.

"Times have sure changed," Carla muttered, stepping to one side of the door. The car started up, throwing gravel as it went down the drive. "Used to be you could answer the door without carrying."

"One must adapt." From the other side, Francesca squinted at the retreating vehicle. "No plate." She took her cell and called Gino at the packing shed. "We had a visitor," she said. "Black car, no plate. Possibly a Toyota. Left a box on the front porch."

"Don't open the door. Call Morrie." Judging by the short breaths, Gino was on the move. "I'm going after him." He disconnected.

The next sound was the roar of the Maserati tearing down the drive. "Oh shit. Oh shit. Oh dear God." Francesca's eyes were wild.

"No. Stop. You're going to do exactly what Gino said. For all you know, there's somebody else here, or that's a booby trap on the porch. No. Do not open the door."

At that moment, the sound of breaking glass came from the back of the house. Francesca froze, then turned to shut off the oven so the pie wouldn't burn, an action that most certainly saved her life when the bullet slammed into the wall where she'd been standing a second before.

"Now what?" Carla said through gritted teeth.

"Plan C. For cellar – the wine cellar. Hurry!"

***

"Not even DeLuna's battering ram could get this open," Francesca said, punching the code into the keypad. The five or so seconds it took for the lock to release seemed forever, but release it did, and Francesca pulled the massive door open just enough for them to slip through and it closed behind them. "The lock will reset automatically," she reassured Carla who was looking way beyond concerned.

"Son of a bitch," Carla said. "Those apples did what the pumpkin did. They saved your life. They keep telling you fruit is essential. They don't know the half of it. You don't suppose we'd be lucky enough that Bruce does his bit again, do you?"

"Possible. Not likely."

Carla nodded. "So, now what?"

"Now, we wait. We certainly won't die of thirst." She looked at the stock and there was a fleeting indecision in her eyes. Instinctively, her hand went to her stomach. "If whoever's here cuts the power to the main house," she continued, "this room has its own power, ventilation system, thermostatic controls. It's got everything."

"Everything except cell service," Carla said, scowling at her phone. "We can't get the word out."

"Got that covered too." Francesca moved to the control panel on the far wall, opened the door, and pressed the alarm button. "This goes straight to Gino, wherever he is. This room is his life. He even monitored it when we were in Italy." She rested her hand on Carla's shoulder. "He'll know there's somebody here and we're in hiding. He won't return alone. Have faith."

"Always." Carla grinned. "And this helps, too." She set her gun on the marble side table next to an overstuffed easy chair. "If I've got to be scared out of my freaking mind, this is definitely the place for it."

"There's even a bathroom. No shower, but it's got the essentials until the rescue squad arrives. So, now to the reason why we're here. Who is in the house trying to kill me, you, or both of us? And who was in the car that took off outside? And why did the other guy that's in the house get left behind? And I'm pregnant." Francesca glared at the massive door, willing her eyes to see through it.

Carla's eyes glowed. "I know."

# CHAPTER TWENTY-NINE

*The Santa Cruz Mountains and Dark Mountain*

There is a learning curve to almost everything in life, and sometimes you don't learn fast enough and suffer the consequences. Sometimes you don't get another chance. Negotiating the roads in the Santa Cruz Mountains at high speeds requires a combination of skill, knowledge, and often, luck. If you live there, you learn the roads and know when to lean into a curve and when to hit the brakes. Do it right, and you live another day. The driver of the black Toyota didn't live long enough to learn that lesson. He'd underestimated the degree of curvature and overestimated his abilities. By the time Gino came on the scene of the accident, there was nothing to do but call 911. The car had barreled off the road and collided with a redwood tree that had been a sapling when the Roman Empire had fallen. The tree had won.

There's a saying in the mountains that the volunteer fire department has a 100% success record of saving your neighbor's foundation in the event of a structure fire at your home. In short, you're screwed. The same holds true for law enforcement. Response times vary, depending on whether they're coming from Santa Cruz or Scotts Valley or Los Gatos. There aren't any points in between if you live near Summit Road. Gino knew he'd have at least fifteen, maybe twenty minutes before the volunteer EMTs arrived and another chunk of time before the sheriff joined them.

Adjusting his driving gloves, Gino scrambled down the hillside to the car. He checked the driver's pockets. Not surprisingly, there was no wallet. The glove box was empty, as well. He snapped a photo of the remains of the right side of the driver's face. The guy had been probably in his late twenties, white, skinny, black hair, pockmarked face, and a nose that had been broken at some time in the past. Black t-shirt and pants. Running shoes. Standard issue. Gino took photos of the gold chains around the neck and the oversized pinky ring on the right hand, signs of the guy's aspirations of moving into the big time in the Mob but lacking the brains. Then, Gino scrambled back up though the underbrush to wait for the EMTs. He'd called in the accident, and that meant they had his number. It was best to remain the conscientious good citizen he was until he'd given his statement. After all, he really didn't know anything. Nothing at all. But then, the alarm at the wine cellar went off, and his gut told him he was no longer a conscientious, good citizen. It would have been a poor act, anyway. He climbed back into the Maserati and raced towards home.

Everything was quiet. Too quiet. Italian homes are never quiet, not even when there's been a death in the family. *Especially* when there's been a death in the family. He scanned the yard. A bike—a crotch rocket—had been stashed off to the side of the driveway. No other vehicles. Just the silence. Leaving the Maserati at the packing shed, he circled around to the side of the house. The window to the far bedroom had been shattered. A few splinters of glass littered the ground, but most of the broken glass lay on the bedroom floor. An entry then, not an exit. Wishing he'd kept his leather gloves on, he hoisted himself up and over the window sill, avoiding most of the splinters but not all. One sliced his palm, and he left a bloody hand print on the wall.

The bedroom door was open. Bruce was in his drawer. *I did my part. Do yours.* Gino closed the door. The click was barely audible, but the sound carried in the stillness, and a bullet thudded into the wall to his left.

Gino ducked. Until he knew where Francesca was, he didn't dare fire, but the shooter had his position and fired again. This time, there was a searing pain in his side, and Gino knew he'd been hit. Gritting his teeth, he charged up the hall and into the Great Room where he found the intruder at the door to the wine cellar, firing into the keypad in a futile attempt to open the door.

Once, and not that long ago, Gino would have hesitated, but that time belonged to the past. Francesca meant more to him than his own life, but the room was wavering and beginning to lose shape. He blinked hard, and using both hands to steady his weapon, fired and then fired again. The second shot hadn't been necessary. He'd gotten a clean head shot the first time. Fighting the weakness that was sweeping over him, he pulled the body away from the door. Taking the key fob from his pocket, he punched the emergency release button. Then, there was Francesca's face, pale and worried, bending over him, calling him back from some distant place.

***

"There are some things you're not telling me." Detective Virginia DeLuna was making a hospital call. "It's time to come clean for all our sakes. You know, the body in your home? The gunshot wound you sustained that came pretty close to turning out the lights for you? The accident you called in and then left before the authorities got there? That sort of stuff? And I'm guessing there's more." She pulled the plastic chair over to Gino's bedside and settled in. "Quite a bit more. Like the package on your front porch. Yes, to answer your unvoiced question. I had a warrant. It was a test tube labeled *thallium sulfate*. That's a deadly poison. But the lab analyzed it. It was water. Ordinary tap water. Maybe bottled. That part's still not clear." She leaned forward. "Talk to me. The doctor said I can stay fifteen minutes. I'm all ears."

"Self-defense," Gino mumbled.

"Probably. Details would be good here. I've had my condo torched, and your friends had the same experience. We've got extortion, murder, and God knows what else, and I get the serious feeling that you all are being slightly less than honest with me."

If it hadn't been for the shards of glass on the floor of the bedroom next to Bruce's bedroom, and the bullet hole in the door frame, Gino might have taken a more hardline approach to DeLuna's overture, but all things considered, she was right. They owed her an explanation. Well, a partial explanation. He took a breath and faced his opponent. The match had begun.

"Just to show that I'm not holding anything back," DeLuna began. "We've got a fairly good idea who your intruder was. After you left the scene of the accident," she held up her hand to ward off Gino's objection, "we sent the prints off. Our corpse wasn't the careful sort. He might have been a quick replacement for a more seasoned driver." She shrugged. "Regardless, his name is—was—Bruno Calcetti. Minor thug with a lengthy rap sheet. Sort of a handyman type."

"Did he work for Johnny?" Gino said.

"Don't get ahead of me." DeLuna's tone was frosty. "The victim—"

Francesca, furious, interrupted. "Be careful who you call the *victim* here, Detective. We were being hunted like animals by that thug who wanted to kill one or both of us. Who's the victim here?"

DeLuna hesitated. "I understand what—"

"Do you? Do you really?" Francesca was shaking with rage and the realization of what might have happened to her, her unborn baby, and Carla and Gino.

The nurse selected that moment to enter the hospital room. "You're all going to have to leave now." Her tone meant there'd be no arguing.

DeLuna let out a heavy sigh but picked up her bag. "This isn't done." She left the room. Judging by the look on her face, if she could have slammed the door, she would have.

Francesca leaned in to kiss Gino and Carla touched his hand. "*Omerta*," she whispered, and Gino, eyes now closed, squeezed her hand.

***

The next day promised a fresh start, and Detective DeLuna was optimistic. She admitted to herself, although she'd never say it publicly, she had come on too strong at the hospital yesterday. This group required special handling. Push too hard, and they pushed right back. Especially the women. She made a mental note to keep that in mind for the future.

The report on yesterday's events at *Dark Mountain* was on her desk, and it bore all the earmarks of a home invasion. There'd been a distraction at the front door, and entry to the home had been gained by smashing a window in the rear. The intruder had fired at Francesca, narrowly missing her. Had she not turned away, the shot would most likely have been fatal. The women then took refuge in the wine cellar and pushed the alarm to summon help.

According to Gino's statement, upon receiving the alarm, he left the accident scene and returned home. Worried, he went around the side of the house to check for trespassers. Seeing the window smashed, he entered the house the same way the intruder had. He was fired upon twice, the second bullet striking him in the right side. He ran towards the shooter and fired twice, hitting the intruder both times as the shooter was attempting to destroy the keypad to gain entry to the hiding place of the two women. The first shot to the head killed the intruder instantly. The second shot hit him in the right arm, corroborating Gino's assertion that he had not shot the man in the back. Not that she would have blamed him. He had purchased the gun legally, and the courts would determine he had the right to defend himself and his wife with deadly force. She set the report aside. That case, as far as prosecution was concerned, was closed. What she wanted to know, and what the report didn't tell her, was *why*. It was time for another hospital call, but in light of the last one, another twenty-four hours might give tempers time to cool. Deciding instead to interview more of the women in the shelter, she was almost out the door when a phone call sent her in another direction.

Tommaso had finished decoding the financials for Enzo Puglisi. He had the names, the dates, and the amounts. Included were invoices, receipts, and records of subsequent investments of those funds. Tommaso had everything ready for her to pick up, and she said she'd be at the rectory within the hour. She disconnected and stared at her cell. Tommaso might be clean, and he'd done what he said he'd do, but he was still a Puglisi, and she still didn't trust him.

With both sets of books, not only did they have an airtight case for trafficking, but money laundering and tax evasion, as well. However, Enzo and Gennaro were dead, and the last two indictments would be mere formalities against the Puglisi estate, unless further digging revealed the involvement of Alphonse and Dominic.

It was unlikely Nicolo knew anything about the business end of the operations. His role would be accessory both before and after the fact in that regard. But she'd get him on arson and multiple counts of murder. How he'd managed to avoid the BOLO vexed her. And add Cesar Torres and Eddie "The Weasel" to the missing list. They had to be getting help from someone. Probably Johnny Vincento, although why would Vincento want to keep two liabilities around.? He was focused on building a new crime family on the still smoldering ashes of the old. It wasn't over yet. Getting Johnny Vincento was also a goal, and time was growing short. She knew where he was now, and where he would be each Friday night he remained in California. He never missed a poker game. She'd call Carla today and find out what she'd meant about knowing a professional player.

***

The priest who greeted Detective DeLuna at the rectory, Father Anthony Puglisi, bore a strong resemblance to his brother, Tommaso, and she commented on that as they walked to the library. "We used to have fun with that when we were kids. We're six years apart, but Tommy always looked older, and I had a baby face. Still do." He laughed. "It always provided one or the other of us with a foolproof alibi, although Tommy needed it more often than I did. Here we are." He stood aside and gestured for her to have a seat. "I'll get Tommy."

The library wasn't large, but the shelves were full. She walked to the bookcase behind the desk and read the titles. Or tried to. Everything was in Latin. At least in this section. The next section was in Greek.

"They're the same volumes, just there for comparison. They're Jesuits, after all."

She turned to face the voice. "Isn't Tommaso available?" she asked. "We had an appointment."

"Yes, we did. And we do. Hold on. Everything is in the cupboard behind the desk." He pushed on one of the Latin books and the bookcase swung out, revealing a large cupboard behind. He took a briefcase from the bottom shelf and handed it to her with a wink.

"Tommaso."

"Yes. I've found the perfect refuge, and I'll be staying here until it's safe to leave." He nodded at the briefcase. "I hope it doesn't take forever. This collar is a bit restrictive. My brother has a smaller neck."

"I don't believe it! You could be twins."

"That would have been more interesting, but no. Still, it's a good approximation. Even fooled the housekeeper here, but getting back to the business at hand. That briefcase is worth a fortune. All that information." Tommaso paused. "If it should fall into the wrong hands, that would be catastrophic. I think I should go with you to headquarters, sort of a guardian angel. I'm dressed for it." He moved to take the briefcase from her hand. "I can carry it."

Tightening her grip on the handle, Detective DeLuna declined. "Very generous, but not necessary. I didn't come alone." Thanking him, she left the library without a backward glance, let herself out, and walked to the unmarked car where two plain clothes detectives waited on the sidewalk by the passenger door.

Inside the rectory, the smile left Tommaso's face. He returned to the cupboard, took a second briefcase from the bottom shelf, closed the bookcase, and returned to his room. He tried again, without success, to loosen the clerical collar. It reminded him of being hung by a noose. He ripped it off.

Nanette had managed to get hold of a cell for just a few minutes, but in those precious minutes, she'd been able to tell him where she was. He'd been hoping to buy a little time with the detective, but it would be all right. They would be focused on organizing the raids against the massage parlors and the clubs. Dealing with the financial fallout from the family's dealings was down the road, and when the IRS was involved, everything took longer than necessary. "He's a genius," his mother used to brag to anyone who would listen. "He can do anything with numbers." He could still hear the pride in her voice. He looked up at the ceiling, or it might have been heaven and the plaster just got in the way, but his resolve strengthened. He just needed enough time for it all to work.

"Yeah." Gino had gotten less and less friendly answering his cell as time moved on.

"It's Tommaso. I've given the briefcase to DeLuna, but I need your help. I mean, I seriously need your help."

"I'm listening."

"I gave her everything she needs to nail the family on all the charges she's pursuing. You can check that out. I'm telling you the truth."

"All right."

"But...I...Look. It's got...layers."

"Just get to the point."

"There are just a few...irregularities in the financials that won't affect their case. I swear. It's just that I needed a bit of...compensation. Anyway, I need to leave. I'm booking a flight tonight and I'm taking Nanette with me."

"How?"

"I love her and she loves me. We're going back to Italy. We're going to have a baby. I got her passport from her apartment. DeLuna has mine, but I've got Anthony's. It will work. But the reason I'm calling. We need a place to stay when we get there. We can't get all the way there just to fall into a trap." The desperate hope in his voice was palpable, and Gino did the only thing he could.

"I'll text you the number. When you land, call it. And for God's sakes, don't go to the rental counter. The guy is connected. You'll be met by the man I trust more than anyone else in the world. Aldo Borgese. He'll have one of those freaking signs. It will say *Esposito Tours*. Just hand him your bags, and when you get to the house, tell Celestina I'll be home shortly. And Tommaso..."

"Yes?"

"*Omerta.*"

"*Si, Gino.*"

# CHAPTER THIRTY

*SFO and San Jose*

Being of mixed racial heritage has its advantages, but there's a downside. Sang Young Boucher's current passport, identifying him as Mario Rossi, an Italian national, albeit one with decidedly Asian facial features, had worked effortlessly to leave Sardinia, but the cognitive dissonance was causing problems as he dealt with a no-nonsense, unwoke customs agent at SFO who wasn't buying it. Even the halting English with the thick Italian accent wasn't going over as well as Sang had hoped. Ultimately, with the backup of travelers exceeding the posted occupancy limits of the room, a supervisor appeared.

With a barrage of hand gestures and verbal insults directed at the agent, delivered in the loudest voice he had, Sang stared the supervisor down. After one cursory glance, the supervisor grabbed the passport from the agent's hand, stamped the visa, and motioned Mario Rossi, still letting out a string of Italian expletives, through the line, with his apologies. You can either disappear into a crowd or be the cause of one. Either way works.

Timing is everything. Had Sang's plane landed an hour later, the supervisor, Jordon Linzer, would have already sorted through the morning's emails, alerts, and general garbage. As it turned out, however, it was an hour before he had a break and could play catch-up. He ran the cursor down the screen, getting into a rhythmic click and delete and nearly deleted the only thing of importance in the two hundred messages clogging his inbox. He took off his glasses, rubbed his eyes, and replaced his glasses. Nothing had changed. He was still staring at an Interpol most-wanted poster with a perfect likeness of Mario Rossi, his morning's pain in the ass. But the man on the poster wasn't Mario Rossi. He was Sang Joon Boucher. The man had lied about his name, but he hadn't lied when he'd told the customs agent he was here on business. According to the caption on the poster, Boucher was a contract killer with a last known address in Sardinia, Italy.

His blood pressure seriously elevated, Linzer called the number at the bottom of the poster and worked his way through the automated system. Finally, reaching the correct extension, he hit option #15 and waited. They put him on hold.

***

A police investigation in its initial states has some similarities to dumping a thousand- piece jigsaw puzzle on the table and moving the pieces around until you make the first join. From there, the border and limits are delineated, a few key central points mesh, and then comes the laborious task of sifting through the rest of the pieces, one by one, until finally, the key piece is found and the rest fall into place. This morning, Agent/Detective/Officer Virginia DeLuna, back at her desk at SJPD headquarters, was eyeing the unexpected gift from Rodriguez of a box of twelve donuts, and she was savoring the moment. The news release had flashed across the screen not five minutes earlier.

*Last night federal agencies in cooperation with local law enforcement conducted a synchronized raid on thirty-three social clubs and massage parlors in an operation that spanned both coasts and covered the greater San Francisco Bay Area as well as cities in parts of Massachusetts, Connecticut, and New Jersey. The raid was the culmination of two years of investigation by the FBI and lead investigator, Federal Agent Virginia DeLuna. Over two hundred victims of human trafficking, adults and juveniles, were freed. Some juveniles had been on the Missing and Exploited Children list. There were seventy-three arrests of operators of the facilities, in addition to the arrests of three members of the Puglisi crime family on human trafficking charges. Those arrested included Dominic Puglisi, owner of Waste Collection and Recycling, and his sons, Luigi and Paolo Puglisi. Alphonse Puglisi, currently incarcerated at the Federal Penitentiary in Leavenworth has also been implicated. Further details will be released as they become available.*

It was a sweet moment, but nothing lasts forever. The trafficking case was one prong of a three-pronged fork, with arson and racketeering the other two. Just as she'd decided on a chocolate donut with crushed walnuts and double chocolate frosting, the phone rang. She took her reward out of the box and set it on a paper towel as far away from the box as she could. She knew cops. She'd leave for the bathroom and come back to crumbs and innocent faces.

"DeLuna," she answered, wiping the corners of her mouth with a rough napkin. She'd expanded the geographical parameters of her ongoing racketeering investigation in the wake of the home invasion at *Dark Mountain*. They still hadn't identified the shooter, so on a hunch—educated guess, whatever—she'd checked with Interpol and gotten passenger lists on flights from Sardinia to SFO for the last week. It was a crap shoot, but it was a place to start if Johnny Vincento was importing talent.

The results of DeLuna's search were instructive, if not helpful. Five individuals named *Mario Rossi*, the Italian equivalent of John Smith or John Doe, had made the trip to San Francisco, with two of them being on the same flight. *Coincidence?* She asked herself. *I think not.* And it was a given that they would have been met, issued American passports and other necessary identification, and then melted into the general populace, with the exception of the *Dark Mountain* shooter, she wagered, who had melted into the morgue.

***

With a sworn promise not to upset the patient, Detective Virginia DeLuna was granted the usual fifteen-minute time slot for her interview with Gino Esposito. Upon entering the hospital room, she found a crowd, no open chairs, and the object of her investigation absorbed in ingesting somewhere in the neighborhood of 2,000-plus calories of cannelloni, a salad that seemed to be wilting for lack of attention, and a glass of red wine on the side.

"Do you people rent a bus to travel together? I mean, seriously, you move in tandem like some sort of Russian Olympic weightlifting team."

"Greetings to you, too," Gino said, between mouthfuls. "Kudos on last night." He raised his glass in a toast.

Her initial plan of attacking from a position of strength destroyed, she accepted a plate of pasta, with bread, and a small salad, handed to her by Carla, along with the admonition, "*Mangia! Mangia!* Eat! Eat!"

"Gino's being released tomorrow!" Francesca said, "and we're celebrating. And you should too!" She poured DeLuna a generous glass of *vino*. "You need to eat more. You are too thin. Men don't like skinny women."

An intelligent person, when faced with an insurmountable blockade, must adapt. Detective DeLuna adapted. "I am not Italian. My family comes from Spain. *¡Arriba, abajo, al centro, pa' dentro!*" To the interested faces, she offered a translation and another chance to take a drink. "Glasses up! Glasses down! Glasses to the center! Now drink!"

Everyone obliged, and with the mood lighter than at their previous encounter, the decibel level was also moderated. DeLuna plunged in. "There are a few things I'd like to talk with you about, but first, you'll be glad to know that Ginger and Nanette have been released from protective custody. We have their statements, and they will be called to testify when the case comes to trial." With that announcement received with smiles all around, she continued. "Now, let's talk about what happened at *Dark Mountain*, shall we?" The smiles faded, but there was no perceptible mutiny brewing, so she pressed on. "You are in danger." She gave a pointed look at Gino in the hospital bed and then turned to face Francesca and Carla and spread her arms heavenward. "As God as my witness, I do understand the history here. I've done the homework. You're paying Vincento the *pizzo* in Italy. But this is not Italy. And not all the police are corrupt here. Some, yes. But not the majority. You can't continue with the Lone Ranger act. *Omerta*. Yes, I know it. I know why it exists. But it exists in Italy. You came here to be free of it."

There was silence when she paused. Whether it was a silence that was telling her she was done and needed to leave, or a silence that meant maybe she had made a small dent in the armor, it was too soon to tell. She waited.

"Johnny Vincento had my mother and father killed." Gino said. "In Italy, when I was a boy, because my grandfather would not pay the *pizzo*. He won. He has always won. Now, he is here and he wants my vineyard. He is trying to beat me down. Will he kill me? Probably not, but he will do his best to kill Francesca to be strong on me." Gino took a reflective sip of his wine, carefully setting it back on the small table by his bed before turning his gaze to DeLuna. "The Puglisis are neutralized, for the most part. And we celebrate that. But it is not over. There's the test tube with the poison, and I have another with a virus that would destroy my vineyard. Warnings. Threats. Violence. No. He will not kill my wife, and he will not break me. There is only one thing for it." He shrugged. "Johnny Vincento must die." Gino's voice was calm, matter of fact. The pronouncement was delivered as a statement of fact—not a threat, but something of necessity that must come about, somehow, in some fashion, if the rest of them were to survive.

DeLuna took a last bite of the cannelloni and washed it down with a bit of wine. She set her empty plate on the hospital tray by the door. Finally, she walked the three steps back to the group and looked at each of the faces, now fixed on her own, waiting. "I do not consider that to be a threat of intent to violence," she said. "It is an observation of one way this could all be resolved, but it is not the only way to destroy Johnny Vincento." She held up a hand. "We can talk about that in just a minute. For now, does the name Sang Joon Boucher mean anything to you?" With blank looks from everyone, she turned to Gino. "You need to talk to your friend Chan. His brother's just off a plane at SFO.

"So? What's unusual about that?"

"He came from Sardinia this morning under the name Mario Rossi."

"That's a common name," Carla said.

"Too common. That's why he used it. He wanted to slip in and out of the country without ever having been here after he'd finished his business." She took a deep breath and exhaled with force. "He's a contract assassin who does frequent work for the Mafia. Connect the dots, and you'll understand why it's a concern. My thinking is that Vincento is ready to make his move and is done with cheap, local talent and substandard imports. Boucher is the best." DeLuna cast a longing glance at the wine bottle. "We need to move cautiously, but quickly. If Chan has any influence over his brother, we may have dodged the bullet for now. If he doesn't, we may not have much time."

The nurse picked that moment to push open the door, but seeing the intent looks, and hearing nothing but normal conversation, looked at Gino who seemed engaged and not overtired, and she left. During the observation, Detective DeLuna gabbed the plastic chair and sat. "I've been up for going on thirty hours. I'll make this brief. And private." With her eyes on Gino, she waited.

"I get it," Carla said. "Come on children. They want to be alone."

"It's for your own safety," DeLuna said. "What you don't know can't hurt him."

***

Even without the noise of conversation, just the presence of a group of people seems to create sound. After everyone had left, the room seemed to close in on itself. Detective DeLuna finally gave in to thirst or comfort and poured each of them an inch of wine. It was all that was left. "I've had a couple of short conversations with your cousin Carla," DeLuna began. "We have another investigation ongoing in San Francisco. This one you'll appreciate as it's focused on Johnny Vincento. I need a poker player. A good one. Actually, I need professional level."

"I'm listening," Gino said.

"There's a restaurant frequented by certain Mafia members. *FrankieG's Cocina Italiana* off Green Street. The Mafiosos don't go there to eat. There's a card room in the back, and lately it's been getting a lot of use, midweek, but mostly on weekends. Some locals occasionally, but a recent addition to the regulars is Johnny Vincento. Since Johnny's been at the poker table, the kingpins have been showing up on Friday nights. They're coming from the east coast. A lot of money changes hands, business is discussed, deals are made."

"How do you know all this?"

"In a minute. Hear me out. I want Vincento gone almost as much as you do." She gave Gino a serious look. "We're a match made if not in heaven, maybe somewhere close. You've got a gambling reputation. I know about your past problem, but I need you to get back in the game one last time and start losing big over the next week. You know, you're about to go off the deep end with everything Johnny's thrown at you. You've reverted. Johnny will jump all over that. We'll take care of the rest."

"Whoa! That last part. No. No way. Are you crazy?"

"You'll be playing with our money."

"Your money?" Gino's interest level increased noticeably.

"Technically, the taxpayers' money, but it's in our budget and it's for a good cause."

Skeptical, but moving quickly past that and into curiosity, Gino nodded. "Go on."

"Right. We have grounds for a righteous bust. The house is taking a percentage, the cards are marked, and the restaurant is serving alcohol to underaged customers. I could go on. All you have to do is play poker. Lose some and then start winning until you clean them all out. After the last hand, good luck on that, by the way—sincerely— you get up and leave and we'll pay a call on the others. Ships that pass in the night, so to speak. Just keep going until you're out the door. There will be three of them, possibly four. You get to bring a friend, if you wish. We've got your back. That's it. Johnny goes down. Will you do it?" She played her last card. "We've got one of ours inside. It's the cocktail waitress. She'll bring the drinks, the cigars, and the new decks," DeLuna smiled. "They'll be clean."

"Any idea how the house decks are marked?"

"Almost forgot about that. Invisible ink." She reached into her bag for a small envelope and handed it to him. "I came prepared, just in case. Contacts. They'll read infrared."

Gino's expression had gone from one of intense interest to one of total blankness. It was as if he'd flipped a switch. There was no furrowed brow, no hint of a smile or a frown, nothing in his eyes, no color in his cheeks, no twitch, no tic, no nothing. His posture was relaxed, his breathing regular, his hands folded across his chest. In short, he'd put on his poker face and had brought the rest of his body along.

That was all the answer Agent/Detective/Officer Virginia DeLuna needed. "Thank you," she said.

*****

Released from the hospital the next morning, with orders to rest for the next week, Gino returned to *Dark Mountain*, alone, to begin a crash course back into the life he had left behind. Francesca was safe with Carla. If this plan of DeLuna's worked, the nightmare would be over for good.

Gamblers who skirt the law tend not to hang around long in one location. With one exception, all of his old contacts had either moved on to other work, been arrested, or were dead, but Gino got the word out through that one contact that he was looking for some action. While he waited, he passed the time with hours of practice, handling the cards, regaining the feel of them, cold stacking, riffling, dealing, followed by more of the same, and he was reminded how quickly skills deteriorate when not used. By Day Three, however, he was back. He practiced during the day and played every night at a different room in a place run by the Mob. Mostly losing, but making sure he won occasionally, he added his winnings to the roll of cash he carried and displayed.

On Day Five, he got the call he'd been waiting for and sent word to DeLuna. It was going to be old school 7-Card Stud at *FrankieG's*. The elite would be there and the bust would go down.

Worried about Francesca and realizing that everything they had or would ever have had come down to this one night had left dark circles under his eyes and his color wasn't good. His complexion had taken on a grayish hue, he had a five-day growth of beard, had worn the same shirt all week, and he looked like shit. He looked the part of someone who needed the adrenaline boost of a win, but nothing had been working out, and this would be his last chance. The reality was this had once been him. He hadn't had to try. This was the role he was born to play.

# CHAPTER THIRTY-ONE

*San Francisco*

After everyone had left the hospital, relocated to the loft, and found seating on the floor, speculation about DeLuna's plans for Gino began in earnest. At least, it appeared that would be the case, until the doorbell rang. Being on the floor above the emptiness that would one day sort itself out into shops and cafes and whatever else some enterprising entrepreneurs envisioned, meant that now and for the foreseeable future, there was absolutely nobody around who should be ringing the doorbell. Nobody at all. Except, as it turned out, Ginger, who had been sprung from police custody and who had nowhere else to go and was frantic about the health and well-being of Bruce.

Morrie pushed the button that allowed her into the gated front hall, and she ran up the stairs to the third loft on the left where Carla waited by the door, arms open wide. "He's more than a snake," Ginger said, her voice trembling, "he's my...he's my dance partner. He's not a pet. I mean, I'm not emotionally attached to him or anything."

Carla gathered Ginger into her arms. "It's all right. I understand. We all do." She gave a threatening look at the rest of the assemblage who took the warning and nodded with encouragement.

"It's just that there's been so much lately, and I don't know what's happening any more." She collapsed into a heap on the floor and her sobs filled the room.

"PTSD," Francesca said. "Somebody needs to go get Bruce." She looked at Morrie. "Now!" she pleaded, and Morrie jumped up, grabbed his car keys, and was out the door before she could say another word.

The trip to retrieve Bruce also gave Morrie the chance to have a quick meetup with Gino and the details of the undercover operation. If DeLuna honestly thought they'd let this pass and blindly obey instructions, she wasn't as smart as he thought she was. He found Gino already at work. Three decks of cards waited on the dining room table. A fourth was fanned out, and Gino was doing some masterful moves with it.

"Impressive," Morrie said, watching Gino shuffle, cut, shuffle, cut until, satisfied, he dealt five hands. He motioned for Morrie to turn over the hole cards. Three hands had nothing, but the last two were a straight flush in one hand and four aces in the other. "I repeat, impressive. DeLuna sending you to Vegas?"

"No. San Francisco. Restaurant. All I need is an invitation from Vincento, and it's been a tough week doing the background work to earn that invite." Gino returned to the cards. "Keep this close to the vest. DeLuna's right on this one. I should be all right, but just in case, you know? Keep the girls out of this. I need to know they're safe. It'll all be over, one way or another on Friday."

"Word." Morrie stuffed Bruce into his carrier and left Gino absorbed, fanning and shuffling, riffling and dealing. He didn't look up as Morrie left.

***

There are those who say reptiles have no capacity for emotional connection, and that people who believe they do, suffer from overactive imaginations. However, as soon as Bruce saw his dance partner, his entire snake body did the hootchie-kootchie, and he reached out as far as his lengthy reptilian body would allow to drape himself, without constriction, from Ginger's neck and make a loose coil around her shoulders. If a snake could have smiled, Bruce would have won the audition for a dental commercial. If he'd been a feline, he would have purred his way to stardom in a cat food commercial.

"I'll be damned," Morrie said, watching in disbelief. "That snake loves her."

"And we love Bruce," Carla said. "He saved our lives." She looked at Morrie. "We need mice."

For the second time in three hours, Morrie Landow was on the road, searching for a place that sold mice. Things weren't looking all that great. *What about road kill?* Morrie drove around a possum in its natural state, splayed out and quite dead. No. Had to be live. The thrill of the kill. Finally, he had a small brainstorm. Not actually a storm. More of a brief shower. He was driving past a strip mall in downtown San Carlos when he spotted it. The sign said *Pet Store*. Just what he needed. Nothing fancy. Just the basics. Puppies, kittens, goldfish, and mice. He bought all the mice they had, along with a small bag of food. Despite the urging of the sales clerk that nine mice needed the economy-sized bag, he held firm. After all, how long were they going to need it?

Back in the car, the mice and the bag of food on the back seat, his thoughts turned to what DeLuna had said about Chan's brother. It wasn't much of a detour, and a face to face would be better than a call or a text. Besides, he was hungry and Chan was back to cooking at *Seoul Food*. Not open for business yet, but Chan was taking the down time to work on some new recipes. Helping out a buddy by offering to sample the food seemed the right thing to do. He texted Carla and told her he'd be back in a bit, and yes, he had the mice.

Once he'd gotten into the old neighborhood, his driving went on auto pilot—one of those times when you get where you're going but you don't remember driving there. He pulled up in front of *Seoul Food*, hesitated, and on a whim crossed the street to see what was happening at the site of the old apartment. Construction had stopped. No surprise there, with most of the Puglisis either dead or in the slammer. And then, in the scant shelter offered by a stack of pallets, he saw a small black dog curled up where the front door had been. The dog was the right size. It couldn't be, but it was. Pierre. After nearly two weeks. Morrie crouched down and called his name. At first, hesitance, but then, recognition. Pierre's little tail thumped on the cement. Morrie scooped him up and took him back to the car, and without a backward glance, started the engine. Pierre in his lap, his ears pricked forward, knew he was going home. Steering with one hand and scratching Pierre's ears with the other, Morrie's eyes stung, and he used his sleeve to wipe away the dampness. *Carla...you were right.* After a couple of settling breaths, he used the voice option to call Chan.

"Saw the car. What's up? Thought you were coming in." Chan's words were muffled.

"I can hardly understand you."

"Sorry. Had a spoon in my teeth. I'm experimenting with some *kimchi*. It's not hot enough."

"I'm sure. I was coming in but then the weirdest shit happened. I found Carla's dog. He was sleeping by the old apartment. I have to get him home. Carla is not going to believe it. He was just *there*. She's looked and looked, but nothing. She comes here every day and walks the neighborhood."

"We get a lot of strays. The cats don't stay long." He hesitated. "I know what evil thought just crossed your mind. Don't even go there. I guess dogs are more loyal to places. So, what brought you over here if it wasn't my exceptional cooking?"

"Your brother."

Silence. Then, "What about him?"

"DeLuna says he's here. On business. Know anything about that? You didn't mention his other occupation."

"No. It's not something I discuss. It's got nothing to do with me, although there is fallout from time to time. On paper, he's still associated with the family business. In reality, I haven't seen him in years. If he's here, I don't know why."

Morrie, just about at the loft, slowed, and Pierre stirred. "I suspect he's here to kill Gino. Word is he's working for Johnny Vincento."

"I'll see what I can turn up," Chan said, then disconnected.

***

It was a day for animal reunions. First Bruce, with his happy dance, and then Pierre, who seemed to understand exactly where he was going and who was going to be there when he arrived. Morrie pulled up to the loft and honked the car horn three times in rapid succession. Then he did it again. Pierre in his arms, he got out of the car, stood in front of the loft, and held Pierre up to show Carla, who had gone to the window to investigate the source of the racket. Her shriek traveled through the window glass and down the two stories to the street. Somewhere in the vicinity of thirty seconds later, Carla had the door open, her arms wrapped around Pierre, and was wiping away the tears with the tissue Morrie had handed her. Sobbing and laughing at the same time, she leaned into Morrie and he stroked her hair.

"Where?" she finally asked.

"At the apartment. He was sleeping by some construction pallets. Waiting."

Carla was holding Pierre as if she'd lose him again if she ever let him go.

"I suspect he's been visiting the restaurants for handouts out back. He doesn't look all the worse for wear. He's home now. That's all that matters."

Carla, overjoyed, took Pierre on a tour of the loft. The introduction to Bruce was short and well-chaperoned. They seemed to arrive at an understanding that boiled down to *you've got your person and I've got mine. Let's just ignore each other.* Still, precautions would be necessary. Bruce was returned to his carrier.

Carla had bought a new bed for Pierre as an act of faith that he would come home, and she'd set it at the foot of the bed, his familiar place. There was a basket of toys waiting, and she set him down so he could explore while she went to fill his new water bowl and then realized he must be hungry at the same moment Morrie did. They exchanged glances.

"I know. I know," Morrie said. "On it. Dog food's going to be a lot easier to find than mice," he said. "I left the mice in the car, anyway." He scratched Pierre's ears and left for the third and, he hoped, last time that night.

# CHAPTER THIRTY-TWO

*Dark Mountain and San Francisco*

It was mid-afternoon on Day Six. One more day of practice. One more day of waiting. Tomorrow it would all play out. The sky had clouded up, and it looked for all the world like rain. Gino had taken a break and moved to the back deck, where he'd done a series of pushups and some lifting. Regardless of his appearance, he needed stamina, and he'd been squeezing in a half-hour workout every afternoon. The last thing he wanted was company, but then he heard Chan's Jeep pull up outside. Chan didn't waste any time getting to the point of his visit.

"There is no way you're going to be able to pull this off," had been Gino's response when Chan had told him what he'd planned. "You're going to get killed. You're going to get *me* killed."

Chan was having none of it. "None of them have ever seen my brother, Sang Joon. And there's a family resemblance, although I am more handsome. Besides. It's done." Chan waved off Gino's objections. "All Sang wanted after being made when he got here was to get the hell out, and by now I figure he's somewhere over Singapore. It doesn't matter. He wanted the money. I paid him, and I threw in an extra ten grand to get him on the first flight out of here. Done. It's just you and me, my friend."

"Look. This may seem like a poker game, but it's not," Gino said. "It's Johnny's power play and he wants me broken and dead. He's playing with his goombahs. The decks are marked, and there's no way out except the front door. DeLuna and her team will be there, but that won't control what happens inside. It's a tough game to beat. Besides, Morrie said you don't gamble."

"What I *said* was, 'unlike most Asians, I don't gamble' and that's true. When it's not a gamble, but a sure thing, however, I have been known to make an exception. So. I repeat. Relax. We can take turns winning, and Johnny won't be the wiser."

"I repeat. The deck is marked."

"Of course it is. I assume you'll be wearing contacts. So will I."

"This is nuts."

"This is poker."

"All right," Gino said. "I'm leaving in an hour. There's a game in San Bruno. It's the last one before tomorrow's make or break. Come on inside. I'll get us a drink. It's a necessary prop these days." He took a bottle of Jack from the cupboard and a couple of glasses from the dishwasher. "They're clean," he said in answer to Chan's skeptical look. "It's actually interesting, going undercover. It would be even more interesting if I knew I'd survive the experience." He poured the drinks, pushed the cards out of the way, and motioned for Chan to have a seat at the table.

"Here's what you need to know. The server with the drinks, cigars, and fresh decks is a Fed. The first deal that's yours after the third hand, I need you to spill your drink on your cards or do some other kind of damage so we get a new deck. Her decks are unmarked. Johnny will lobby for one of his decks. I've been told he keeps a few on the table for replacements.

"If I use Johnny's deck and deal him a winning hand, he'll know not to bet. He'll be able to see that I've dealt myself a better one. He'll know that I know and that will mean game over and lights out for me. It was a problem I was struggling with, but with a new deck, all I'll need is some time to shuffle and stack. It won't matter about the rest of the cards. I can make sure nobody else gets anything other than three of a kind or a pair. Regardless. I won't be the one who requested the new deck. He won't do anything to you if he wants to keep breathing. You are the hired killer, after all. On the last hand, we clean everyone out and then we leave. That's going to be the hard part."

"Not that hard. You doubt me." Chan looked offended.

"We won't have any weapons," Gino said.

"We won't have any *guns*," Chan said. "You've never seen my Kung Fu moves."

"Kung Fu is Chinese."

"Whatever. Don't worry. I mean it. Don't."

Gino shot a glance heavenward. If God were listening, this would be a good time to send a sign. Gino waited. Nothing. He was on his own. "The game is 7-Card Stud. I'll be learning their tells the first couple of hands. I know yours already."

"My face is inscrutable. I have no tells."

Gino cleared his throat. "Not your face. Your hands. When you're thinking, you tap your right index finger on whatever is in front of you. Positive, you tap faster. Negative, slower. Don't think in this game. Just play unless you need to communicate."

"No shit. Hmm. That explains a lot. All right. No thinking. I'll just play what you deal me and tell you when you need to be aware."

"And when I deal you something you can work with, work with it."

"Should be fun."

"That's probably the only word I wouldn't have used."

***

*FrankieG's Cocina Italiana* was a relic, a survivor. While other restaurants had adapted to changing times and adopted a minimalist approach with a more subtle and understated décor, Frankie's held on to the past with a death grip. Its garish exterior left no doubt as to its identity or its menu, both of which were proudly proclaimed across the two front windows in mile-high lettering. *AUTHENTIC ITALIAN FOOD* shouted one window, while its partner on the other side of the wood and glass door with the air conditioning unit jammed in the space above, replied *COCKTAILS*. They'd managed to cram in a phone number, some additional menu items, and a *HAPPY HOUR* announcement before they ran out of space. It was a vision to be sure, but it also served a more important purpose. It blocked anyone from having a clear view of the interior and the patrons. This was a decided benefit in the event it became the venue for a Mob hit. It was actually a stroke of genius. Another stroke of genius was the barber shop next door, also run by the Mob, and the door that connected both businesses, camouflaged by the supply cabinet that could be moved quickly out of the way should an emergency exit be required. Gino had noted its location from DeLuna's sketch of the interior.

When the black Bronco Sport pulled away from the curb, allowing Gino to pull in, it was game on. So far, so good. DeLuna had done her prep work. From this point, he was on his own.

It was the changing of the guard at *FrankieG's*. The last handful of legit diners were paying their bills and gathering up hats and jackets. By nine o'clock, the restaurant was empty, the door locked, the blinds shut, and the sign flipped from *Open* to *Closed*. In the private back room, the poker table waited for the first deal of the night. No last names, no guns, and no cell phones were the ground rules. FrankieG, the proprietor and host for the night's game, searched everyone upon entry to ensure compliance.

Gino stood in the doorway, getting his bearings. Tonight's game was cash-only, with rules that had been bent so much, they'd broken. The ante would be $25, the buy-in 1K, the small bet $125, and the big bet, $250. Conceivably, the winner could walk away with well over a million.

FrankieG was pushing seventy. Mostly bald, he'd covered the remains of his white hair with a brown driving cap that clashed openly with his purple slacks and jacket. He wore enough gold bling to add a good five pounds to his skinny frame, and with a nose that almost reached his chin, he left a less than favorable visual impression.

The regulars had claimed their usual places. Gino took the one open seat, putting Chan on his right and FrankieG to his left. Bennie "The Mechanic" was seated to Chan's right. He was the other cigar smoker, easily weighing in the vicinity of three hundred pounds. Probably late forties, he had a scar running diagonally across his face from his forehead to his jaw and was missing the pinky on his left hand. Then came Johnny, a sartorial seminar in his tailored gray Italian suit, gray silk shirt, and tasseled loafers.

"I'll be dealer tonight, if there are no objections," Johnny said, reaching to claim the deck in the center of the table before he gave an Academy Award-winning smile that showed a mouthful of perfectly capped, and probably implanted teeth at a painful level of whiteness. It was blinding. Gino could almost feel a migraine coming on.

"It's a friendly game," Chan said, nothing friendly in his tone. "We'll share the wealth." He handed the deck to FrankieG, his eyes still on Johnny who was trapped. Johnny could leave, which would not only be bad form, but suspicious, and would most likely result in a close examination of the deck, which would have serious consequences. Plus, it would deprive Johnny of his main goal, bankrupting Gino. His only other option was to accept the change, but it really was no choice. He smiled again and bowed his head in acknowledgment of the change in plan.

*Damn.* Gino picked up the faint quick tapping of Chan's index finger on his whiskey glass. With a friend like Chan, you didn't have enemies. The game proceeded, each player having a turn at the deal. Johnny won when he had the deal. The rest of the time, he didn't lose. When it was Chan's deal, he set his drink glass on one of the cards, but when he picked up the glass, the card stuck, and he creased it as he was trying to peel it away.

With no apology, Chan gathered up the cards and motioned for the server to collect them. "I'll need a new deck," he said, reaching for one on her tray.

"You don't need to do that," Johnny said, picking up one of the extra decks from the table and shooting it over to Chan. "It happens. I already got a couple from her. We got to be prepared. Right?" He laughed and set his cigar down on the ashtray. His mood had improved. He waved the girl away.

"I've already got this one," Chan said, tipping the girl for the deck. He slit open the cellophane wrap, dumped the cards on the table, and spread them out before the shuffle.

"If you shuffle good enough, you don't need to wash the cards," Johnny said, but Chan ignored him. He gathered the cards, shuffled, cut, and slid the deck to Bennie who cut again.

Sometimes Lady Luck smiles on you, and Johnny might have thought she was smiling at him when Chan dealt him two pair that turned out to be the winning hand, but Lady Luck is fickle. Sometimes, she just sets you up for the fall to come. The cards weren't marked, and Johnny'd still won. And that made him cocky. Never a good trait in a poker game.

"I never had much appreciation before for washing the deck," Johnny said. "But when you're lucky, you're lucky."

"Better to be lucky than good," Bennie grumbled, staring at his hand that held absolutely nothing. All he had was high card and it was a six of diamonds.

The last deal of the night went to Gino. "I can feel it," Gino said. "This time, I'm going to have the luck. I'm overdue."

"You're overdue for dealing," Chan said. "Get on with it."

"I'm not going home with anything if I don't take this one," Bennie said, the cigar rolling around his mouth.

Finally, after shuffling until he was satisfied, with some chatter to distract from the time he was taking, and after a few cuts, Gino pushed the deck to Chan. He tapped. The ante, then the deal—two hole cards and then Third Street.

Gino dealt FrankieG the 9 of Hearts, but even with a pair of 8's as his hole cards, he folded, lit a cigar, and leaned back in his chair as if the only reason he was there was to get out of the house and watch a game. The rest of the door cards saw Bennie with the 9 of Diamonds, Johnny—the 8 of Diamonds, Chan – the 5 of Spades, and Gino dealt himself the 3 of Diamonds. As lowest card, Gino was the buy in.

Johnny's play had become predictable in the first round they'd played that night. He checked every hand. It didn't seem to be a cautious move, Gino observed, more what Johnny considered to be a way of exerting dominance. He called when it came back to him. He never folded. He never raised, although he called every raise. He was waiting for The River.

The action, or what there wasn't of it, put FrankieG to sleep. His head slumped on his chest, his snores the only other sounds apart from the steady drip, drip, drip from a broken water pipe in the kitchen. It was the quietest game Gino had ever played, but the tension was palpable. There was a steady, slow build until Gino dealt the final cards for Seventh Street—the River.

The last deal was a hole card with no limits on the betting. As if someone had turned on the light switch in a dark room, everything came alive. Everyone still in the game was hoping for some magic.

Johnny's door cards were the 8 of Diamonds, 10 of Hearts, Ace of Spades, 4 of Diamonds. Everything would depend on his three hole cards. At the moment, all he had was Ace high.

Chan's door cards were the 9 of Hearts, Queen of Clubs, Queen of Spades, 5 of Spades. With a pair of Queens, his was the highest hand showing which made him the bring-in.

Gino held the 10 of Diamonds, 3 of Clubs, 4 of Hearts, 3 of Hearts. A pair of 3's wouldn't do much. It didn't look all that promising.

The betting went around the table five times. Johnny abandoned his check pattern in a frenzy of calling and raising without any restraint. His left eye twitch was in fifth gear. He couldn't wait to throw more money down. Finally, Gino had had enough. "I'm all in," he said, shoving everything he had to the center of the table.

"All right," Johnny said. "I'm all in."

Chan tapped his index finger on his cards in rapid mode, a tell that went unnoticed by Johnny. He too went all in. His hole cards were the Queen of Diamonds, 9 of hearts, and 9 of Clubs. He had a full house.

"Good hand," Johnny said. "Just not good enough." His hole cards were the remaining three Aces, giving him an almost unbeatable hand. Almost unbeatable, because it played out the way it does in every B movie ever made about poker. Johnny reached to claim the pot. And, just as in every B movie, when it's time for the hero to step up, Gino shook his head and spread his cards on the table. With the addition of his hole cards, he had the 3,4,5,6, and 7 of Hearts. He had a straight flush, and he said those words that turned the universe back on a true course. "Not so fast, Johnny. A straight flush beats four of a kind." He lifted Johny's two hands, now nothing but dead weights at the ends of his arms, from the prize and claimed the pot.

Johnny, hate oozing from every pore in his body and his eyes glittering like some sort of demon from the depths of hell, shoved back his chair, stood, and pulled a .38 from a shoulder holster. "You son of a bitch. You cheated me. That's my pot and you're dead." In the nanosecond between that last word and squeezing the trigger, he fell back, toppling his chair on the way down, the knife protruding from his right shoulder, blood streaming down his arm, his gun hand now rendered useless.

"Don't worry," Chan said to Gino. "It was a throwaway. I keep some for cleanup. Don't need it back." He glared at Johnny. "Don't want it back. I don't use contaminated equipment." Keeping his eyes on FrankieG and Bennie, neither of whom showed any desire to join Johnny, Gino got up from his chair and he and Chan passed DeLuna and her team coming in on their way out. "I told you not to worry," Chan said.

***

"The problem with playing poker with a Mafioso," Gino said to Chan, "apart from the obvious risk involved, is that you can't trust him. Once you understand that, things get a little easier. FrankieG made a show of checking Johnny for a gun, but it was a foregone conclusion I was never going to walk out of that game alive, win or lose. If the hitman didn't take care of me, Johnny would. That was Johnny's thinking, but it was flawed, because the hitman was somewhere over the Pacific at an altitude of 42,000 feet."

"You trusted *me*," Chan said.

"Different Mafia."

The next day, a similar raid occurred in Sardinia. It was the culmination of nearly two years of work and it went down splendidly. When the Feds here had finished with him, Johnny would be extradited to Italy to await trial. Potentially, he would be about 125 years old at that time. In the meantime, his land holdings in Sardinia were seized, becoming the property of the government to eventually be turned into a park for all the citizens to enjoy. There would be no admission fee. No *pizzo*. Even in Italy, change is possible. It was over. It was done.

# CHAPTER THIRTY-THREE

*Dark Mountain and San Francisco*

Except it wasn't over and done with as long as Nico was loose, and this was one of the topics of discussion at the celebration dinner at *Dark Mountain*, after everyone had assembled and Gino had shaved and taken a much-needed shower.

"We got to get rid of that little gnat once and for all," Carla said. She'd set the grocery bags on the island in the kitchen and was scratching an itch on her elbow.

"Don't forget Cesar," Francesca added. "You know, I don't like how this is stealing our joy. I say that tonight we celebrate our victory and leave tomorrow's worries to tomorrow."

"I agree," Ginger said. Nobody asked Bruce his opinion. He was back in his dresser drawer, asleep.

"Johnny's down for good. The protection racket is done. The trafficking operation is over," Carla said. "All we got are just a couple of minor inconveniences."

***

It was as if the Higher Powers had been listening, because, somewhere between the hors d'oeuvres and the salad, Morrie got a text. The beep that had disturbed their peaceful munching was forgiven when he reported the latest news item from Agent/Detective/Officer Virginia DeLuna.

"God ain't finished with us yet," Carla said, listening to what Morrie read to the group.

*Police units responded to a garage fire this evening at the residence of Superior Court Justice Alan Faucett. The fire, which was confirmed to be arson and confined to the interior of the adjoining garage, resulted in considerable damage to that structure, but firewalls between the garage and the residence kept the fire from spreading. Authorities found human remains inside the charred residue of one of the owner's classic vehicles, a 1952 MG TD. The identity of the victim is not known at this time.*

"That's the judge from the arraignment. I've no doubt that body will prove to be Nico. The hit is out, and a fitting way for him to die. A bloody shame about that car, though," Morrie said. "I have a friend who collects those. And I suspect Cesar Torres has also been dealt with. He is, after all, among the 'missing' and we have some experience with that."

***

Gino, understandably preoccupied for the past two weeks, finally noticed that Francesca had been ignoring the wine. "Why aren't you drinking?" he asked.

"I am." Francesca lifted the glass of ice tea to her mouth and her eyes twinkled. "Don't fret. I'll be back with wine after a bit."

A previous online course, *Understanding Women: What They Say and What They Mean,* had given one piece of information that had stuck with Gino. *Women tend to talk around a topic instead of getting to the point immediately.*

Francesca took pity on him. She set the glass down, leaned forward, looked into his eyes, and asked, "Should we have the baby here or at *Castel del Mare?*"

After the applause, and after lifting glasses to Francesca and the baby, Gino made the toast. *"alla famiglia!"*

At that moment, a gentle breeze drifted in from the open kitchen window, and Carla reached up, letting the filaments of air pass through her fingers. She looked at Morrie, and the expression on her face was one of contentment and satisfaction. "It comes on the wind," she said, raising her glass.

*"alla famiglia!"*
*To Family!*

# ABOUT THE AUTHOR

Karen K. Brees is the Amazon #1 bestselling author of *The World War II Adventures of MI6 Agent Katrin Nissen* series, *The Esposito Family Chronicles*, and numerous nonfiction titles. She holds a master's degree in history and a doctorate in adult education. She has been a bookmobile librarian, university professor, classroom teacher, cattle rancher, goat herder, and sheep wrangler. An obsessed gardener and sporadic knitter, she currently resides in the Pacific Northwest on a small farm with her horses and her husband.

THE
ESPOSITO
CAPER
KAREN K. BREES

# NOTE FROM KAREN K. BREES

Word-of-mouth is crucial for any author to succeed. If you enjoyed *Disorganized Crime*, please leave a review online—anywhere you are able. Even if it's just a sentence or two. It would make all the difference and would be very much appreciated.

Thanks!
Karen K. Brees

We hope you enjoyed reading this title from:

www.blackrosewriting.com

Subscribe to our mailing list – *The Rosevine* – and receive **FREE** books, daily deals, and stay current with news about upcoming releases and our hottest authors.
Scan the QR code below to sign up.

Already a subscriber? Please accept a sincere thank you for being a fan of Black Rose Writing authors.

View other Black Rose Writing titles at www.blackrosewriting.com/books and use promo code **PRINT** to receive a **20% discount** when purchasing.

www.ingramcontent.com/pod-product-compliance
Lightning Source LLC
Chambersburg PA
CBHW030816210726
48290CB00002B/613